Worth

MW01610646

By K. Constantine

Copyright © 2019 K. Constantine

Constantine

All Rights Reserved.

Chapter 1

First contact

Star System: Virgil's Star (VGL 191)

Force: Marine Company One — dispatched from the Alcmene naval

vessel Nemean

Location: Two klicks inside the Structure

"Fall Back!" Major Lewis shouted into the general channel. "All units fall back!"

His Marines raced through the tight corridors, flashes of green laser light mixing with their headlamps to illuminate the darkness.

Gravity here was heavy, but the Marine EVA suits were designed to compensate so that the wearer would feel Earth-normal. Despite that, Lewis felt his feet dragging.

He switched to the command channel and began giving orders.

"Wessler! Duffy! You've got four squads coming your way. Unidentified hostiles on our tail. Have your men ready to fall back behind the squads. Execute defensive retreat. Don't try to hold your line once we are through!"

"Corporal Duffy here, sir! Acknowledged."

"We'll be crossing your position in about sixty seconds. Wessler, acknowledge!"

"Sir," said Duffy over the comm, static muffling his voice. "Wessler took a squad to explore one of the side corridors. We lost contact with his unit about ten minutes ago, sir."

"Shit!"

"Should we send scouts after them, sir?"

"No time. Execute as ordered. Once the squads are through, you are to fall back in full defensive retreat. Understood?"

"Yes sir!"

Lewis closed the command channel and gave a signal to Waverly.

Waverly was his command's official liaison to ISAT, the Institute of Science and Technology, a pan-governmental organization whose original function was to monitor and control potentially destructive technologies. These days ISAT had a monopoly on technology and dolled it out — or forbid it — as it saw fit.

Lewis opened a private channel to Waverly. "Waverly, we need to slow those hostiles down. What have you got in your TSAC?"

Waverly placed a hand on his backpack and another on his utility belt, thought for a moment and replied, "A round of GGs ought to slow those things down."

"Great! I'll cover you from here. Martinez and Lotte will cover your flanks. Get those things ready now!"

Lewis gave orders to Martinez and Lotte to lay down fire to the left and right of Waverly, while Lewis took point just off their central line of attack.

"Wait for my order, Waverly!"

"Yes sir!"

"Last squad to cross perimeter one," Lewis shouted into the general channel, "call out your position when you are through. Duffy and his team will cover your retreat back to the shuttles."

Electronic acknowledgements flashed green on Lewis' heads-up display.

Lewis glanced at his watch. They should be getting through in ten seconds.

Five seconds.

"Waverly, get ready!

Three seconds.

Waverly began taking aim.

Two seconds.

Lewis took in a deep breath to steady his nerves.

One second.

"Squad four through, sir!"

"Waverly, now!"

Waverly steadied what looked like a two-foot tube on his shoulder, his fingers dancing over a red keypad, and fired.

The GG landing zone seemed to turn pitch black, as gravity within a ten-meter area increased tenfold.

"Good job! Waverly, get your ass back to the shuttle. Martinez, Lotte, hold your positions and keep firing at those bogies! Run like hell when I give the word."

Lewis turned his attention to his heads-up display, turned on the SITMAP and watched icons representing each squad make their way back to the shuttle landing point. Even with the SITMAP on, he couldn't see Wessler's team.

They knew coming in that this structure was heavily shielded, and communications would be difficult. But he didn't expect anyone to disobey orders and get themselves lost.

Not wanting to leave anyone behind, he reluctantly gave the order to Martinez and Lotte to retreat.

"Get back to the shuttle. NOW!"

Lotte and Martinez retreated in staggered fashion, with each Marine running ten meters, stopping to lay cover fire while the other Marine ran ten meters and so on, until they could get out of the hostiles' firing range.

Crouched behind a twisted piece of steel, Lewis opened the general channel and called to Wessler again.

No answer.

"Sir! We've got a problem." That was Lotte.

Before Lewis could answer, a deafening roar blasted static through his EVA comm and blinded his heads-up display.

It took seconds for his visor to correct and restore his vision, coming in shadowy at first, before the visor adjusted to the lighting and compensated for damage to his EVA suit's external visual sensors.

The corridor ahead of them was blocked by tons of debris.

He saw Martinez's name tag among the debris but no other signs of him.

Lotte was lying over the jagged edge of a boulder, his back bent at a painfully dangerous angle.

Lewis made his way to Lotte, plugged his suit into the Marine's EVA and checked for vitals: still breathing, heart rate low, unconscious, being pumped with recovery nanos by the suit's onboard medical computer.

Lotte would survive the explosion.

But with the effects of the gravity grenades fading, and blasts of green laser fire coming their way again, Lewis wasn't so sure they'd be getting out of this alive.

Dragging a piece of metal in front of their position, Lewis placed Lotte flat on the ground behind the sheet and took aim with his rifle.

Whoever — whatever — they were, they were coming.

Search and Rescue

System: Virgil's star (VGL 191)

Location: The Structure, 350 meters from the landing zone

Corporal Duffy watched the two shuttles take off from the Structure's hangar bay and fly back into open space.

Their mission to explore the Structure had quickly become a search-and-rescue mission. Duffy felt a surge of pride when he asked for three volunteers to stay behind to help him carry out the mission, and every member of his squad who wasn't wounded stepped up for the task.

Despite his ample pick of volunteers, he knew immediately who he wanted.

Private First-Class Laura Chan, formerly attached to the Flying Hornets, a combat engineering unit that specialized in rescuing commercial spacers trapped in shoddy mines dug by shady companies in Alcmene's in-system asteroid mining belt.

Senior Private Michelle Hauser, a medical doctor by training who'd joined the Marines out of her deep desire to see the stars — or at least that's what she'd tell Duffy whenever they'd drink too much and fall asleep in each other's arms.

And finally, William "Buff" Layton, arguably the fittest Marine Duffy had ever encountered. Rumor had it that a fully suited Marine wearing EVA-strength augmentation gear, which was standard on such missions, would still lose to Layton in an arm wrestle.

Duffy called into the command comm, still in range of the shuttles.

"Falcons One and Two. This is Corporal Duffy. Get back to the Nemean and give a full report to Captain Gregory. Give us six hours to conduct our search, and then ask the captain to come and get us."

Green acknowledgements flashed in his heads-up display. The two Falcon shuttles accelerated away from the structure bound for the Nemean, station keeping one AU away.

Back to the task at hand, Duffy surveyed their surroundings with a sweep of his head. Things looked quiet — a far cry from the chaos a few moments ago, when the entire Marine recon force was making a headlong retreat from an unknown, heavily armed enemy.

Still, as the ranking officer it was his duty to stay back and retrieve anyone left behind.

Luckily, the Falcons were equipped with portable excavation equipment, which the Marines could supplement with their EVA suit's augmented lifting capacities.

The job here was big, but Duffy figured between the four of them and their equipment they'd be able to dig out anyone who was under all that debris.

"Laura, would you do the honors, please?" said Duffy into his teams' channel, gesturing at the excavation equipment resting by Private First-Class Laura Chan's feet.

"The pleasure is all mine," Chan replied.

Chan and Duffy had attended university together and joined the Marines at the same time. They'd been longtime friends, and while never pursuing a romantic relationship, deeply cared for each other.

They had promised to be each other's best man or woman at their respective weddings — assuming either of them got around to doing that.

While Chan set up the excavation equipment near the beginning of the debris field, Duffy turned his attention to Senior Private Michelle Hauser.

Hauser was already using her MEDKIT to scan for life signs within the debris field.

"Anything?" Duffy asked her.

Silently examining her MEDKIT display, she paused for a moment before shaking her head. "No. Nothing so far."

"OK, keep at it. They could have survived if their EVA suits weren't damaged before the collapse."

Layton was already at work, digging through the debris himself, using his suit's augmented strength to move the heavier, more dense pieces of debris and his gloved fist to smash through smaller, more brittle pieces.

"Joining you, Buff," Duffy said, and began hand-digging through the field.

It would be a few minutes before Chan had the excavation equipment ready to go, and even with it running, the debris field was large enough to keep a single excavator from finishing the job in time for their scheduled pickup.

Duffy would have requested more volunteers and more equipment, but he was already pushing things as it was by disobeying direct orders to retreat along with the rest of the recon force to the shuttles and the Nemean.

Beyond that, he didn't want to risk any more Marines than he had to. Duffy figured that his small team of four could more easily evade any hostile force they might encounter; a large team would be easier to spot and engage immediately, as had happened with the original recon force.

"All set here, Corporal," called Chan. "I'm turning on the excavator. You guys stay clear over there on your end while this thing is on. Don't want to pulverize your lovely EVAs," she said with a smile.

The main body of an excavator sat on a tracked chassis allowing it to maneuver over most types of terrain. The front of the device looked like a protruding cone with jagged teeth. The excavator was guided by the operator, as it slowly moved forward along its tracks and into the material being extracted. Through a combination of heat, grinding and chemistry, it could chew through most rocky and metallic material, boring out a hole one meter in diameter.

The chassis allowed the boring mechanism to track for three meters before it had to be reversed and backed out of the hole to either allow personnel access into the tunnel or reset so that another section could be cut out.

In this case, since the debris field was around ten meters wide, Chan would bore out the six meters to the right while Duffy and Buff would hand-dig their side of the field, until they got through to the other side or found survivors.

"Corporal, what if the excavator accidently bores through the major or any of our guys unlucky enough to be stuck under this mess?" Layton asked.

"Good question. Laura, are you sure about your readings? Are you one hundred percent certain that there is no one trapped under this stuff?"

"I'm taking continual readings as the excavator does its thing. I've set its forward speed to a foot per minute. At that rate, the excavator scanner should be able to identify life signs before the nozzle gets to within a foot of anyone who might be under there."

"Understood. Michele, how certain are you that your MEDKIT can reliably scan through this stuff?"

"It doesn't appear to be made of any exotic material. Basic reinforced steel, basalt rock and some crystalline material I haven't identified yet. I think the MEDKIT is working fine."

"These walls were playing havoc with our comm during the firefight," Layton said. "What if this place is also affecting the MEDKIT scans?"

Duffy thought about that for a moment. Turning to Laura, he asked, "OK, how many Lifter Sets did you bring?"

The sets attached to an EVA suit, augmenting the wearer's ability to both lift and move large, heavy, bulky objects that would otherwise be impossible for a human to handle on their own.

"Just two," Laura answered.

"Great! Buff, grab one. I'll take the other. Michele, keep your scans peeled and close to Laura's excavator. Augment the excavator scans with your MEDKIT scans. Sync them up and see if they produce the same results. If there's even a hint of a doubt that what that machine is about to touch is organic or made of Marine-issued material, full stop — and we dig out that area by hand. We don't want to pulverize the major. That won't look too good on any of our records."

Just a little levity, Duffy thought, to help calm their nerves. Or rather, it was his nerves he was trying to calm.

Fastening his Lifter Set to his EVA suit, Corporal Duffy joined Layton as they continued to dig out their side of the debris field.

Squad 17, commanded by Sergeant Wessler

System: Virgil's star (VGL 191)

Location: Somewhere inside the Structure

Sergeant Wessler had ordered his squad to reconnoiter the corridor as a precaution against a flanking attack on the Marines making their way into the structure. He and Duffy had been ordered to establish defensive perimeters to protect the main force's advance and, if needed, its retreat, and to maintain comm with the shuttles. But there wasn't much standing in the way of his squad and any attack coming from his side of the ingress point. Sure, he had assigned a fire team to watch the entryway, and the ISAT sensors deployed were not picking up any hostiles in that direction, but his gut told him otherwise.

So over Corporal Duffy's protests, he ordered his force in to look around.

From the outside, the corridor didn't appear to be that deep. The main run looked to be about three hundred meters deep with some adjacent, smaller corridors branching off along the way. That would have taken his squad a few minutes at most to recon and secure.

His watch indicated it was now four hours since they had first entered the corridor's entrance, and they had yet to find a way back out. Somewhere along their scouting mission they had lost sight of the entrance, and their sensors were not very helpful either. They could record the path they were walking along just fine with their SITMAP displays but were unable to position themselves in relation to the rest of the force, the shuttles, the corridor entrance and, for that matter, anywhere else in space.

The good news so far was that they had encountered no hostiles, and their supplies were holding up fine. The bad news was that he could tell the squad was getting edgy as the clock ticked and had still been unable to link up with the main force.

Having been trained to think of the big picture during his tenure as a Marine, he found the big picture nowhere in sight.

"Sergeant," called Rodriguez from Fire Team One, "we think we have something."

A corner of Wessler's heads-up appeared magnified in his visor, and he could see what Rodriguez was seeing.

"That looks like an energy source," said Wessler.

"It looks bigger and hotter than anything I've ever seen in here so far," said Rodriguez. "Should we investigate?"

"Let's keep the fire teams together," said Wessler. "Take point. Fire Teams Two, Three and Four, eyes on Rodriguez. Single file until we get close, then stagger your advance until circumstances tell you otherwise."

Acknowledgements flashed green on Wessler's heads-up display, indicating that each fire-team leader had received the orders and confirmed their intent to execute.

The corridor was dark and only slightly backlit by a pale blue hue that seemed to emanate from the wall material. It wasn't entirely unlike phosphorescence in terms of the effect. While their EVA suits compensated for the low light levels, the darkness still gave Wessler an uneasy feeling.

He had always been afraid of the dark as a child, a fact that made his joining of Alcmene's Marine force all the more amazing, given that space was generally…black.

All four fire teams followed Rodriguez and Wessler in single files, each team spaced two meters apart.

Wessler noted that the surface they'd been walking on had changed from smooth and metallic to rough and rocky, like the desert surface of a terrestrial world.

And while their path had so far been on level ground, they were now entering what appeared to be hilly territory, starting with an incline that continued for twenty meters.

"Full stop," Wessler called into the squad channel. "Teams Three and Four, watch our six. Teams One and Two, forward firing positions."

"What are you thinking, sir?" asked Rodriguez.

"I'm thinking we are now high up on a hill and exposed from both directions — plus whatever may or may not be inside these walls," he said, pointing to the corridor to their left and right. "Switch to your SCOPE and let's see what's down this hill."

Rodriguez activated the SCOPE icon on his display, and another screen dropped over his main viewer. The extra screen overlay magnified things by a factor of fifty at the highest setting. In these low-light conditions, even with the compensation provided by the suit, magnification fell to about a factor of twenty.

Still, that meant anything not well camouflaged within about seventy meters of their position should be visible.

Wessler tapped into Rodriguez's display so they could share the same magnified view. As the leader of the unit, it was essential for Wessler to be able to take in multiple points of view and types of information without tying up his heads-up display functions with the same protocol.

A side corridor came into view about twenty meters to the left of the main corridor they were in. It was positioned in such a way that Rodriguez's SCOPE could see partially inside, maybe a meter deep. The walls there emitted a reddish hue rather than the blue they'd encountered so far. Wessler's thermal sensors also detected elevated heat levels.

Other than that, there was nothing else in sight along the main corridor.

"What do you think?" asked Rodriguez.

"You take Fire Team One. I'll take Two. Let's go investigate that gash in the wall. Teams Three and Four hold position here."

Rodriguez went first, running low and fast for five meters. He then crouched, looked around and waved his team forward. Wessler followed, running five meters past Team One's position on the opposite side of the corridor, then waving Team Two forward.

The two fire teams covered the total distance in a few seconds and were now positioned five meters from the side entryway, crouched low with weapons drawn.

"How's our six looking?" he called to teams Three and Four.

Green lights appeared in his heads-up display, indicating all clear.

"OK, get ready. I'll take point. Let's move in. Slowly," said Wessler.

Wessler led the two fire teams into the mouth of the side corridor, Rodriguez following closely behind him and the rest of the two fire teams bringing up the rear.

They could immediately feel the external temperature of their EVAs rising and their visors compensating for the new light, but it was nothing the suits couldn't handle.

Wessler's feet began to drag, but his suit indicated it was compensating for any local variations in gravity by adjusting to Earth-normal.

"Rodriguez, how do you feel?"

"Heavy, sir."

"Me too."

Still they moved forward, the corridor twisting and turning at sharp angles and the space getting more and more claustrophobic as they made their way in deeper.

A sudden turn to the right brought the fire teams to a tunnel crossing.

"We're not following this crossing," Wessler said into the general channel. "Let's just see how far we can explore this branch we're on now and get back to the main corridor."

Wessler knew they were entering dangerous territory. Standard military doctrine called for placing a guard at every intersection, every ambush position and every vital line of retreat. They could not afford getting cut off from the rest of the squad, especially as they were already cut off from the main Marine force he hoped was still somewhere in the Structure.

Just as the last fire team crossed the intersection, the ground began to rumble.

Wessler didn't know what was happening, but he took this as a cue that it was time to get out — now!

"Fall back!" shouted Wessler into the squad channel. "Fall back now! Back to the hill!"

Teams Three and Four where closest to the intersection and were the first to cross it. To their left and right, the Marines could see the ground bubbling up with what appeared to be miniature tanks flopping through the holes in the ground and firing on the Marines' positions. The red-hued walls made the tanks look all the more murderous in their attack.

The fire teams were now separated by the corridor filling with mini tanks.

Wessler and Rodriguez were with teams One and Two on the far side of the intersection, while teams Three and Four held the side nearest the exit and the hill, where the rest of the squad had been told to wait.

All four teams opened fire on the mini tanks, while the tanks returned fire with pinpoints of hot, visible light.

Lasers.

That is a blessing, Wessler thought. Had they been human tanks, they'd be firing explosives, which would have blown them to bits in the tight quarters of the corridor.

The Marines' return rifle fire was having very little effect. Individual blasts would seem to slow or stun the tanks but weren't doing enough damage.

Wessler had an idea.

"Rodriguez! Have Team One slave their weapons to yours. Tomly, have Team Three slave theirs to your weapon. Team Two, you will slave your rifles to mine. Team Four, slave your weapons to Young's"

Wessler knew his squad's strengths and weaknesses well. Rodriguez, Tomly and Young were the best marksmen in the squad, while he was almost as good as Young.

Slaving a fire team's weapon to another Marine's weapon meant that all could be aimed and fired in unison. They'd all be hitting the exact same spot at the exact same time, packing a much more powerful punch.

Rodriguez took aim first, waiting the two seconds for all his team's weapons to sync together. Steadying his sights on one of the mini tanks ten meters down the left corridor, he pulled the trigger and fired.

Molten metal splattered from the mini tank's armored flank, flying onto the corridor walls and stopping it dead in its tracks.

"It's working, sir!" said Rodriguez.

Slaving the fire team's weapons together was having the intended affect. Each beam that hit the minis had four times the power of a single rifle. But it was slow going, with the squad being able to engage just four targets at a time, while the minis emerged from the ground at a rate of ten per second.

"Change of plan!" shouted Wessler into the squad comm. "Fire Teams Three and Four, unslave your weapons and fire at the nearest tank access points to your position. Maybe we can shut them in. Teams One and Two, keep firing on the nearest tanks."

Both fire teams unloaded their magazines at the nearest access points, with promising results.

The rocky ground cover around each access point melted and bubbled over, pouring into the interior of the access holes and burning into the mini tanks as they tried to emerge.

A number of the small tanks did manage to climb out of their holes but were soon slowed as the molten rock began to cool on their surfaces and in the nooks and crannies of their tracked undercarriages.

After several minutes of continuous fire from all teams, new mini tanks stopped emerging from the ground and the remaining units were dispatched by the slaved weapons of Fire Teams One and Two.

"Good job, people!" Wessler said. "Now let's get back to the hill and link up with the rest of the squad."

Wessler motioned for Rodriguez to lead the teams out and back into the main corridor.

Rodriguez looked at Wessler, who was now standing about a foot from one of the red, glowing walls.
"I'll be right behind you. Signal me once the team is in the main corridor."

"Yes sir," replied Rodriguez and jogged back to the head of the retreating force.

Wessler pressed a button on his left wrist, which opened a small compartment in the arm of his EVA suit. He pulled out a long, slender probe and pressed the tip against the wall. Holding it there with his left hand, he keyed in some commands with his right hand on the pad housed along with the probe.

His heads-up display lit with information regarding the red, backlit wall.

According to his instruments, the wall was a basalt-like rocky compound, with an apparent melting temperature of one thousand degrees Celsius, which meant that to melt one kilogram of the material, he'd need to pump it with about nine hundred kilo joules of energy.

Standard Marine laser rifles fired rounds that yielded approximately three hundred kilo joules of energy per one-second bursts. In theory, the squad could melt the walls to prevent further mini tanks from emerging into the corridor, but that would be impractical and too difficult to pull off. It would be hard to ensure that all or even most of the melted material pooled properly to form a significant barrier for the tanks.

Wessler signaled to Rodriguez using his heads-up. "Teams all clear?"

A few seconds went by before Rodriguez replied, "Just through, sir. We've just emerged into the main corridor. Have visual and radio contact with the rest of the squad. Do you need assistance, sir?"

"No. Move the squad back to our hill position. I'm going to make it hard for any more of those mini tanks to follow us once they figure out how to open their fox holes again."

"Understood, sir. Teams One through Four heading back to the hill."

"Good," said Wessler, and closed the channel.

Reaching an arm behind him and pressing a knuckle into a curve on the lower back of his EVA opened a compartment positioned midway up the spine of the suit. From there, he pulled out two smooth, black, six-inch-diameter disks.

The blast discs were designed to pack a variable explosive yield, up to about two thousand five hundred kilo joules, or the equivalent of ten standard issue infantry grenades. Two blast discs would yield twice that output and the blast effects would be magnified in the close confines of the red, glowing corridors.

That was the main reason they hadn't tried using explosives during their battle with the mini tanks.

He set one blast disc at the base of each corridor wall — one on the left and one on the right.

By his calculations, the blast would completely collapse this portion of the tunnel intersection and extend for several meters in all directions. Assuming the mini tanks could only make egress from where they first met them — and Wessler admitted to himself that was a dangerous gamble to make — the collapse would prevent the minis from emerging from this location and attacking them again.

He set the timers to sixty seconds and ran back the way they had come.

When he emerged into the main, blue-lit corridor, he flashed a "DOWN!" command to the squads waiting at the peak of the hill.

As ordered, their heads went down for cover, and as his clock ran down to fifty-eight seconds, he dove towards the ground, executing a flip in the air and landing on his back. From there, he positioned his feet flat on the ground with his shins perpendicular to the floor, using the EVA's thick, hardened boots as shielding against the blast that would be going off … NOW!

A shockwave rumbled out of the red corridor, showering the immediate area just outside with small boulders, shards and dust of red, glowing material.

A metal shard, possibly used to reinforce the structure internally, lodged itself two inches into Wessler's left boot shin. Taught to every Alcmene Marine recruit, use of the shield-in-place technique had saved Wessler's EVA suit vitals from a potentially damaging blow.

With the problem of the mini tanks put on ice (at least temporarily), the squad was now ready to resume their march through this Structure, find their way back to their colleagues and, Wessler hoped, get out of what was increasingly starting to feel like a prison.

Marine Private Alexander Lotte

System: Virgil's star (VGL 191)

Location: A cubed chamber somewhere inside the Structure

Marine Private Alexander Lotte felt a deep cold penetrating his bones. He was floating somewhere, alone, feeling not exactly lost but having no idea where he was. Drifting as he was in a floating sea of cold tranquility, he forced his mind to focus. Having nothing external to focus on, he remembered his yoga training, and focused on his breathing.

Minutes — no, hours — or maybe days passed for Alex as he drifted along in that floating dream state, his breath the only reminder that there was a world outside this place.

He dreamed so many dreams that he could hardly remember what it was like *not* to dream. And finally, after dreaming one monstrously incomprehensible dream, his eyes slowly fluttered open, protesting at the need to adjust to the faint blue light of his surroundings.

He was now firmly in the physical world. He was lying on his back, on a hard, cool surface. He looked down towards his feet and saw that he was completely naked. His EVA suit was nowhere in sight and his coveralls were gone, as were his rifle and other equipment.

Sitting up, he felt a deep ache in his back. He looked around and realized he was in some type of chamber. It was a clean cube, judging it to be perhaps thirty meters on each side. Each wall of the cube was equally lit by a soft blue even light, not unlike the walls he'd last seen when he, Major Lewis and Private Martinez were retreating back towards the shuttles.

That felt like a long time ago. Even years ago, although he doubted it had been that long. The last thing he remembered was running towards Martinez while Martinez laid down cover fire, and then feeling a rush of heat and a shock wave that threw him violently into the air. He recalled a horrible crash and a searing pain in his back, and then things went to black.

Alex shook his head. Whatever had happened after that must have been recent, he thought, given that his fingernails hadn't grown since he'd last looked at them, and his hair was still cut short, military-crew style. He recalled very clearly having shaved about an hour before their final mission briefing, which was three hours before he and his squad boarded Falcon One to explore the Structure.

Judging by the roughness of his face, whatever had happened to him must have happened just a few hours ago.

Alex got up on his feet and slowly walked around the perimeter of the chamber, counting his steps. Sure enough, the space was indeed thirty meters on a side. Looking up toward the ceiling, he estimated the same distance in that direction.

"OK," Alex thought. "What else do I know?"

He made a mental list.

Someone took my EVA suit and all my equipment. I'm literally naked.

There are no friendlies here. And no hostiles here either. I'm alone.

The environment here is suitable for humans. But I'm cold.

"Not a good situation to be in," he mumbled to himself.

He knew, however, that *someone* must have brought him here. And whoever *that* was knew enough about humans to provide Alex with a breathable atmosphere. That meant that his captors wanted something from him, which meant they'd need him alive, for a time at least.

So there was hope.

Having nothing else to do, he decided to run through some yoga asanas to help warm up and focus his mind.

He began with a series of ten sun salutations. After the tenth, he got into downward dog position and rocked back and forth on his heels. That gave him a good stretch and he was now feeling warmer and more limber. The ache in his back was still there but not as bothersome, for which he was grateful.

Steadying his downward dog position, he went into a plank and lifted into an upward facing dog.

Feels good, Alex thought as his muscles warmed, and his body stretched in a satisfying way.

After a few rounds of a down dog to plank to up dog sequence, Alex stood up, reached his arms overhead and yawned.

He was refreshed and more alert now. Stronger and more confident. And while he might be vulnerable, he realized that he didn't feel any fear. Despite being alone, naked and in what he knew to be a very dangerous situation, for some reason he could not fathom he felt no fear.

Almost on cue with his thoughts, a panel in the far wall from where Alex was facing slid up about six inches. Nothing happened immediately, and Alex thought it might be a way out. However, that idea was dashed as a six-inch cylindrical object crawled out from the panel, the door slamming shut after it cleared the panel's threshold.

Whatever the cylinder was, it appeared to be walking on dozens of thin spindly legs that were about three inches long. Though it was silvery and appeared metallic, there was a quality to its shape and movement that made Alex immediately think of a centipede.

The cylinder-centipede began moving towards Alex at a slow but steady pace. Alex looked around the chamber but there was literally nothing he could use as a tool or weapon. Unwilling to let it get near him, he began walking backwards in a direct line away from the centipede, figuring it would follow him in a straight line whatever direction he went. That way, Alex could keep backing away from it while also keeping enough maneuvering space to his left or right as needed, to keep it at distance. As if it sensed his strategy, the centipede began moving faster, quickly closing the distance to about five meters. At this close range, Alex saw that the cylinder was not one continuous piece of material but rather made up of six one-inch-wide sections. Each section bent and rotated with some independence from the others, which presumably allowed the centipede to more easily walk over obstacles or rough terrain.

Alex continued backing away, walking along the perimeter of the chamber, left hand feeling against the wall while he kept his eyes on the centipede.

It closed the distance again, this time to just under a meter. The thing was frightening to look at, and Alex now felt very exposed and vulnerable. Instinctively, he lowered his right hand to cover his groin area, while keeping the left hand on the wall to guide himself as he continued to back away.

When the centipede closed the distance to half a meter, Alex decided that he'd treat this like any other bug.

He took a deep breath, one long look at the centipede and then made a running leap for it. The centipede seemed confused and froze in place for half a second, just enough time for Alex to land on its back, heel first, smashing the spindly legs that supported it and crushing the three middle sections of the cylinder.

"Oorah!" Alex exclaimed. Followed by, "That hurt!" as he lifted his foot and rubbed the striking heel with his hand.

Shaking out his legs, he bent over and picked up the cylinder. Definitely not organic. A robotic centipede? For what? Whatever the reason for its construction, it gave Alex an idea.

He pulled apart the cylinder sections and laid them on the floor. They looked like large metallic rings that would fit snuggly on his hand, had he been wearing his EVA suit.

Next, he reached inside the sections and pulled out rubber-like belts that bound the sections together. Tearing those lengthwise, he made several thin rubbery cords, then threading the cords inside the sections, stringing them together like beads.

Alex then placed the beads across his right knuckles and used the two cord ends to secure the threaded cylinder sections to his hand. After wrapping a few more pieces of cord around his hand, he stopped and held it up to his face.

Not bad.

He now had a rudimentary set of brass knuckles. Alex swung his brass-knuckled hand around, simulating punches and chops, getting a feel for the heft and balance of his new weapon.

It felt good.

I could easily knock someone out with one punch wearing these knuckles, he thought to himself.

With a weapon now in hand, he felt less vulnerable.

Having nothing else to do, he sat down, lotus style, and meditated.

Chapter 2

The *Nemean* was a Hercules-class naval reconnaissance and light attack vessel.

Hercules-class vessels were designed primarily for stealth and speed but could also pack a punch. Propulsion consisted of two hyperlight pods, one below the bow and one astern, enabling her to cover one light year in eighteen hours. Sub-light drives were attached off her port and starboard quarters, allowing for in-system travel or travel in regions of space where entry into hyperlight mode was too dangerous.

Her main weapons were mounted on a retractable platform covering a quarter of her belly and consisted of three laser cannons and four missile batteries.

The *Nemean* could also be used to house and transport a full company of Marines for covert or overt operations. Her hangar bays had enough room for three Falcons, one search-and-rescue space tug and an ultra-stealth reconnaissance flyer.

With her weapons bay deployed, the Nemean came in at one thousand twelve feet in length and at her widest was five hundred thirty-two feet across and four hundred eighty-four feet high — not including hyperlight pods or sub-light drives.

Her crew consisted of one hundred and fifty, including command and support staff. That number jumped to two hundred and thirty with a full Marine company aboard. If necessary, the *Nemean* could in theory accommodate a total of three hundred personnel if a mission called for it.

However, quarters would then be cramped, and it was unlikely that Naval Command would ever order a mission with so many aboard a Hercules-class ship.

Since Hercules-class ships were fast, the extra capacity was added to her design to take advantage of her speed in rescue and evacuation missions.

On the other hand, scuttlebutt had it that naval command staff just liked having roomy accommodations when traveling, and that's why they tended to hitch rides on Hercules-class ships.

Whatever the reason, when not deployed on recon missions, as the *Nemean* was now, the Hercules class was indeed a favorite for diplomatic missions and for travel among top brass and civilian leaders.

In the eyes of Captain Gregory, the *Nemean* represented one of the finest achievements of Alcmene's advances in naval design and engineering. In fact, the design was so successful that it was eventually shared with the rest of the human worlds, something that had, until recently, been rare.

Stationed at Orbital One, Alcmene's primary shipyards, Captain Gregory had watched the *Nemean*'s construction firsthand. The ISAT officers also observing her coming together had remarked how impressed they were with her design and with the skill of Alcmene's engineers.

So when he was told that he would be commanding the *Nemean*, he was overjoyed and filled with pride.

Now, out here, one hundred thirty nine light years from home and maintaining station a safe distance away from the Structure, he still had pride in his ship, but could not help feeling a bit small as data about the size and complexity of the Structure rolled in on his personal command display.

As far as artificial objects went, the Structure was large — four thousand kilometers in diameter — and enormously complex. A mixture of familiar rocks, metals and crystal substances combined to form a much more durable material than the constituent parts suggested. Probing scans tended to bounce off the exterior, with only hints of data about the interior returning when the *Nemean*'s scanners played over openings in its surface.

Captain Gregory had spoken to the ranking ISAT officer aboard the *Nemean*, Field Agent Romanov Collins, about enhancing the ship's sensors to get a deeper look into the Structure, but the agent had been mostly unhelpful in offering a solution.

Without any better options at his disposal, the captain had decided the best way to learn more about the Structure, its purpose and who built it would be by examining it directly. He ordered Major Lewis to take his company of Marines in for a closer look, along with several xeno-specialists and their field equipment. They were given strict orders to abort the mission if they met any hostile forces. Captain Gregory had no idea if the Structure was inhabited, but if it was, he wanted to avoid starting a conflict at all costs.

Preliminary reports from the two Falcons heading for the *Nemean* were spotty — the Structure was emitting energy in the form of neutrinos and other particles that interfered with communications.

Despite that, the captain didn't need any specific details to know by the messages which did make it through that his force had been attacked, and that they had evacuated the Structure under duress.

The shuttles were still thirty minutes out. Captain Gregory called a staff meeting in anticipation of the news the Falcons were bringing them.

Before leaving for the staff conference room, he ordered Lieutenant Paris to keep working on improving the comm signal between the ship and the Falcons. "Report if anything new comes in."

"Aye, Captain," said Paris.

Gregory took the chair at the head of the conference table.

To his right sat ISAT Field Agent Collins. Commander Peters, his executive officer, sat to his left, and along the rest of the table were Lieutenant Alicia Harris, the *Nemean*'s navigation officer, Lieutenant Commander James Marker, ship's weapons officer and Dr. Smith, head of shipboard medical operations.

Looking around the room, Gregory cleared his throat and started.

"As you all know, as of right now, we have been station keeping out here for seventy-two hours." He pressed a button on the pad in front of him and a three-dimensional image of the Structure floated above the conference table. Pointing to it, he said, "And we have not seen any activity from that since then. Our scans couldn't materially penetrate its hull. Agent Collins, can you give us any insight into why that thing out there is able to resist our scans so thoroughly?"

Field Agent Collins cleared his throat as if to speak, but instead looked up at the 3-D Structure, frowned and shrugged. "I can't say anything with any certainty at this time. It appears to be impenetrable to conventional shipboard-scanning technology. When Waverly gets back here, I'm sure we'll have more to go on."

Peters was about to say something, but the captain gave him a discrete hand signal and he sat back in his chair.

"Thank you, Field Agent," said Gregory.

"Given our situation, I want to be ready for anything. Ms. Harris, I want you to plot a pre-programmed RAND course, away from the Structure. Keep it on standby just in case we have to execute it at a moment's notice."

RAND courses were pre-programmed flight paths making heavy use of randomly generated vectors and small, random changes to hull shape to evade detection and attack. They were used in extreme situations when human reflexes and decision making were not fast enough, and when casualties made normal ship-piloting duties impossible.

Gregory hoped it wouldn't come to that, but he wanted to be ready.

"Understood, sir," said Harris.

The captain gave her a nod and then looked at his tactical officer, James Marker.

"Mr. Marker. Status of our weapons systems?"

"Nominal, sir. Power cells are operating at ninety-two percent efficiency, so our cannons should have no difficulty cycling through three hundred volleys before needing a recharge. The power losses are within spec but being investigated."

"We need cannon efficiency at ninety-seven percent minimum," said the XO. "We are in a potentially hostile situation here, and we may need all the firepower we can muster."

"Understood sir," replied Marker.

"Missiles?" asked the captain.

"We have a full complement of AKE-5 missiles and the atomic warheads to load them with if needed."

"Good," said Gregory. "Let's split them in half. Pre-load forty with atomics and keep the other forty in KE mode."

Military vessels used AKE-5 missiles to perform double duty. When loaded with atomic warheads, they could be used as tactical nuclear missiles, typically against large, heavily armored targets, like capital ships at mid-range.

In KE mode, the atomic warheads could be swapped out and replaced with high-density-mass (HDM) rounds and fired using an electromagnetic rail system capable of accelerating them to over two million kilometers per hour. KEs were best used against large, static or slow-moving targets, often solid space debris or other large mass, large surface area targets at significant range, as onboard engines continued to provide thrust until impact.

"KE mode?" asked Peters. "We'll would need to initiate bombardment from well out system for those to be effective."

"Exactly, Commander. I want us to be ready to fire from standoff distance or at range, depending upon what the situation calls for. However, I'm hoping we won't need to use any of our weapons. We are here are here to gather facts and possibly make contact with sentient beings. I'd rather we make history than start a war."

Gregory turned his attention to Dr. Smith. "Doctor, what's the status of your sick bay?"

"Fully functional. The medical team is ready to receive casualties from those two Falcons heading our way," he said, pointing to the visual schematic on the screen tracking the shuttles' flight back to the *Nemean.*

"Good. Have your teams meet the shuttles in the hangar bay in five minutes."

Glancing at his watch, Gregory said, "They'll be here in ten, and I want those Marines looked after and taken care of to the best of this ship's ability. Understood?"

Dr. Smith nodded in agreement. "Understood, Captain."

"That will be all. Dismissed."

As everyone got up to leave, the captain motioned for Field Agent Collins to hang back. The captain didn't waste any time getting to his point.

"Mr. Collins, to be blunt my impression is that you are holding back on us. I want to trust you. I really do. But there are times, especially like during this briefing session, when I have my doubts. I know you have your loyalties to ISAT, that is understood. That's the way it's been for a long time. ISAT is a sovereign entity unto itself. We all know that. But ISAT needs each and every one of the worlds in the Union. And I'll remind you, while Alcmene isn't Earth, it isn't a backwater power either."

"I have nothing but respect for Alcmene, its people, its navy and of course you, Captain. Like every other ISAT officer attached to your naval ships, I am here at your discretion, to serve the needs of your ship and the mission. However, I am also charged with looking after the interests of ISAT. I agree that sometimes this is a delicate balancing act to perform."

The captain studied Collins silently for a moment before replying. "My point here, Mr. Collins, is this: I need your full cooperation and I need transparency. I want direct answers to my questions."

Field Agent Collins took a long look at Captain Gregory before answering. Clearing his throat, he said, "You'll have my full cooperation at all times, within the limits of my mandate. That goes for transparency as well."

Glancing at his watch, the captain stood. "Let's hope so, Mr. Collins. I now have two shuttles to greet." And with that the captain left the conference room and headed for the bridge.

Collins remained seated, leaned back and closed his eyes.

He would have to talk with Waverly first, before any of the captain's officers got to him.

Falcons return to the *Nemean*

System: Virgil's star (VGL 191)

Location: Aboard the Alcmene naval vessel Nemean

Commander Peters and a dozen navy personnel, along with Dr. Smith and his medical team, awaited the docking of the two Marine transport shuttles.

Falcon One came in first, landing softly onto the hangar bay's pad, automatic docking clamps engaging to secure the craft.

All Marine shuttles had one large door in the rear of the ship that allowed for the rapid deployment, or loading, of people and cargo. It also had two doors, one port and one starboard, typically reserved for pilots or officers, or for a small number of people requiring exit and entry.

Presently, Lance Corporal Eugene Felix stepped out of the starboard side door, where he was greeted by Commander Peters and his staff. Peters noted that Felix's EVA suit had been badly damaged, with dents and charred burn marks across the legs, chest and shoulders.

"Permission to come aboard, sir," said Felix, saluting the commander.

"Permission granted," replied Peters. "Where is Major Lewis?"

"MIA, sir, along with Wessler's squad and Private Martinez."

"What's the status of MC1?"

MC1 stood for Marine Company One, the official military designation of the Marine force aboard the *Nemean*.

"Still operational sir. Although depleted in strength. Presently, Falcon One has twenty-one injured requiring immediate medical attention. Falcon Two has seventeen injured requiring medical care. Many of those not injured will require repairs to their EVA suits, and the company will require a resupply of munitions and equipment."

"Understood. The master of the barracks will give you everything you need. See her immediately with your company's needs. After that, have the doctor check you out and then you are to report to debriefing at 16:00 sharp."

"Thank you, sir," said Felix. "Permission to debark the Falcons?"

"Granted."

Felix gave a hand signal to the Marine piloting Falcon One, and a moment later the main rear door of the craft slid open. Marines able to walk helped carry out their injured colleagues, while others limped off the shuttle on their own. The medical crew quickly sorted the exiting Marines into groups, with those requiring the most urgent care immediately whisked away to sick bay. Some were treated on the spot, while others were put in queue for further evaluation.

Meanwhile, the hanger crew began evaluating the shuttle for damage and taking inventory of the ship's power and other vitals.

Peter's naval personnel escorted non-injured Marines to various parts of the ship, some to the ship's workshop for assistance with EVA suit removal or repair, and others for interviews and personal debriefs.

--

Falcon Two held station half a kilometer from the *Nemean*'s docking facilities.

Sitting up front just behind the pilot's nest gave Waverly a good view of the shuttle's surroundings. From this distance, the *Nemean* looked sleek, powerful and athletic. It was clear that the ship had been designed to perform, as well as impress.

He wondered what the aliens aboard the Structure thought of the *Nemean* and her crew.

The Structure's defenders had just routed a full Marine company, equipped with state-of-the-art combat armor, weapons and sensor systems. And they'd made it look easy. Who knew what they could do to the *Nemean* if they launched a spaceborne attack? Who knew what kind of spacecraft the Structure's defenders could field if they wanted to?

That thought made Waverly nervous. Until today, he had always been confident in his capabilities as an ISAT combat officer. Now, he wasn't so sure of himself. He found himself shivering at the thought of another engagement with those things on the Structure and hoped no one noticed.

As activity around Falcon One wound down, it was Falcon Two's turn to land and begin the process all over again, with medical teams assigned to evaluate injured Marines for appropriate prioritization and treatment, while other personnel were waiting to look after the mechanical needs of the Falcon and the Marines' equipment.

Luckily, as Waverly felt his stomach getting ready to convulse the morning's breakfast all over the ship's deck, the Falcon's pilot engaged the drive system, lurching Waverly backwards, which somehow quieted his stomach.

With finesse, the pilot eased the Falcon towards the waiting doors of the *Nemean*'s landing bay and quietly landed the ship on the hangar deck.

There was a clanging sound as the Falcon was secured to the deck and the main cargo-bay door slid open. Out poured the Marines into the waiting arms of the ship's medical and technical personnel. Marines with injuries were given top priority. Those with EVA mechanical issues were given second birth, while everyone else — the non-injured and those with equipment issues — were out last.

Waverly was among the non-injured and his gear was intact, and so he was one of the last to get off the Falcon. The deck was filled with scores of people, a mixture of Marines and medical personnel, hangar crew, mechanics, officers, and others.

As he stepped off the Falcon, Waverly's personal comm buzzed in his ear. It was Field Agent Collins.

"Waverly. Meet me in docking bay lounge east."

Waverly buzzed back with an acknowledgement signal and headed off towards the lounge.

Docking bay lounge east was a spacious, open area near the docking bay where crew and visitors could relax in more plush surroundings. There were two such lounges on the ship, the other one imaginatively named mess hall lounge west.

Agent Collins sat in a deep leather chair near a corner of the lounge. In front of him was a low table with a bowl of snacks, two glasses and a bottle of unopened Apfelwein. Seeing Waverly walk into the lounge, Collins waved him over and invited him to a chair opposite his.

Seeing the setup, Waverly winced at the invitation. He still wore his EVA suit and there were injured Marines being wheeled around the ship. This just didn't feel right to him. However, ISAT agents did things their way, and Collins was his superior, so he sat down and nodded.

"You wanted to see me, sir?"

Collins looked around, retrieved a small cube from an inside pocket, kicked the edge of the table in front of him and said, "No one should be able to hear our conversation now."

Waverly gestured towards the cube in Collins' hand. "What's that?"

"It generates a sound-dampening field. Lets us speak privately without anyone overhearing our conversation."

Waverly took an exaggerated look around the lounge. "Sir. There's no one here. Marine Company One just got its ass kicked by some very mean aliens aboard that thing out there. I don't think anyone is thinking about us right now."

"We still have to be careful. ISAT protocols. Waverly, I think you've been spending too much time with your Marine unit. After this mission, I'm going to recommend some desk duty for you. We don't want you to drift too far from our core ISAT principles."

That stung. Waverly reminded himself yet again that Collins was his superior officer and changed the subject. He reached down, poured himself a half glass of the apple cider and took a sip.

"Very good. Are you ready for my debrief, sir?"

Collins smiled. "I want to see all the data you recorded while aboard the Structure. The combat parts of your mission are of no concern to me right now."

Collins handed Waverly a three-inch long slender silver tube. "Here. Download your mission recordings onto this memory tube. I'll call you to discuss later, after I've had a chance to analyze it."

The two ISAT officers sat in silence for a minute, as the cylinder downloaded the data contained in Waverly's EVA suit instruments.

"Did you use any items from your TSAC?"

"Gravity grenades against hostiles. The ESA System and the Sampler. Didn't have time for much else."

"Good. Give me the ESA and Sampler. I'll analyze that data as well. How did the GGs perform against the hostiles?"

"Hard to say, sir. It seemed to slow them down for a few minutes, but then they resumed their attack at the same intensity as before."

Collins nodded. "As you know, ISAT's overarching goal is to protect humanity. From itself, but also from outside forces. Right now…humanity is in the cross hairs of its own worst inclinations, as well as the cross hairs of whoever built that thing out there."

"Sir. I'm not sure I'm following," said Waverly. "I agree the aliens we encountered could do us serious damage. We don't know their full capabilities yet, or their intentions, and I wouldn't be surprised if they have the capacity to destroy this ship. But I don't follow on the other point you made."

Collins leaned forward. "I've already seen enough, Waverly, to know that the captain and his team are putting the entire Union in jeopardy. All of *our* worlds. They are in over their heads. They don't know what they are dealing with. *Yes*, that thing out there can most likely destroy this ship with one shot. However, what I'm concerned about is that the captain, in his ignorance, has the potential to precipitate humanity's destruction."

Waverly had never seen Collins look so intense and focused before. "How could the captain cause humanity's destruction?

The field agent didn't answer, instead pouring himself a cup of the Apfelwein.

"If I may speak freely?" said Waverly.

Collins nodded.

"You are making this sound a bit overly dramatic—"

"It's is all very simple," replied Collins, cutting him short. "Think about the types of actions that the captain is most likely to take. He will either take steps, out here, that could lead to civil war among the Union planets, or he may issue a foolish order that prompts the aliens aboard the ship out there to wipe us out for good. Those are the actions that are in line with Naval Command's thinking — a style of thinking ingrained in Gregory. Unfortunately, they really don't know what they are dealing with. ISAT did try to dissuade them from undertaking this mission. Obviously, that didn't work."

Waverly remained silent.

Collins continued, "Talk to the Marine grunts. Talk to the enlisted personnel. What I want you to do is convince the lower ranks that it's time to leave this place and get everyone back home. Find out who agrees with you and who could help make that happen...if it came to it."

"Mutiny, sir? You're asking me to help start a mutiny?"

"Your job is to take the crew's temperature. Now that the Falcons have returned and they know what happened aboard the Structure, see how they feel. Do they want to stick around here, or would they rather go home to their families? And if it comes to it, if it really comes to it...who among them are willing to help make that happen."

"And you, sir, what will you be doing?"

"I will be doing the same thing as you," Collins answered, "among the command and executive staff. Starting with the captain."

"And if the captain decides to remain here?"

"He would be validating my opinion of him."

Lance Corporal Felix

System: Virgil's star (VGL 191)

Location: Aboard the Alcmene naval vessel Nemean

Lance Corporal Felix removed the final piece of his EVA suit and handed it to the waiting technician. The barracks master had assigned three technicians to see to the corporal's personal needs, while she oversaw the resupply of MC1.

"We are going to look into upgrading the EVAs when we get back to Alcmene. Based on the battle damage we've seen on this mission, the techs have some ideas on how the suits can be improved. I'd appreciate it if you could put the word out to the members of MC1 that their suggestions and gripes on the present version are welcomed."

"Thank you, sir" said Felix. "You guys in the BC are always looking out for us."

"BC" stood for Barracks Command and consisted of the various personnel that supplied and maintained the Marines' gear and equipment. The BC always made sure that the Marines got replacements in a timely manner and received new iterations of equipment as soon as they became available. Barracks Command cut through the red tape put up by other government bureaucracies, making it easier for the Marines to focus on what they did best.

"Well, I'm not exactly a *guy* corporal," said Lauren Vella, the *Nemean*'s barracks master. "Or is this uniform as unflattering as I've been told?"

They laughed at that.

"I had Sub-Lieutenant Dean retrieve a fresh uniform for you. I don't think you want to present yourself to the captain looking like that."

"Good thinking." Felix removed the coveralls that all Marines wore under their EVA suits and put on the uniform.

He saluted and turned to go, softly singing the lyrics to an old Marine marching song *"BC girls go all the way, they give you want you need to stay, strong in the field and throughout the day, give me a BC girl right away!"*

"Lance Corporal Felix!" Vella shouted in the sternest voice she could muster.

Felix turned, genuinely worried that he had taken their flirtation a bit too far with that old song.

"Sir?" he said, saluting.

Vella, stone faced, stared at him for several seconds before breaking into a smile and saying, "Nice vocals, Corporal. You should try out for the *Nemean*'s acapella group. They've been a big hit with the BC girls, you know. You're welcome for the uniform."

Felix smiled and dropped his salute. "Thank you, sir! You've been very kind. Please also give my regards to the sub-lieutenant. I'll give the singing group a try sometime."

Glancing at his watch, he added, "It's almost 15:00, and I've got a meeting with the captain. Catch you at the mess hall lounge tonight?"

"Maybe, Corporal. Good luck with the meeting."

Felix gave Vella an exaggerated bow before waving goodbye. She smiled and blew him a kiss.

Catching her kiss in the air with his right hand, he placed it on his heart and turned to go. He had ten minutes to make it to the captain's meeting room, and he still had to shave.

The captain's meeting room

It had taken Lance Corporal Felix three minutes to sprint from the ship's supply and maintenance area to his quarters. It took him another minute to shave, thirty seconds to wash his face and thirty more seconds to dry his face and crisp up his uniform. It had taken him another minute to change into a clean pair of shoes.

That left him five minutes, which he used to walk to the captain's meeting room. He got there in three and waited outside the door for two minutes before knocking.

"Enter."

Felix entered the meeting room, saw the captain sitting at the head of the table and saluted.

"At ease, Lance Corporal. Have a seat."

Commander Peters sat to the left of the Captain, and the *Nemean*'s tactical officer, James Marker, sat to his right, while Navigator Alicia Harris was to the right of Marker.

"Thank you, sir." Felix looked around the table at each of the four officers. "Before we begin, I'd like to bring everyone's attention to the countdown clock. Duffy and his team expect extract from the Structure in a little less than two hours."

Corporal Duffy's decision to go back and look for survivors had been immediately reported to the *Nemean*'s command staff upon Felix's return to the ship, and the crew had set up a visual clock to count down the minutes remaining before they'd have to break station keeping and start heading in towards the Structure to retrieve the team.

The clock was presently showing 112 minutes.

Falcons were equipped with two drive systems. Ion drives were used for atmospheric flight, docking maneuvers, ship-to-ship combat, troop deployments and other routine activities requiring relatively short trips through normal space. At maximum speed, a Falcon could cover one AU in about six days using its ion drive.

However, Falcons didn't have enough power to operate a traditional hyperlight drive. Instead, for longer journeys requiring speed they used hybrid jump-propulsion drives, enabling Falcons to cover a distance of one AU in about fourteen hours. Hybrid drives used micro jumps to traverse part of the distance in jump space and the rest in normal space. Due to the disorienting effects humans experienced coming out of jump space, jumps were reserved for the first leg of a trip, giving the passengers and crew sufficient time to recover. The maximum range of a Falcon's hybrid drive was three AU. More than that and the effects of the jumps would likely kill everyone aboard as well as burn out the engines.

The *Nemean*, on the other hand, was equipped with two full capacity hyperlight pods, enabling the ship to traverse through normal space while wrapped in a protective bubble of space time. Even with the hyperlight pods engaged, passengers aboard the *Nemean* experienced the same sensation as if the ship were motionless in normal space, with none of the ill effects of the hybrid drives.

At full speed and relying only on the hyperlight pods, the *Nemean* could cover one light year in eighteen hours. The only limitation hyperlight pods faced was that they could not be safely used near masses generating a gravitational field equivalent to the force exerted by a quarter solar mass half an astronomical unit away from the pods.

The primary star in this system was a super massive red giant known as Virgil's star, or VGL 191, and had a radius equivalent to thirteen hundred solar radii. At the *Nemean*'s current distance from the star, the force of gravity exerted on the ship was well above the threshold for hyperlight pod usage.

Moving the ship away from the star would enable her to use the pods, but that would just increase the distance to the Structure. Unless the Structure moved out system, there was no way of using the hyperlight pods to extract Duffy's team.

That left the sub-light drives. They allowed the ship to operate in normal space and could accelerate the ship to ten percent the speed of light. Using the sub-lights, the *Nemean* could rendezvous with Duffy's team in about eighty-three minutes.

The captain pressed a button on the console, opening a channel to the bridge. Lieutenant Bailey, the *Nemean*'s officer of the deck, answered the call. "Yes, Captain?"

"Lieutenant Bailey, set course for the Structure. Use preprogramed RAND course Alpha Seven One. Set speed zero point zero nine light."

"Understood, sir. Initiating now."

The captain closed the channel.

Looking around the room, he said, "That should get us there about twenty minutes early, enough time to ferry them back via Falcon and minimize our time near the Structure."

"Now, Corporal, tell us what happened. Start from the beginning."

The Lance Corporal nodded and clearing his throat.

"About one hundred kilometers out from the Structure, we were able to visually confirm that it did, indeed, have an open landing bay at the coordinates supplied by the bridge sensor team and later validated by Field Agent Collins.

"Were the bay doors open?" asked the captain. "Or did you have to force your way inside?"

"Open sir. The bay was large enough for both Falcons to fly in simultaneously, but Major Lewis thought that was too risky. So we sent in Falcon One first, while Falcon Two remained outside the bay doors. Once the first Falcon landed safely, Major Lewis set up a defensive perimeter around the landing area and signaled for the second Falcon to come in."

The captain nodded approvingly.

"Marines from the second Falcon were used to bolster the defensive line. Both pilot crews were ordered to remain in the Falcons, while the rest of the force was formed into squads and led by their non-coms towards the interior of the Structure."

"Did you notice anything unusual in the landing bay?" asked Peters.

"Not really. Everything was quiet. There were no signs of hostiles or any living thing on the Structure. If it wasn't for the fact that it was artificial, it felt just like boot camp, where you and your squad must spend a week living on an asteroid with nothing but your EVA suit and the gear on your back.

"We found strange markings on some of the interior walls, large internal structures that didn't have any obvious use to us, and everything seemed to be illuminated by a pale blue light. Not light like we're used to, but a light that seemed to emanate from the objects and walls themselves."

"Like phosphorescence?" asked Ms. Harris.

Felix nodded. "Yes, something like that."

"After about five hundred meters, we came to an opening. The main path we had been on split into three, with corridors and passageways branching off to the left and right.

"The major ordered several squads to hold that position, and to guard against any attacks from our left and right flanks. The main force continued down the original path.

"We walked for another five hundred meters. It wasn't a straight path. There were straight sections but there were also long, winding sections. In some places, things became very narrow, where we had to walk single file, and in other places we could walk shoulder to shoulder, maybe five across.

"From time to time we'd come into large openings, chambers where the ceiling was fifty meters high.

"If you look at the reports I've already filed and the reports of the others, you'll see that we ran into quite a few small objects. I'm sure some of the Marines picked them up and kept them as souvenirs."

"We'll want those objects examined by the science teams," said Peters. He used the console in front of him to issue orders to all non-coms that all objects found and retrieved by their units were to be turned in to the *Nemean*'s science office immediately.

"Did *you* bring back any souvenirs, Corporal?" asked the captain.

"No sir. Honestly, I just wanted to get the hell out of there."

The captain nodded.

"Anyway, we found a chamber that glowed green instead of blue. Besides the color, there was a different feel to the place. It was a huge space, with multiple levels around the central platform area, running up and down the Structure."

"A transport hub?" asked Marker. "Where you can change floors?"

Felix shrugged. "We didn't get a chance to find out. Our tactical motion sensors picked up something and the major ordered the squads to take up defensive positions behind anything we could find. We had the area well covered. We could have shot at anything from multiple angles.

"We stayed in that defensive posture for a few minutes. Keeping still and only communicating using our point-to-point comm links. The number of objects on the motion sensors kept increasing and then the shooting started."

"Who shot at you?" asked Marker.

Felix pressed a button on the console in front of him. A grainy image appeared, showing a tall, angular figure leaping down from a ledge while emitting a powerful green laser from a weapon.

Felix pointed to the image.

"That's what shot at us. By the time Major Lewis issued the order to retreat, my motion sensor counted four hundred hostiles within range. I am sure there were many more heading our way."

Looking toward his commanding officers, he added, "We fought, sirs. We fought hard. We took a lot of casualties, but we caused them a lot of damage too. The thing is, those things were strong. I mean physically. I tackled one that was bearing on Major Lewis. It backhanded me and I skidded to a halt five meters away. It left that big dent on my EVA's left shoulder."

"We've reviewed the footage from the unit, sir" said Lieutenant Marker. "Those things are deadly accurate shots too. Incredibly precise."

"Machines."

"Sir?" asked Marker.

"Those are machines, Lieutenant. AI soldiers. Automated defenders. Whatever you want to call them. They're machines."

"What happened after that, Corporal?" asked Peters. "Did you see what happened to the major?"

"Bad as it was, we all made it back to the second defensive line. We found Duffy's squad still holding position but Wessler's team was gone. There was shooting all around us. Total chaos.

"The last I saw, the major took up positions against the hostiles, along with Agent Waverly and two Marines. Many of us volunteered to stay with him, but he ordered us to keep going. I believe he was trying to slow the hostiles down, to give as many of us a chance to get aboard the Falcons as possible.

"A lot of the Marines took a beating, either getting shot or beaten up like I was. I think the major knew that by the time we got to Duffy's line, a lot of us couldn't move that quickly anymore due to our suit damage.

"After that, things became a bit hazy. I got aboard Falcon One and helped a couple of Marines secure themselves to their seats. I went into the pilot's nest and asked if he'd seen the major. The pilot said we had just picked up Waverly, but the major and the two Marines with him were missing.

"Something exploded about twenty meters forward of the landing bay. I saw Corporal Duffy and three other Marines on the comm link speaking to the Falcon pilots, ordering them back to the *Nemean* and asking for a pick-up in three hours.

"Once the Falcons cleared the Structure's landing bay, we jumped. A lot of the guys puked when we re-entered normal space. They looked terrible. The pilots put the Falcons on maximum burn, and we came back here."

"Thank you, Corporal," said the captain. "Prepare an extraction team. Once we get close enough, I want you and your team to take one of the Falcons back into that landing bay and get Duffy and his volunteers out of there. If they haven't found any of our missing crew, you, Duffy and the others are to double time it back to the *Nemean*. Search-and-rescue operations will cease the moment you step aboard that Structure."

"Understood, sir."

Lance Corporal Felix was glad to be done with his debrief. He was tired and needed to rest badly. With fifty minutes to go before he'd have to board the Falcon, he walked to his quarters, opened the door and collapsed onto his bed. Sleeping in his uniform was against regulations, but he didn't have time to care, as he fell asleep the moment his head touched the bed.

On the bridge of the *Nemean*

Collins walked onto the bridge and headed straight for the captain's command console. Saluting, he said, "Captain Gregory, I must have a word with you."

"Agent Collins," said Gregory, "we're on course for the Structure; we'll be arriving in sixty minutes and launching an extraction mission to recover Duffy's team and any other survivors. Is there something urgent you'd like to discuss, or can it wait?"

"That's fine, Captain. I can tell you right here, in front of the rest of the bridge crew, that you are making a terrible mistake by taking this ship in any closer."

The captain looked up from his console, as did several other bridge officers.

"I believe, Captain, that we are playing with something we don't understand, and it's in our best interest to leave this place immediately."

"There are Marines still out there, Collins," replied the captain. "I am not leaving anyone behind. You saw what happened to our expeditionary force."

"Exactly. We all saw. And what do you think they'll do if we attempt to land another shuttle in their hangar bay?"

"I understand the risks. We all do. But I will not leave anyone behind — not if it can be helped. Furthermore, this is an exploratory mission, and there are still many unanswered questions here. I am here to find answers."

"Please, Captain, don't let your pride get in the way!" Collins said. "The reality is you have no idea what you are dealing with here. You are, to be frank, completely in over your head."

"As I already explained," Gregory insisted, "we understand the risks. This is a risky business we're in, but without risk there's no glory, as the saying goes."

Raising his voice so that everyone could hear, Collins said, "Captain, don't be a stubborn fool. I strongly urge you to abort the mission and return home."

The field agent's hands trembled as he struggled to contain his mounting anger. He had read that Captain Gregory could be obstinate, but how could he so *completely* ignore the advice of his senior ISAT officer?

Trying to sound more reasonable, Collins added, "We've learned enough for now. There will be other opportunities to return here. After we've analyzed the information your teams have already obtained, we'll be able to come back better prepared. You really have no idea how dangerous this mission is quickly becoming and for very little in return."

Remaining calm, Gregory said, "Your concerns are noted, Field Agent Collins. I have a broad mandate on how I conduct this mission. I've made my decision. This is no longer up for debate. Now, you can either take your station or leave the bridge."

Collins looked around at the bridge crew, who were all looking at him in disbelief. Nodding, he mumbled to himself and stormed off the bridge.

Commander Peters walked over to the captain's console and in a low whisper said, "That man is dangerous."

Gregory shrugged. "He's certainly no diplomat."

"With respect, sir," said Marker, "Collins made some valid points. We really have no idea what to expect, sir. They may not take kindly to us landing a force there again."

"Agreed," said Gregory. "That's why we are only sending in one Falcon with a small extraction team. That's also why I want you all to be ready for anything. I don't want to go in with guns blazing. Keep the weapons platform ready for deployment and the cannon primed but out of sight."

"Aye sir," said Marker. "I'll be ready."

"Good." Turning to Peters, Gregory ordered, "Check in with the Lance Corporal. Make sure they are ready to launch the Falcon as soon as we are within range."

"Aye sir," replied the commander.

Chapter 3

Questions of a restless mind

System: Virgil's star (VGL 191)

Location: Alexander Lotte, weightless somewhere inside the Structure

Marine Private Lotte felt exhausted. He no longer had a good sense of time nor how long he'd been away from his unit. He dimly remembered fighting alongside Major Lewis and Private Rodriguez. That seemed like ages ago now.

He wasn't sure exactly where he was anymore, but he knew he wasn't in the cube chamber.

A sense of weightlessness told him that he must be floating in space somewhere. But once again, he was not wearing any gear and felt naked, even though he couldn't look down at his body, nor run his hands over it.

While not feeling like a prisoner, he also knew he was not free to go.

And had he been free, *where would he go? Which way was home? What was home's name? Who would he see there? Did they miss him? Did he miss them? Did he have a mate waiting for him? Did he have progeny? What was the rest of his military unit doing? What where they planning? How many of them where there? Was the* Nemean *the only ship? Or where there more like it? Why had he come here? What had he hoped to gain? Was he frightened?*

All these questions flooded his mind at once in a jumble, disorienting him and overwhelming his ability to focus. He couldn't understand why he kept wondering about these things. *I must be going insane,* he thought.

Does that happen often? Losing control of my mind? What about my focus techniques? Can't yoga help me now? If not, why did I study it? Who did I study with? Where is my teacher now? Where is my teacher's home? What else can the teacher teach?

Lotte shook his head. Each question led to another question, piling upon each other in an endless chain. The questions came to him from deep within, hearing his voice in his head, hearing and *feeling* the questions.

Fearing he might be losing his grip on reality, Lotte shouted, "I don't know, damn it! I don't know!"

A moment later there was silence. His mind was a place of stillness, calmness and tranquility. There were no more questions, no more thoughts.

He was in a state of nirvana…a state of perfect peace, of harmony and happiness.

A thought invaded that peace.

The capacity is thus within you.

"What?" Lotte said out loud.

His mind spoke back to him.

The word nirvana relates to religious enlightenment. In the ancient language of Sanskrit, it means to be extinct, to disappear, as it relates to the individual. Suffering and desire all disappear. It takes many years of meditation to reach this state, and few individuals ever do.

Then the questions started again.

What are the origins of Sanskrit? An ancient language from where? Is it the place you call home?

"I'm going insane," Lotte thought again.

Stay for a while. There is no time here. You may go if you wish. You remain here because it is your wish.

Lotte wasn't sure what was going on, but he felt like he was talking to himself, inside his mind, his mind asking and answering its own questions.

He tried to focus his awareness on the only thing he could physically control….his breath.

Lotte inhaled deeply to a count of three, held his breath for a count of three, exhaled for a count of three and held his breath for a count of three.

Sama Vritti Pranayama. Four-part breath.

"Yes," Lotte replied. "Four-part breathing. Now let me breathe!"

His mind began to speak again: *Sama Vritti Pranayama is Sanskrit. The enlightened ones teach their charges to breath in four steps. It makes you aware of the prana flow. This is the four-step cycle, observe: Puraka, inhalation, Antar Kumbhaka, retention of air after inhalation, Rechaka, exhalation, Bahya Kumbhaka retention after exhalation.*

"Shut up!" Lotte shouted. "You annoying pain in the ass! Where am I?"

Pain. Physical suffering or discomfort caused by illness or injury. Physical injuries have been healed. There is no such causative agent. Mental pain, anguish. This is pain too. Your practice is rooted in removing such pain. Continue with your practice and let the pain leave you.

Lotte continued his four-part breath, moving up to a count of four, then five, then six and finally seven.

The last thing Lotte remembered was completing a third round of a four-square breathing cycle, counting to seven and then waking up on the floor of the cube chamber, face up, staring at the ceiling.

In some sense, being here was a relief. At least here he could hear himself think without any intruding voices in his head.

However, his relief was short lived — as the far side door slid open, and a man-shaped being stood at the threshold with a long, rod-like object in its hand.

Alexander quickly got to his feet and looked around. His brass knuckles where nowhere in sight, but he did see a Marine combat baton lying against the near wall. Keeping his eye on his visitor, he walked over to the wall and picked up the baton.

It had good balance and the heft felt right. He'd trained with these before but never really used them in combat, preferring his rifle.

As the man-shaped being walked into the cube room, Lotte crouched low, watching to see if the alien's weapon was a projectile or a blunt-force tool like his baton.

A moment later the alien roared and charged, its muscular arms hefting the rod over its head.

The distance the alien had to cover was about thirty meters, plenty of time for Alexander to angle and move into an advantageous position.

However, the last twenty meters were a blur, as the alien sprinted and covered the distance in less than two seconds, barely enough time for Alexander to roll out of the way, the rod weapon narrowly missing his head.

Alexander repositioned himself to face the alien and could now see how he had covered that distance so fast. The alien's legs were heavily muscled and twice as thick as Alexander's. Most of its power was probably in its lower body, although its arms and torso looked strong too.

Alexander hefted the baton and looked directly at the alien. Whatever it was, it was two feet taller than he, and aside from the rod-weapon and a sash tied around its midsection, it was unclothed. Its skin was grayish white and looked tough and leathery.

Its face was triangular, with a visor-like device positioned at roughly eye level, just above a round fleshy bump that Alexander assumed was a nose. A faint line below the nose looked like a mouth — or a zipper. It was hard to say.

The alien took one quick step forward and swung its weapon through the air, aiming for Alexander's head. Alexander ducked and stepped to his right. The alien's rod clipped his left shoulder, causing Alexander to lose his balance and stumble to the floor.

Again, the alien raised its weapon high and aimed for Alexander's head.

Alexander raise the baton and blocked the blow.

CLANG!

The alien's blow struck with so much force it bent the baton. The bones in Alexander's arm ached, as he used one hand to regain his footing and the other to swing the baton at the alien's legs.

The baton landed on hard flesh with a muted thud, making the alien groan and step away.

Back on his feet, Alexander swung to the left and right, creating a danger zone to keep the alien at a safe distance.

However, that didn't deter the creature, which sprinted forward, knocking Alexander to the ground.

It roared again, the sound echoing off the cube chamber's walls.

Alexander attempted to put space between him and his attacker, but the alien thrust out its hand and grabbed Alexander by the flesh of his collar bones, dragging him to his feet before tossing him against the nearest wall.

Alexander heard something crack and felt as though the skin around his neck was boiling off. He groaned in pain as the alien sprinted again to close the distance, kicking Alexander in the ribs.

Another *CRACK!*

This time more audible than the first.

Alexander was on his knees, doubled over in pain when he heard a hissing sound. Looking up, he saw the alien's zipper mouth wide open, jagged teeth showing, as it hissed and spewed a slimy substance from deep inside its throat.

The view down the alien's throat seemed to clear Alexander's foggy head, because a moment later he found the strength to ram his baton into the alien's mouth, crashing it into the roof and causing a geyser of purple blood to spew from the hole left behind.

The alien howled in pain as it gurgled on its blood, convulsing and stumbling away.

Taking the initiative, Alexander charged his assailant, striking the alien across the face with the blood-covered end of his baton.

The alien again swung wildly with its rod-weapon, clipping Alexander on the neck, the force momentary interrupting the blood supply to the Marine's brain and sending him to his knees.

The alien staggered forward, intent on finishing his opponent, but was unable to steady himself as purple blood kept flowing from its mouth.

A few plodding steps more and the alien was again staring down at Alexander, who was just regaining his bearings after suffering a momentary blackout.

SMACK!

The alien swung an open hand across Alexander's face, causing him to fall again, his side now exposed. Rod-weapon still in hand, it attempted to roar before blood choked its airway and it began to lose balance.

Alexander rolled to his knees and took hold of the rod with two hands, yanking it from the alien's grip.

The alien continued to heave and gasp for air, as Alexander swung the rod wide with two hands and brought it crashing down on the left side of the alien's head.

Blood still pouring from its mouth but no longer struggling to breathe, the alien collapsed in a heap.

It was finished.

Alexander was relieved but also felt mounting remorse.

Throwing the rod across the chamber, he sat down on the floor holding his midsection before falling onto his back and drifting off into unconsciousness.

ISAT Junior Field Agent Malcom Waverly

System: Virgil's star (VGL 191)

Location: Aboard the Alcmene naval vessel Nemean

Waverly didn't like the assignment Collins had given him. Well…calling it a formal assignment wasn't exactly right. It wasn't a formal order but an unofficial directive he really couldn't refuse. ISAT agents had considerable leeway in terms of what they could order their subordinates to do, especially if it even vaguely served to uphold ISAT's three golden rules.

Rule number one: ISAT shall preserve and protect all technological knowledge to the betterment of all Humanity.

Rule number two: ISAT shall carefully control access to new technologies until such time as the Council of Master Engineers rules that it can be freely shared among all Human worlds.

Rule number three: ISAT agents posted to Union world ships, facilities and other military and government organizations shall perform all duties assigned by the host world representatives, so long as they do not violate ISAT rules one and two.

So in theory, Collins could always cite rules one and two for issuing his orders, and he'd be technically right.

Even so, Waverly just didn't like the idea of trying to undermine the captain or causing division among the crew…and especially among the Marines. He'd trained with them, served with them and fought alongside them. In fact, Major Lewis, as well as Privates Lotte and Martinez had sacrificed themselves so that he could get back to the ship.

How could he do anything to sew division among such people?

But how could he refuse a clear and technically lawful order from a direct ISAT superior?

Forced into doing something he didn't want to do for someone he didn't want to do it for, he decided to take the middle ground.

He'd casually ask around to see how the enlisted felt with regards to the progress of this mission and find out if they really wanted to go home.

Rationalizing, he concluded that this would be useful information to have. He could even share it with the captain if any significant currents of opinion turned up that could impact the mission.

Waverly glanced at his watch, noting that he had to give Agent Collins a status report in about five hours.

That gave him enough time to go visit the ship's training center. Training with MC1 was something he enjoyed, as it kept his combat skills sharp and gave him a chance to fraternize with the friends he had made aboard this ship. What was more, it would also give him a chance to see how the enlisted really felt about things.

--

The training center was adjacent to the Marine barracks. Officially it came under the "jurisdiction" of Barracks Command, which meant that it was always well maintained and stocked with the latest training equipment.

The facility and training grounds weren't huge — by volume they represented about two percent of the *Nemean*'s internal space. However, given that much of the ship's interior was taken up by vital equipment like life support, engines, weapons systems, wiring and circuitry, conduits and ducting, not to mention the bridge, engine room and living space for the ship's crew, that percentage of the ship's interior represented a significant commitment of valuable real estate and an example of how much Alcmene's Naval Command valued its troops.

In terms of distances, the grounds were perfect for running, sprinting and field games like soccer, football and even baseball, which the Marines and crew sometimes enjoyed. Even more popular were mock battles between units and squads, where the terrain and atmosphere could be adjusted to simulate different types of environments and allow for training in and out of EVA suits.

Presently, Waverly took up one of the private running lanes along the perimeter of the facility's open area, and began to slowly jog, warming up his muscles before adopting a faster pace.

Running felt good. It was how Waverly dealt with stress; it also gave him a sense of freedom and hope. Not that he wasn't satisfied with how his life was going right now, but, at his core, Waverly was a dreamer, and he always looked forward to better days.

That was one reason he really didn't like working with Field Agent Collins. Collins was a pessimist and a cynic, and always suspicious of others. Not entirely bad traits to have in Collins' line of work, Waverly thought. But that wasn't who *he* was. He just couldn't fit the mold that Collins was setting for him.

After running a few laps, Waverly stopped to get a sip of water from one of several waterspouts strategically ringing the training facility.

Other Marines were out on the field, some formally training under the watchful eye of a non-comm, while others seemed to be training on their own, probably during their down time.

He spotted Vehicle Specialist Sarah Parker headed towards the water station he was using and decided to stick around to strike up a conversation with her.

Sipping from a cup, he nodded as she approached. She returned the acknowledgement with a smile. Pointing to the waterspout, she asked, "May I?"

"Sure, be my guest," said Waverly, smiling back.

Waverly had an extra cup in his training gear and offered it to Parker.

"No, that's OK," she said. "I don't mind taking a walk to the spouts when I get thirsty. But thanks for the offer."

"Ah, OK." Offering his hand, he said, "I'm Malcom Waverly by the way."

"Yeah, I know you. You're the ISAT attaché to the MC1. I've heard your name around the barracks. Rumor has it you single handedly fought off those hostiles aboard the Structure few days ago, allowing the rest of us to fall back to the Falcons."

"I did?" Waverly said, truly caught by surprise.

Parker tapped his right shoulder. "Come on now, Mr. ISAT. I'm kidding you. We got our asses kicked. But no, you did a good job. That was a crazy deployment. We'll be ready for them next time."

"I'm not looking forward to facing those guys again anytime soon."

"I like you, Waverly. You're honest. But you won't catch a Marine saying that."

"Why, are *you* looking forward to going out to that thing again and mixing it up with the hostiles?"

"I'm a soldier. I follow orders. If I'm told I've got to gear up and go over there again, I'll take every chance I can get to extract some blood from those bastards for what they did to us the first time around."

"Pretty sure they don't have any blood," replied Waverly. "The consensus was that they were automated bots, wasn't it?"

"Yeah, whatever they are…Next time they're gonna have my rifle up their asses if I have my way."

Waverly smiled and noticed the tattoo on her arm. It depicted an eagle with a sword in one claw and a rifle in the other. The word '*honor*' was emblazoned in a crest surrounding the artwork. "Hope I don't get on your bad side!"

"Nah, you're all right. Look, I have to get back. My training session is almost over. I'll see you around."

"Thanks. See you around."

Parker smiled and waved as she walked back out to the training area and to her training partners.

One data point.

Parker didn't speak for all the Marines, but he suspected her take on the situation probably wasn't uncommon among the military.

Still, she represented just one data point.

After taking a few more laps around the lanes, Waverly toweled off and headed back to his quarters. He had a meeting with Collins soon and wanted to make sure he was ready with his recommendations.

--

Waverly pressed the buzzer outside Collins' stateroom. Junior ISAT officers were generally not permitted to enter an official ISAT stateroom without supervision. This was now only the second time Waverly had gotten a chance to see the interior.

Collins opened the door, invited Waverly in with a sweep of his arm and locked it behind them.

"Have a seat, Waverly," Collins said, directing the junior officer to a chair in front of his work desk.

Collins took his chair, the huge desk separating the two ISAT men, and noted the movement of Waverly's eyes over the contours of the desk.

"I see you like this piece of furniture," said Collins.

"It's impressive, sir."

"It's more than impressive. It's imposing. It's expensive. Tell me, how much do you think a desk like this would cost in the open markets of Alcmene?"

"Twenty thousand Alcmene Denii?"

"Not a bad guess. But no. This would cost more than your entire salary for a year."

Waverly gasped. "With respect, sir, what use can a desk like this possibly serve to pay that much for it?"

"I'll tell you, Waverly. This is a replica of a nineteenth-century oak roll-top desk. These were originally created by master craftsmen, the kind that don't exist anymore. This specific design was modeled after an old desk found in the maintenance room of the ancient Humphrey Scottish Rite Masonic Center building, in the old United States, on Earth."

Waverly nodded, unsure where this discussion was going.

"This desk was originally designed by one Anton Petersen, who founded the A. Petersen & Co company. They were masters at creating desks and other large furniture objects. You can see Petersen's heritage right here," said Collins, pointing to relief carvings all over the desk. "And I have an assignment for you, Waverly. I want you to do some research on Aton Petersen."

"I don't understand, sir. Why should I spend time researching an ancient desk maker?"

"Ask me that same question after you've done some research."

"Understood, sir. I'll check the ship's library first thing when I get back to my quarters."

Collins laughed. "You won't find anything there. You'll do that when you get back home. Speaking of home… I'm hopeful you've made some progress with the crew."

"I can't say I have, sir. I need more time. So far, the feedback among the Marines is that they will do as ordered. And if they are ordered to return to the Structure and fight the inhabitants there, they will. In fact, I think some of them are even eager for a fight—to extract a measure of revenge for the losses they took the first time around."

"That's bravado speaking," said Collins. "Marines will never admit that they are afraid or that they want to go home. Especially not to an outsider. Keep working your angles, Waverly. I want pressure from the lower ranks to force the captain's hand."

"Have you had any success with the officers?" asked Waverly.

"I spoke to Commander Peters in the mess hall lounge. He is standing by the captain. At least for now. Is that all you have to report, Waverly?"

"Yes sir."

"Fine. Let's have our next status report in eight hours. I want you to be more aggressive, Waverly. Spell it out for them. Be crystal clear what it is you want from them."

"What would that be, sir?"

Collins leaned forward across the antique desk, spread his arms wide and said, "To leave this place immediately. We do not belong here. Like I said, this captain is in over his head."

Waverly nodded and stood to leave.

As he approached the stateroom's door, Collins called for him to remain a moment.

"Waverly, one day, if you move up the ranks, you'll have a desk like this too."

The desk didn't particularly interest Waverly, but he knew Collins was a bit eccentric and so humored him. "Something to look forward to, sir."

"Not just something! This is more than a desk, Waverly. This is ISAT. This is what you and I have given an oath to protect."

"Does that desk contain the technologies the captain says you won't share with him?"

"Does your TSAC contain technologies you won't share with the Marines?"

"No sir. My TSAC contains technology that I'm bound to use to assist the Marines during combat missions."

"And are the Marines permitted to use the devices in your TSAC? Or is that authorization restricted to you and you alone?"

"Me, sir."

"Tell me, why does ISAT only allow you to use those systems and weapons, and not the Alcmene Marines?"

Waverly had to be careful here. He didn't want to jeopardize his relationship with his superior officer nor his future with ISAT.

"I'm trained to use the technology. And the technology is currently controlled and restricted to ISAT personnel. But its existence isn't secret. It's all in the treaty governing joint Union / ISAT operations."

Collins looked satisfied with Waverly's answer. "Excellent! This desk," said Collins, as he gently rubbed its surface, "is not included under such treaties. There are things whose use is not just restricted to ISAT personnel. There are things whose very existence can never be revealed outside ISAT walls."

"Never, sir?" asked Waverly, almost rhetorically.

"Many such things are at the discretion of an authorized ISAT representative. For other things, Mr. Waverly, the answer is never."

"Thank you, sir. I think I understand things better now."

Collins nodded. "Eight hours, Mr. Waverly."

"Understood, sir." Waverly saluted and quickly left the stateroom.

Outside, he was glad to be among the crew, walking the halls of the *Nemean*. Collins was increasingly becoming…*strang*e, and that gave him an uneasy feeling.

Feeling hungry, he decided to go to the mess hall for some lunch. That would also give him an opportunity to talk to some more of the enlisted and complete the assignment given to him. He was not planning on fermenting any discord among the crew — no matter what Collins wanted him to do — but he had no issues with gathering opinions. Gathering information. That's what ISAT did best.

Mess hall lounge west

System: Virgil's star (VGL 191)
Location: Aboard the Alcmene naval vessel Nemean

Commander Peters had two hours of down time to get some rest and relaxation. This mission was probably the most exciting, yet disappointing, Peters had ever been on. He needed a break, and when the captain had offered him a couple of hours off, he gladly accepted.

Changing into a fresh uniform, he left his quarters and headed to mess hall lounge west. He was looking forward to a hot meal, a good drink and some soft music.

There were a few officers having dinner at the lounge, and a group of four Marines were enjoying drinks at the bar. Peters took a table by himself by one of the corners of the lounge, offering him a good view of the rest of the floor.

The service was fast and professional. A waiter took his order — spaghetti and tuna fish, with a sprinkling of lemon, dill and a flask of iced tea — and returned within ten minutes.

The food was delicious. Tuna was plentiful on Alcmene ships, and this was one way the chefs aboard could elevate the ingredient from boring everyday fare to a delicious and sophisticated meal. Peters hadn't eaten so well in weeks, and he savored every moment of it. After devouring his meal, he leaned back in his chair, spinning an ice cube in his glass around and around, watching it slowly melt and subtly change the tea's color from its original deep golden peach to a lighter, more watery consistency. He downed the diluted tea and poured himself another glass.

Glancing at his watch told him he still had an hour before he was due back on the bridge, and he intended to sit there, quietly enjoying his tea.

But Collins entered to the right of Peters' periphery vision. Looking that way, Peters gave him a nod of acknowledgement, prompting Collins to say, "Good to see you, Commander. May I join you?"

Reluctantly, the commander agreed and motioned for Collins to take the seat in front of him.

"How have you been Mr. Collins?"

"Personally, I've been fine. Professionally, I've been rather dismayed."

"Why so?"

"*This* mission, Commander. It hasn't been going very well. I've seen some of the reports by the Marines who returned from the Structure. They were completely unprepared for the aliens' hostile response."

"That has been difficult on the Marines," replied Peters. "We sent the MC1 in prepared for a fight but with orders to talk first and retreat at the first signs of shooting. They did as ordered. They performed extremely well under the circumstances. And the hostiles they encountered…they are unlike anything we've seen before. Our guys were badly outnumbered and outgunned and on unfamiliar territory. They did as well as could be expected."

"Oh, I agree, Commander. I am not faulting the MC1. They did a fine job. I'm more concerned about how this mission is being managed. I really think it's time we call it a day and report back to our superiors."

Peters watched as Collins began taking napkins and carefully folding them in two, stacking them in front of him, almost absentmindedly.

Peters reached for one of the napkins, wiped his mouth and said "I've been told by a few other officers that you feel that way. I was also there when the captain kicked you off the bridge. The captain's been clear — we are not leaving just yet."

Agent Collins fidgeted in his seat, about to say something, but Peters waved his hand to stop him and continued, "Look, Collins, we all want to get home as soon as possible. However, we have people who are still out there, somewhere inside that Structure, and we want to do everything in our power to get them back. Secondly, we came here to learn about the Structure and the people who built it. Who they are, their intentions, whether they are a threat to the Union. We still don't know any of that."

"Commander, would you say that the attack on the MC1 was a hostile act?"

"Yes."

"Then that answers one of your questions, and I would argue that as far as your most important question — *are they a threat?* — the facts speak for themselves."

Peters leaned back in his chair and thought for a moment. "That's partly true. However, it ignores context. We did send an armed force to their doorstep. They didn't take kindly to it. We'd likely do the same."

Collins nodded. "That brings me to another point of concern. I ask you, Commander, *why* did we send such a large armed force? An *entire company of Marines*? Were we perhaps guilty of provoking the beast?"

"That's something the executive staff debated on the way to this system. How best to make contact and explore the Structure. Remember, before the attack on the MC1 we had no idea if that thing out there was even inhabited."

"We could have sent in a smaller force. Or continued trying to communicate via our comm. There are other things we could have done."

"The captain asked you repeatedly for assistance in scanning that thing," Peters pointed out. "The executive staff asked you many times for any technological assistance you could bring to bear on the issue of communicating with, or studying, the Structure. And you refused each time. We were left with few choices and we selected the best and most reliable one — the MC1."

Collins looked around the lounge and noticed that the Marines at the bar had been watching him.

"Yes, they are looking at *you* Collins," said Peters. "A lot of the soldiers hold you partly responsible for what happened out there. They've heard how you denied assisting us. And they've served in combat with Waverly, who's been an example of how ISAT operatives are supposed to support Alcmene and Union teams. You cite ISAT regulations that prevent you from helping — and then they look at Waverly, who does what's needed rather than hide behind regulations."

"Waverly is a junior officer. He is not privy to the same things that I am privy to. Commander, I formally recommend that we leave this system at once. Those aliens out there are not going to allow us to keep poking our noses here."

"We will leave when the captain says it's time to leave," replied Peters.

"I hope that's soon, Commander. Your captain is in over his head here. Mark my words."

Agent Collins stood up, thanked the commander and left the lounge.

Peters thought about what Collins had said. Where they in over their heads? He decided that, yes, they probably were, but that was the nature of such missions. This was a first for all of them, and mistakes were inevitable. Better to fail now, out here, then wait until those aliens found the Union worlds to learn about their intentions.

His break time over, the commander stood up, waved thanks to the waiter and headed for the bridge.

The Marauders

System: Virgil's star (VGL 191)

Location: aboard the Alcmene naval vessel Nemean

Waverly walked into the mess hall around noon ship's time. The aromas wafting from the kitchen made his mouth water. Eager to get some food in his stomach, he picked up a tray and walked straight to the chow line.

Three Marines were ahead of him, scooping up mashed potatoes and slices of meatloaf onto their plates, with a healthy helping of steamed broccoli, carrots and peas. The chef had prepared lime pie for dessert, and there was ample iced tea for the troops. Classic American, this type of meal was called, a staple of the military for hundreds of years now because it was healthy, easy to freeze and to prepare.

Alcmene's settlers had mainly been from the old United States and brought many of their traditions with them. And while Waverly was not a native Alcmene, he admired the people and culture, and saw himself as an honorary citizen of the colony.

Filling up his plate with the same fare as the Marines in front of him, Waverly followed them to a table and asked to join them.

They waved for him to take a seat, and after exchanging a few friendly nods around the table, the Marines dug into their food like hungry beasts. Waverly took the cue and dove into his meal as well, scooping up heaps of mashed potatoes, soaking them in gravy and stuffing his mouth like the others were doing.

Once Waverly and the three Marines finished their meals, they leaned back to let digestion take its course before diving into their pieces of lime pie.

Taking a sip from his glass, Waverly cleared his throat and said, "So, what squad are you guys with?"

"Fire Team Six. Starkley's Marauders," said the Marine sitting closest to Waverly.

"Nice to meet you. Who's Starkley?" asked Waverly.

"That's Starkley," said the Marine, pointing to the man sitting across from him. "He's our squad leader."

Corporal Starkley nodded and stuck out his hand across the table. Waverly shook it and said, "Nice to meet you, sir."

"At ease, Field Agent. I'm not your commanding officer."

"Call me Billows," said the Marine sitting next to Waverly. "And that's Tubbs," he said, pointing to the Marine next to Starkley.

"Good to meet all of you," said Waverly. The three Marines nodded.

Corporal Starkley took a bite of his lime pie and said, "You're the last man who saw Major Lewis alive, aren't you? Back on that thing out there?"

"I was with him when he ordered the retreat. Private Lotte and Rodriguez were there too. They were laying down cover fire for me so I could launch some GGs at them."

"Grav grenades?" asked Billows.

"Yes, gravity grenades."

"I heard about those. Would be handy if we could have those standard issue."

Waverly spread his arms open in a gesture of apology. "Not my call. Right now, their use is restricted to authorized ISAT personnel."

"Can you at least let us play around with a couple of them?" asked Tubs. "We won't tell your superiors."

"Not a bad idea," said Billows, his lips turning up in a mischievous smile. "How about after we get done here we go to the training room and toss some of those GGs around?"

Waverly shook his head.

"Come on, man," said Billows, putting his arm around Waverly's shoulders. "Just want to see one up close and personal."

"That's enough!" shouted Starkley. "We are not violating any regulations here. And let's not put this man in a difficult situation. He's got orders. Now that's *it* about the gravity grenades."

Billows began to sulk, causing Tubs to flick a piece of lime pie at him before all three Marines broke out in laughter.

"These boys here are just messing with you, Field Agent," said Starkley. "We're happy to have ISAT attached to our unit. I personally don't want to mess with anything that messes with gravity. Just give me a rifle and my EVA gear and I'm set."

"Hear, hear!" said Tubs, raising his glass of iced tea in an exaggerated toast to the corporal.

"Hear, hear! Billows repeated, also raising his glass.

"A toast to the MC1," Waverly said, and raised his glass as well.

The corporal stood, raised his glass again, paused for a moment to look at Waverly and the two seated Marines and said, "Here's to the grunts, leathernecks and grimy devil dogs who raise their rifles together. Next time make sure you lime-eating lizards point your barrels at the enemy!"

"HAHAHA! OORAH! SEMPER FIDELIS!"

The Marines ate the speech up, jostling and throwing friendly insults at each other, before calming down and drinking the last of their iced teas.

"Hey, Corporal, I vote we make Waverly here an honorary member of the Marauders. What do you think?"

"Good idea, Bellows." Looking at Tubs, Starkley asked, "Will you second that vote?"

"Seconding!"

"Since I cast the deciding vote, you're a Marauder now! Congratulations, man!"

"Thanks, I'm honored guys," Waverly said.

"What should we call him, men?" asked the corporal.

"SAS!" Bellows said instantly.

"SAS?," repeated the corporal.

"Yeah! Official military acronym for the stuff he's got in his TSAC — some amazing shit!"

The three Marines broke out in laughter again. Quieting his men, Corporal Starkley said, "As commanding officer of this unit, I hereby designate you SAS. Welcome aboard, soldier!"

They all earnestly shook Waverly's hand and patted him around his shoulders and back. For all their good-natured ribbing and fun, they seemed sincere in accepting him as one of their own.

"I'm *really* honored to join your ranks, Marauders," said Waverly, while saluting each one of them individually.

Looking at Waverly, Corporal Starkley suddenly asked, "What do you think happened to the major?"

Taking a moment to replay the scene in his mind, Waverly shook his head and said, "I really don't know. I just hope he's still alive, along with the other Marines that were left behind."

"They're not being left behind!" said Bellows. "We *always* go back for our guys."

"Then why haven't we gone back yet?" Tubbs wondered.

"Let me ask you guys something," said Waverly, interrupting the cross talk between the three Marines.

They all stopped to look at him, waiting for his question.

"Do you guys want to—I mean *really* want to go back over there?"

Tubbs was the first to reply. "Tell you the truth, I'd rather be home. Just got married before this deployment, and I'm eager to get back to my wife."

Bellows started playfully jabbing him with his elbows, a wide grin on his face. "I bet you're *eager* to get back," he said.

"No, man, I'm serious! You'll see when you get married and have someone to go back to."

The corporal cleared his throat. "We are Marines. We don't want to ever, I mean *ever*, leave one of our guys behind. I'm sure I speak for all of us here when I say we'll gladly go back to get our brothers and sisters out of there."

"Semper fi!" said the other two Marines, almost in unison.

"Tubs here wants to get back to his wife. That's true. And as much as I like bunking with these grunts, I'd rather be home with my family too. Bellows is young and single and lives alone back home. He may not have no one to go back to, but I can attest to the fact that he'd rather be chasing after coeds than be out here with us. *But!* That doesn't mean we don't want to go back, get our guys back and kick some alien ass!"

"OORAH!" shouted Billows and Tubs.

"Why do you ask? Hope the Marauders didn't just induct a coward or a traitor into our ranks."

"Bellows!" shouted Starkley." Mind your manners!"

"It's OK, Corporal," said Waverly. "I know how my question probably sounded. I guess all of us would rather be home sometimes, but we signed up for this and that's all there is to it. And besides, I personally owe the major, Lotte and Rodriguez my life. If the Major hadn't told me to run while the three of them covered my retreat, I'd be MIA too."

Everyone at the table looked somber after Waverly finished speaking. Bellows was the first to break the silence.

"I don't know," he said.

"What don't you know?" asked Tubs.

"I don't know if I'd go back for Waverly, to be honest."

Waverly felt both insulted and hurt. He thought he'd bonded with these Marines. He was a Marauder too now, or wasn't he?

Corporal Starkley stood and looked directly at Bellows. "Stand up, Private!"

Bellows did.

"Explain yourself."

"Well, sir. I don't think I'd go back for Waverly."

"You already made that clear, soldier! Now speak up. Explain yourself!"

Other Marines at nearby tables were looking in their direction.

"You see, sir. I can't feel nothin' for a guy who won't share his Grav Grenades with us. He's not playing nice."

He stood there, letting the silence hang for a few moments before cracking a huge smile.

"I'm kidding, sir! Of course I'd go back for the runt!"

They all started laughing.

Having managed to get the attention of several female Marines in the mess hall, Bellows began to show off a few of his dance moves, blowing kisses at the women. Tubs reached up, grabbed Bellows by his shirt collar and pulled him back down into his chair.

The corporal pointed at Bellows and said, "This here is an example of how the Marine Corps defends the honor and virtue of womankind all around the Union worlds…by keeping uncouth, undersexed grunts like Bellows lightyears away from anywhere they can do any harm."

They all laughed again, sipped a little more tea and started to clean their table.

It was time to get back to their duty stations, and Waverly had to prepare for his next meeting with Collins.

The three Marines and Waverly went in opposite directions. The Marines gave Waverly bruising hugs and hard pats on the back before parting ways.

Waverly felt good. He'd made some new friends and felt less isolated than before. The truth was he didn't have much in common with Collins on a personal level and just didn't trust the man. With duty calling, Waverly went back to his quarters, changed and made his way to Collins' stateroom.

--

After a brief wait, Collins opened the door and invited Waverly inside.

Instead of sitting at his nineteenth-century antique desk, this time Collins sat in a wide, comfortable leather chair. A stand beside the chair had a leather-bound book resting on it, and beside that a cup of steaming coffee.

"Have a seat, Field Agent," said Collins, pointing to a utility chair opposite from his.

"Thank you, sir."

Collins reached over and picked up the cup of coffee. He blew into the steam and smiled. "Hot coffee makes me happy. What makes you happy Waverly?"

"My family. My friends. Scientific discovery. Exploration."

"You are an idealist. A trait I rather admire. Tell me, do you know what this is?" said Collins, gesturing at the book sitting on the table beside him.

"No sir. I didn't look closely."

"This is a book written by a very famous man. He lived during the European Renaissance. This man was a philosopher, a historian, a politician, a diplomat, a poet and a writer. Tell me, Waverly, why are such men so hard to find these days?"

"What do you mean, sir?"

"Polymaths," said Collins. "Why was there such an apparent abundance of polymaths in the old days, and why are there so few of them now?"

"I'm not sure, sir, that is an accurate statement."

Collins smiled. Waving his hand as if to give Waverly the floor, he said "Go on. Disabuse me of my notion."

"My point, sir, is that there are still many people who have a wide range of interests and areas of expertise."

"And where are these people?" asked Collins." You can't tell me, for example, that any such people are running this ship."

"I don't know enough about the command staff to answer that specifically," said Waverly. "Though that's not my point."

"Shouldn't we know the truth about those who would lead us? Especially those who would lead us on such momentous missions as these?"

Not wanting to get into a debate about the captain with Collins, Waverly pivoted back to what he was originally going to say. "Sir, I believe there are many such people. I don't know if they are commanding naval vessels or selling ice blocks during Io's polar storms. I just think it's a matter of visibility."

Collins raised his eyebrows, sipped some coffee and nodded. "Explain," he said.

Waverly continued. "In ancient times, it was easier for a polymath to stand out —especially if they received patronage from a powerful or wealthy benefactor. Populations were smaller then. It was easier to stand out among a smaller crowd…and the podiums people stood on were smaller, with less room for people on the fringes of society.

"Also, discoveries were less costly to make — especially in terms of energy. Consider how much harder it was, just in terms of pure energy, to work out the physics that make our Gravity Grenades possible, compared to the physics needed to explain the toss of a ball in a gravity field. The former required enormous machines and teams of scientists and engineers to operate them and make sense of the results, while the latter required a ball, a strong arm and a good imagination.

"The other thing is, today there are so many subjects to be an expert on, compared to a relative few in ancient times. Plus, today *dabbling* is no longer as acceptable as it was in the past. Today a dabbler in any serious field would be a liability to the subject he's engaging in. Imagine someone dabbling in medicine or engineering or weapons design. In the past it was OK to be a dabbler and that earned you respect. Not so much today."

"You lack appreciation for the classics," replied Collins. "For the achievements of the past."

"Not at all, sir!" answered Waverly. "I admire what our ancestors have done. They did remarkable things with none of the tools and support structures and luxuries we have. My point is only that — because of *their* great achievements and *their* genius — they have enabled, *in the here and now*, a relatively large portion of our population to be capable of what only a small fraction of theirs could do in the past."

"You are saying that five hundred years ago there could only have been one Isaac Newton, while today we could have thousands?" asked Collins.

"In a sense, yes, that's what I'm saying," replied Waverly.

Collins began to laugh. "There is some sense in what you're saying, but I am not convinced yet. Another assignment for you Waverly — refine your analysis and its presentation."

Go hump an airlock, Waverly thought to himself, while nodding at Collins' new assignment. "I'll get right on it."

"You'll get on it when this mission is through."

"Yes sir," replied Waverly.

Picking up the book next to him, Collins held it in front of him and said, "This book is called *The Prince.* It was written in 1513 by an Italian polymath by the name Niccolo di Bernardo dei Machiavelli. Have you heard of this man?"

"I have," replied Waverly. "*The Prince* was standard reading at the academy."

"Yes, and it remains so today," said Collins. "In fact, I was the one who got the book onto the standard curriculum. Let me ask you, Waverly, what do you think of the maxim '*The end justifies the means?*'"

"Machiavelli never said that, sir," answered Waverly. "Although some people still think that's what he was saying."

Collins smiled and said, "Very good. Let me read you something." Flipping through the pages of the delicate leather-bound book, Collins began:

"Men judge generally more by the eye than by the hand, because it belongs to everybody to see you, to few to come in touch with you. Everyone sees what you appear to be, few really know what you are, and those few dare not oppose themselves to the opinion of the many, who have the majesty of the state to defend them; and in the actions of all men, and especially of princes, which it is not prudent to challenge, one judges by the result.

For that reason, let a prince have the credit of conquering and holding his state, the means will always be considered honest, and he will be praised by everybody because the vulgar are always taken by what a thing seems to be and by what comes of it; and in the world there are only the vulgar, for the few find a place there only when the many have no ground to rest on."

Looking up from the book, Collins asked, "What was Machiavelli saying?"

Waverly cleared his throat. "I believe, sir, that the means, whatever they may be, do in fact, matter. The ends, no matter what they are, don't automatically justify the means. However, despite this, there are times when it is imperative to accept the ramifications of the means used, and the damage such means may do to you or others, if the goal is worthy."

"So are you saying that the ends won't balance out, or cancel, the ill effects of the means?"

"Yes sir. I am saying exactly that. Nevertheless, there are times when the means may be justified — at least partly — to secure a goal that is very important, or worthy, if you will. That's very different than pursuing an end regardless of the means. Now this is very much about politics and politicians. An honest politician may be rare because it's virtually impossible to be completely virtuous and still achieve certain ends. Your hands will always be sullied somehow. Machiavelli believed that opinions matter, and perhaps unfortunately, appearances sometimes matter more than actions."

Collins smiled and nodded. "As I read to you, *'Men judge more by the eye than by the hand…and in the actions of all men, and especially of princes, which it is not prudent to challenge, one judges by the result.'"*

"Yes sir. Basically, appearances matter and don't do whatever it takes to achieve your desired result."

"Very good, Waverly. I knew you'd do well with this. I've seen your marks on this subject. I hope you will remember this conversation, and your lessons, if and when the time comes for you to speak on ISAT's behalf."

"What do you mean, sir?" asked Waverly, puzzled by Collins' statement.

His superior waved off the question. "We'll talk about that another time. Now…onto your status report."

"I think most of the troops are steadfast in their support of this mission, or at least in their duty as soldiers," Waverly said. "Some will admit to wanting to go home, but also feel honor bound to recover the missing Marines and exact some level of revenge on the hostile forces aboard the Structure."

"You see, Waverly, that's why throughout my career I have tried to influence the curriculum at the academy."

"What do you mean, sir?" Waverly asked again.

"The Leninists were right. A proletarian revolution — which is a necessary thing — must be led by what they termed professional revolutionaries. They provide the leadership, intellectual scaffolding and organization to lead the working class in overthrowing the order."

"Sir, I had no idea that you were a Marxist," said Waverly.

"I'm not a Marxist," replied Collins. "But I know how these things work. The Luxemburgists were wrong. They thought that a majority of the working class must be materially and intellectually involved in a revolution for it to happen. That such a large and diverse group of people in the lower rungs of society could be so uniformly and synergistically committed to one goal was foolish of them to believe. Idealistic perhaps, but foolish."

Waverly sat taking it all in, not knowing how to respond.

"Sir, with all due respect, Marxist revolutionary theory seems out of place out here," said Waverly. "What are your orders, sir?"

"Such theories are not out of place here," Collins said smoothly. "I am providing a frame of reference for you. A way to think about our situation. If the enlisted personnel, especially those making up the lower ranks of the military, don't want to change things, then things won't change. Which means we fall back to the Leninists' approach. We provide a driving force for change from the top."

"The captain, sir?" asked Waverly. "Are you going to try to convince the captain to leave again?"

"I've tried that on several occasions and failed every time. I've tried with his immediate subordinates, all members of his command staff. That didn't work either. I am left with just one option."

"And what would that be, sir?"

"You asked about your orders? Your orders are to continue carrying out your duties as an ISAT agent and follow lawful orders given to you by command officers aboard this ship."

Waverly got up to leave. "Thank you, sir. I will see you in eight hours for our next status session."

"No need. We are through with those. Report to me only on those things that require my authorization, my approval or my advice. If I need a meeting with you, I will send you a message."

"Understood." Waverly saluted and left the stateroom.

Outside, he shook his head. He wasn't sure what to think now. Collins wasn't being forthcoming and seemed preoccupied with ancient personalities and theoretical constructs. He glanced at his watch. It was late, and he needed to take a break and find a quiet place to think things through.

Reaching his quarters, he opened the door and sat on his bunk. He was missing something important but couldn't put his finger on exactly what. Looking down at his bunk, he found it rather welcoming and lay on his back.

A few moments before he drifted off to sleep, he thought about what Collins had said about the Leninists.

How was he planning to start a revolution from the top when the captain and the command staff had clearly rejected his advice?

An idea began to form in his cloudy mind, but sleep overtook him before he became fully aware of it.

Perseus Force

System: Virgil's star (VGL 191)
Location: Aboard the Alcmene naval vessel Nemean

Lance Corporal Felix stood in front of a squad of four Marines. They were lined up in a row for inspection, and Felix was going to take his time going through each Marine's EVA and gear. He knew Barracks Command would never allow a faulty EVA to make it onto a Marine, but still, these troops were his responsibility and he wanted to be sure there would be no issues with any of their equipment.

This was not a mission he was looking forward to. Just the thought of being inside that thing again made him sick to his stomach. The place just didn't feel right to him. He certainly didn't want to go up against those hostiles again either.

He was sure many of the other soldiers felt the same way. Time for a pep talk.

"OK, you grunts!" barked Felix. "I want you all to look alive and look sharp. No slackers, slouches or slugs on my watch."

"None here, sir!" replied the squad in unison.

"Good! Now, by the powers vested in me by no one in particular, I hereby designate this squad the Perseus Force."

"OORAH!" replied the squad.

Smiling, Felix asked, "Which one of you grunts knows why?"

"Sir! Because Perseus rescued Andromeda from the sea monster, sir!"

That was Private First Class Josephine Nakamura, one of the best hand-to-hand combatants he had ever faced. She was also an expert in Jojutsu, a Japanese martial art whose practitioners used a short staff called a jo to defend against sword attacks.

Felix was going to recommend Nakamura lead training seminars on how to apply the principles of Jojutsu to the existing curriculum on empty rifle fighting — otherwise known as how to use your rifle to smash the enemy's head when you're out of ammo.

"Does that mean we should stop calling that thing the Structure and start calling it Cetus?" asked another Marine, Private C.C. Smalls, a wide grin on his face.

"Not a bad idea, Private," replied Felix. "And maybe we should call you Medusa!"

That gave the entire squad a good laugh.

Just as the squad was quieting down, Commander Peters walked into the hangar bay.

"Officer on deck!" announced Felix, bringing his squad to stiff attention.

"At ease," said Peters. "The captain just wanted me to check on you. We'll be in launch range in another ten minutes. Looks like you have everything in order here, Corporal. Remember — this is going to be quick. You are going in, picking up as many passengers as you can find, and leaving. Keep your engines running. Head back to the *Nemean* as soon as possible. No sightseeing. No fraternizing with the locals."

"Yes sir," Felix said. He glanced at his watch. "Time to board. On the double, Marines!"

The squad rushed into the Falcon's waiting ramp and strapped into their seats. Felix saluted Peters and followed the squad inside.

"Good luck, soldier!" called Peters behind him.

Felix looked back, saluted again and sealed the Falcon's cargo door.

Moments later the craft lifted off the *Nemean's* hangar deck and exited into open space. The pilot rotated the Falcon to directly face the Structure, lit the ion drive and poured on the thrust.

Felix connected his viewer to the Falcon's cameras. Switching to the aft view, Felix watched the *Nemean* drift away. Even though they were moving away at a good clip, Felix thought that the *Nemean* looked like a huge city skyscraper from the distance. Switching the viewer forward to tap into the craft's bow-mounted cameras, the Structure — *no, Cetus* — loomed incredibly large.

For a second, he wondered who could have built such a thing. And for what purpose. He had a momentary vision of those hostiles. *Hope we don't run into them again.*

He glanced at his watch. "Landing in five minutes!" he shouted over the team frequency.

Two minutes passed.

He gestured to the Marines seated around him, raising his hand and extending three fingers. "Three minutes, Perseus Force! Make sure your EVA's are buttoned up. We're about to go in."

Green acknowledgements lit in his heads-up display. They were ready.

The Falcon tilted a bit to starboard, then to port when the pilot overcorrected to keep the craft aligned as it flew past the threshold of the Structure's hangar-bay doors.

"What happened?" asked Felix.

"We just flew through some kind of force field, sir," answered the pilot. "It put some rotation on us — had to compensate. Seems like we're clear now. Landing in thirty seconds. Hope you guys are strapped in!"

"We're good back here," replied Felix.

A few moments later the Falcon landed, and the cargo door slid open. The Marines rushed out, crouched low and took positions around the Falcon.

Scanning with his motion sensor and checking for contacts on his SITMAP, Felix gave the "Go!" signal, and the Marines fanned out toward Duffy's last known position.

Strange. The Falcon had turned on its auto beacon. Duffy should have seen that and called in by now, Felix thought. Checking with the pilot, Felix confirmed there had been no calls from Duffy's team.

After a few minutes, Perseus Force found the excavation site.

"This is where Duffy's team was conducting its search," said Felix.

Pointing to the clean gap in the debris field, Nakamura added, "Looks like they managed to dig through over here."

"So where are they?" Felix asked.

Private Smalls took point, carefully making his way through the path Duffy's team had excavated. Shining his light around, he saw the excavator, turned over on its side with part of its metal frame deformed and melted.

"Corporal! I've found the excavator. Looks like it's been badly damaged."

Felix and the rest of the squad rushed to Small's position.

"And there's a Lifter Set," said Nakamura, pointing to the other side of the debris field. "That looks mangled too."

Turning on MC1's unit comm, Felix called to Duffy.

"Corporal Duffy! This is Lance Corporal Felix with an extraction team. Please respond."

While the EVAs were equipped with a range of communications frequencies that could be used between various speakers, the UC, or unit comm, was a universal general frequency and could be heard by all members of the unit. Unit comms also superseded all comms so that breakthrough announcements could be made without delay or interference from other conversations that might be going on.

"Corporal Duffy," repeated Felix. "We've brought a Falcon to extract you and your excavation team. If you can't reply, give me a sign. We've got our motion sensors on and SITMAPs set to maximum."

The answer was silence.

"Anything?" Felix duly asked the squad.

They shook their heads.

"I hate leaving them behind like this," said Felix. "But our orders are clear. Get in, retrieve whoever we find and get out — ASAP."

"Hold on, sir," Peering into her motion detector, Nakamura said, "I think I'm seeing something. It's faint, but it's there. Do you see anything on yours?"

Felix looked closely at his screen. And then he saw it. They all saw it. Their motion sensor screens turned red as they registered more contacts than the detectors could individually parse to their EVA HUDs.

"Retreat! Now. Back to the Falcon!"

A microsecond later, the normally dim blue interior of the Structure lit up in harsh, fiery green colors.

C.C. Smalls was the first casualty as something struck him from behind, the impact throwing him ten meters across the chamber before he smashed face first into an unyielding wall.

Nakamura crouched low, firing her rifle with her right hand while priming and throwing a fragmentation grenade with her left.

Felix ducked low behind a column and began firing at targets. About twenty meters away, a phalanx of two-meter tall, three-legged beings marched towards their position. They carried what looked like curved rods that fired green bolts of energy. Each time a bolt passed within two feet of his position, his EVA suit alarm warned of a buildup in static electricity.

He turned the alarm off as it was distracting him from the fight.

Looking to his left, he saw Nakamura with a handful of frag grenades. One by one she threw them at the advancing phalanx. Hostiles were blown to bits, weapons and body parts smashing into the rest of the phalanx, and the grenades seemed to be making an impact.

The phalanx slowed, while its forward line was replenished by soldiers from the rear.

"Good job, Nakamura! How many more of those frags do you have?" asked Felix.

"Three more. I'll be out soon."

The fourth member of their squad, Layton Nichols, had brought a mini R-PIG, or rapid plasma-ignited grenade launcher, to the party.

"Nichols! You still have that PIG?" shouted Felix into the team comm.

"Yes sir!"

"Then use it to turn those tripods into bacon, man!"

Nichols retrieved the R-PIG from his back, inserted the ignitor rods into his EVA's auxiliary power pack and fired.

THUMP! THUMP! THUMP!

Three rounds streamed through the chamber and exploded right on top of the advancing phalanx.

Nakamura threw two more frag grenades while Felix set his rifle to auto and sprayed the phalanx with plasma rounds.

"Nice and crispy," he said. "That's how I like my bacon!"

"OOHRAH!" shouted the three Marines.

Felix caught movement in his periphery. It was Smalls. He was face down, body turned against the wall, and trying to rotate his body so he could see what was going on.

"Smalls, this is Felix. What's your status?"

"Fucked up, sir. I can't feel my legs. My EVA is flashing an environmental warning. I think I've sprung a leak."

"We'll get you out of here. Hang on."

Felix's comm spit out static before a voice broke through. "Perseus Force. This is Falcon One. I'm reading a lot activity. What's your status?"

"Falcon One, we need immediate EVAC! Screw regulations and get that bird in here. We're about fifty meters and to the left of the hangar bay."

"Be right there, sir"

Moments later, a wall and several columns behind the Marines shook, rattled and crumbled, plumes of dust and debris filling the chamber.

Beyond the dust was a three-meter cone, with a smoking, 12.5mm cannon just below the tip.

The Falcon pilot had blasted his way out of the hangar bay and into the chamber. Nichols fired more R-PIGs at the alien phalanx, while Nakamura and Felix ran to Small's position, picked him up and put him on the Falcon.

"Nichols," shouted Felix. "Get down! Now!"

Nichols dropped to the ground just in time to see fire spitting out of the Falcon's 12.5mm gun.

The alien phalanx had already been badly damaged between the PIGs and frag grenades and had gaping holes several lines deep throughout its forward line.

The Falcon's powerful gun chewed up the remaining alien lines, cutting down anything that it crossed paths with, decimating the remaining alien soldiers.

The three-legged hostiles tried to mount a counterattack, but the Falcon's gun was too fast and too powerful. Nichols unloaded his remaining R-PIG rounds at the retreating alien ranks and dashed into the Falcon.

With all aboard, the pilot quickly spun the craft around, leveling more of the already damaged hangar bay walls, aimed for the exit and punched the throttle to maximum.

"*Nemean,* this is Falcon One," said Felix. "We're coming in hot. Keep the light on for us."

"Falcon this is *Nemean* flight command. Acknowledged. We are ready for your arrival."

"Corporal?" said the voice from Nemean's flight deck. "The captain's on the line."

"Put him through."

"Lance Corporal, any survivors?"

"Negative, Captain. We were unable to located any of our Marines. We barely made it out alive ourselves."

"Casualties among your team?"

"One, sir. Private C.C. Smalls. He's alive but badly injured."

"Medics are on standby and will meet you in the hangar bay. Captain out."

Once again, Felix hooked up his EVA HUD to the ship's cameras. Turning to the aft view, he looked at the Structure. Despite hauling ass back to the *Nemean* at the maximum possible speed the ion drive could muster, the Structure was so large it barely made a difference. It remained an enormous sphere in his viewer.

Leaning back in her seat, Nakamura opened her visor, revealing long black hair that framed a beautiful face. Felix had opened his visor too and she told him, "At least we kicked their ass this time. Glad Nichols brought some PIGS along for this party."

Nichols opened his visor, looked at Felix, then Nakamura and said, "Just had a feeling...but the real hero today was the stick jockey in the pilot's nest. We gotta buy that man a beer when we get back."

They raised their right fist into the air at that comment, an Alcmene Marine hand gesture almost as old as the colony itself.

Even Smalls, who was lying down in a crash couch, managed to raise his fist in agreement.

They were lucky to be alive, Felix thought. And they were still light years from home.

Chapter 4

Perseus Force returns to the *Nemean*

System: Virgil's star (VGL 191)

Location: Aboard the Alcmene naval vessel Nemean

As soon as the Falcon touched down and was secured, Private C.C. Smalls was wheeled to sick bay. His vitals held steady and his EVA suit had pumped him full of medical nanos that helped stabilize his condition even before the medics saw him.

Felix, Nakamura and Nichols were quickly debriefed by the command staff and the method of their "victory" noted for any future encounters.

As Nakamura had put in her report, "PIGS and really big GUNS. That's how you defeat the Cetos."

Felix's team had officially taken to calling the Structure *Cetus* and its "inhabitants" the *Cetos*.

Command had nixed that designation, but it had gained traction through the ranks.

"The bastard Cetos!" "Those Cetos can suck my rifle!" "I'd like to shove a frag grenade down those Cetos' throats!"

Those comments or their like were becoming increasingly common in the mess halls and in other common areas where Marines tended to congregate. Even during that morning's training exercises, in full sight of their NCOs and commanders, Marines had been heard shouting *"Cetos scum!"* while firing off simulated rounds with their practice weapons.

While such conduct technically went against regulations and he was bound to discourage it, the captain didn't really mind. The Marines were understandably passionate about the situation.

Despite the setbacks this mission had suffered, the twenty-four missing Marines, the scores of injured soldiers and an equal number of EVA suits and gear that needed repair or replacement, he didn't want to give up on the possibility that the beings who inhabited that Structure could be dealt with in a diplomatic, if not entirely friendly, way.

He called an impromptu informal meeting to discuss the situation. Seated around the table were Commander Peters, ISAT Field Agent Collins, Lance Corporal Felix and Lieutenant Marker.

"Gentlemen, I've called this meeting to gather opinions and bounce around ideas. First, here are the facts.

"We've sent armed boarding parties to the Structure twice. Both times they have been met by hostile forces. Furthermore, in both cases our forces retreated from the hostile response. Only Lance Corporal Felix's team managed to post a 'victory' of sorts against the enemy forces his team encountered, while we can't say that about Major Lewis' encounter."

"Sir, I might also add that the hostiles Major Lewis faced were *different* from the hostiles my team faced," Felix observed.

Marker said, "Right. Lewis' team was raked by robotic forces while you guys went up against living, organic beings."

"Honestly, I think the tripedal beings we faced were easier to deal with than the mechanical ones. The mechanical soldiers were fast, precise, fearless and hard to kill. In our brief encounter with the tripedals, it was obvious they were susceptible to the same things our forces are susceptible to – fear, confusion…"

Collins interrupted. "What you are saying, Corporal, is that they suffer from *organic inefficiencies.*"

"Yes, pretty much sums it up."

The captain cleared his throat. "This brings us to our second fact. That Structure out there is inhabited by at least two different sentient races. One mechanical, one organic. Do they work together? Are they part of the same society? Are they allies or enemies? Did either one build the Structure? Who operates it?"

"We do know that the mechanicals and the tripedals venture into areas of the Structure that are in range of both races," said Peters. "That is to say, the phalanx that the corporal's team faced off against appeared in the same vicinity as the mechanical forces Major Lewis encountered."

"One thing, sir," said Felix. "The MC1 didn't encounter any hostiles until we were at least a klick away from the LZ and inside the Structure. Perseus Force encountered the tripedals just a few hundred meters in, right after we located Duffy's excavation zone. It could be that the mechanicals inhabit a deeper section of the Structure, while the tripedals are closer to the surface."

"Interesting observation, Corporal," said Gregory. "In theory, there could be dozens of races inhabiting different parts of that thing out there."

"I don't think that's just a theoretical possibility, Captain," said Collins. "I think that's a near statistical *certainty*. Structures like this have been theorized to exist by scientists and philosophers for centuries. The most famous are the ringworlds and Dyson spheres, but solid structures like this one make sense too."

"And maybe these are actually more common," said Peters, "as it would be easier for an advanced civilization to take an existing object — like a moon — and convert it into an artificial habitat, like this one appears to be."

"I think this is much more than a habitat, Commander," replied Collins. "This is probably also a type of starship, if our analysis is right. This structure certainly didn't originate in this system. Just by analyzing the chemical composition of the particles on its surface, we can say with a fair amount of certainty that it is covered in material alien to this system."

"So where did it come from, and where is it going?" asked the captain. "Ideas?"

"I think we can speculate all day about that," said Collins. "In my opinion, our best course of action right now is to end the mission and return to Alcmene."

"You've made your opinion on that matter clear already, Field Agent," the captain said. "But we didn't come all this way just to run away at the first sign of trouble. Plus, we still have the matter of the missing Marines to consider. I have no intention of leaving anyone behind if I can do anything about it."

Peters, Marker and Felix nodded in agreement.

"Marines don't leave people behind," said Felix.

"Neither does the Navy," said Peters.

"Nevertheless, leaving *is* an option gentleman," said the captain, addressing his officers. "An option I don't agree with. But still an option for us to take, if it comes to that. For now, however, I think there are better options. Let's go through some of them."

All but Collins began listing ideas without being called upon, the meeting morphing into a free-for-all ideation session.

"We can keep trying to communicate with them."

"We can go back with a larger force and get our guys back."

"We can send a diplomatic mission in, unarmed."

"We can call for reinforcements."

"All good ideas," said the captain after a few moments, bringing some order back to the discussion. A few really stood out to me. We are in no position to call in reinforcements. Politically, that is currently untenable. The President won't authorize sending another ship unless it is in the direct defense of Alcmene or to fulfill Union obligations. Neither of those criteria are currently being fulfilled, so that's out."

"That's unfortunate," said the commander. "Perhaps a show of force would change the dynamic here. But with the presidential election just weeks away and the threat of armed conflict between Alcmene and the Independent Mining League all over the news, a call for reinforcements isn't what the admirals want to hear right now."

"And you can't ask another Union world for help, because your government has kept this a secret," added Collins, an accusatory look on his face.

"Given the Structure's proximity to Alcmene and our outworld colonies, our government deemed it a planetary issue for now."

"This is very clearly going to become a Union issue," said Collins. "Perhaps faster than you can imagine."

"Agreed that this will eventually be brought before the Union to discuss," said Gregory. "But not before we've completed our fact-finding mission."

"And obtained any advantages, say new technologies, for your government before the rest of the Union knows that thing even exists."

"Again, Mr. Collins, this falls under the jurisdiction of the Alcmene government, and so we are taking the lead here."

"Captain, we are light years away from any human world. This is open space, and your government can lay no claim to anything in this system, let alone an alien moon-sized starship inhabited by an assortment of hostile forces."

"This isn't the time to debate politics with the captain," said Peters. "We've got our orders."

Collins smiled. "You've trained your executive officer well, Captain. He even speaks for you when you'd rather not speak."

Marker shot Collins an angry look, while Felix shook his head.

"Gentlemen," the captain said, raising his arms in a gesture of reconciliation. "We are all in this together. Let's keep our focus. So: Reinforcements and leaving are currently non-viable options. What else is left?"

"We can go back with a larger force and attempt a rescue," said Marker.

Collins sat up straight and said, "I strongly advise against such a course of action."

"Agreed," said the captain, which seemed to please the agent. "Collins is right. Each time our soldiers have stepped foot on that thing they've been met with gunfire. At full strength, we can deploy a company of eighty Marines. Marine Company One is down to fifty-six troops. We can augment that with about twenty naval personnel explicitly trained for ground combat, bringing the company back to *almost* full strength. That is realistically the best we could do now. Which means that the best, in terms of boots on the ground, is still slightly less than what Major Lewis had to work with. And that didn't go well, as we know."

"The captain is right," said Peters. "Based on the reports from both expeditions, the Cetos can field far larger forces than we can."

"Then how are we going to rescue the Marines that are still on that thing?" asked Felix. Despite his team's relative success in fighting back against the tripedal phalanx, there was still a sense of failure in not being able to find Duffy's team or the others.

"We're forgetting one thing," said Marker.

"What?" asked Felix.

"The *Nemean*. This ship has considerable firepower. As do the two Falcons. We could use the *Nemean*'s guns and missiles to augment a ground assault — if it comes to that."

"Thank you, Mr. Marker," said Gregory. "Hopefully it won't come to that. The way I see it, we have two basic options that ought to be combined. We can try communicating with them *and* send a diplomatic mission."

"Attempts at communicating with them so far have all failed," said Peters.

"I think I may be able to help here," said Collins. "ISAT has developed a device that will boost comm signals and enable retrofitted comm systems to access additional spectrums that the aliens may be using."

"Why didn't you bring this up before?" asked Peters. "We've been trying to communicate with them since we got here. And you have *now* decided to share that?"

"Because the timing of this technological deployment is *now* appropriate," replied Collins.

Peters was about to say something, but the captain signaled for him to hold off.

"How long will it take you to retrofit the *Nemean*'s comms?" asked Gregory.

"Two hours. I'll need a comm system engineer and two technicians to assist."

"I'll see to it you have all the resources you need. Coordinate with Lieutenant Paris and let's get this done."

Field Agent Collins nodded, excused himself and walked out of the meeting room.

After the door had been shut, Felix said, "I still don't see how we're going to get our guys back. I don't think talking is going to help much."

"Right now, it's our best option. Boots on the ground might work if we knew where our people were. But that thing is huge. Over four thousand kilometers in diameter. Our people could be anywhere in a volume of space nearly thirty-four billion cubic kilometers. That's assuming it's a hollow sphere, which we know it's not. Unless we find some way to look inside that thing, I don't see another option."

The captain's comments seemed to bring everyone to agreement.

The next step was figuring out how to open diplomatic channels with an unknown number of probably hostile aliens whose language nobody knew.

The Rosetta Message and ADAM

System: Virgil's star (VGL 191)

Location: Aboard the Alcmene naval vessel Nemean

Two hours later, Collins completed the installation of the ISAT comms package.

The captain ordered Lieutenant Paris to use the package to scan the enhanced spectrum for incoming messages.

"Mr. Paris, I want you to prepare the Rosetta Message for deployment" Gregory said. "Let's see if we can get their attention."

The Rosetta Message was a coded information package carried by all Alcmene naval vessels, designed to be used in first contact situations. The Rosetta Message contained basic scientific information and pictographic elements designed to indicate friendship and cooperation.

While versions of the message had been deployed many times throughout history, no one had ever been able to broadcast it face to face with an alien entity until now, and there was no telling how it would be received.

"I suggest we go to Alert Level 2, sir," said Commander Peters. "We have no idea how they may interpret Rosetta."

"Agreed," said Gregory. "Set condition to Alert Level 2."

With all departments confirming their alert status, Paris began broadcasting the Rosetta Message through the ISAT comms package.

The diplomatic mission was going to be a trickier affair. Given the aliens' hostile response to human visitors, sending an actual human being to the Structure was out of the question.

Rather, the captain instructed engineering to work with Lieutenant Paris, Field Agent Collins and Commander Peters to prepare an electronic diplomat to be delivered via remote control.

The electronic diplomat, officially an *Advanced Diplomatic Autonomous Machine*, or ADAM for short, was equipped with remote sensors so that its handlers could see and hear everything it did, and contained a suite of other passive sensors for collecting information for later analysis. ADAM contained messaging similar to that of Rosetta, and also contained a special "gift" package consisting of half a kilo of elemental *Leradium*, a metallic substance so rare as to represent less than a tenth of a percent of all the metals produced per year by the combined economies of all Union worlds.

Leradium "gifting" was a key component of the Union worlds' first contact protocols. How do you demonstrate friendship and a desire to trade with someone? You give them something valuable.

While Leradium was extremely valuable among Union worlds, there was no guarantee it would have any value to aliens. However, it was hoped that the rarity of this element would automatically confer value to it across civilizations, regardless of how alien economies functioned.

If that were not so, it was at least hoped that an advanced alien civilization would view the gifting of something so rare as a non-hostile act, and perhaps with a little luck, might also view it as altruistic.

It took about three hours to prepare ADAM, fully charge its power cells, run through diagnostic system checks and load the half kilo of Leradium into its small cargo hold.

"Prepare to launch ADAM," said the captain. "Report on final system checks."

"All systems green, sir," replied the engineer over comm.

Collins, Peters and Paris also reported green from their workstations.

"Launch ADAM."

"ADAM launching from Bay Two in three....two....one....launch," said Paris. "Switching to automatic nav control."

"Nice job, everybody," said Gregory. "How long until he's knocking on their door?"

"Twelve hours, sir."

Electronic diplomats couldn't be launched with high velocities, lest they be misinterpreted as an attack.

Diplomacy, as always, required patience.

"Very well."

The captain stood from his command console. "Commander Peters, you have the bridge."

"Aye sir. I have the bridge."

Fight or flight

System: Virgil's star (VGL 191)

Location: Aboard the Alcmene naval vessel Nemean

The captain and Collins sat across each other, sharing the pot of coffee sitting on the table between them. Mess hall lounge west was mostly empty, aside from the occasional crew member who came in for a quick snack or to chat with the staff.

It had been six hours since they had launched ADAM, and the captain took the lull in bridge activity to see if he could better connect with Collins. The field agent had been so insistent on leaving Virgil's system, but seemingly had a change of heart when he volunteered to upgrade the *Nemean*'s comms package and provide support in prepping ADAM.

The captain had dealt with ISAT agents before, but Collins was different.

"Thank you for your assistance with the upgrades to our communications suite," said Gregory. "I'm hopeful those upgrades will help us better understand our friends out there."

"Captain," replied Collins, "don't fool yourself. They are not our friends. As I've advised many times, extreme caution is needed here. And at the risk of repeating myself for the hundredth time — I *strongly recommend* we return to Alcmene and issue a full mission report."

The captain nodded. "If you feel that strongly about leaving, why did you offer to upgrade our comm systems?"

"As I explained to the commander," replied Collins, "the timing was right. ISAT only deploys new technologies when appropriate. We had reached a stage in our mission when the timing, in my estimation, was appropriate."

"And your assistance with ADAM?" asked the captain.

"ADAM technology is well within your existing technical repertoire, Captain," replied Collins. "I have no reason to withhold assistance in such cases."

Changing the subject, the captain asked, "Tell me, who or *what* do you think built that Structure out there?"

Collins shrugged. "I only know as much as you do, Captain. I am doubtful that any of the hostile creatures encountered by the Marine teams built that. As to its purpose…time will tell, I suppose."

"Which is exactly why we've been sent here," replied the captain, "and why I won't leave until we have at least *some* answers. It's far better for us to find out here, well away from the Union worlds, than to one day wake up with them in orbit around one of our planets."

Collins paused to take a sip of coffee, when suddenly an alarm blared throughout the ship, followed by a deep shudder moments before the deck heaved up and rolled to port, causing the coffee pot to spill onto the floor, the hot coffee in his cup scorching Collins' face.

The captain got up, exited the lounge and ran down the hall. Keying his comm, he shouted "Bridge! Report!"

"A barrage of missiles just struck the ship's starboard side," answered Commander Peters.

"On my way!" shouted the captain, his breath running short as he sprinted to the lift that would take him back to the bridge. Moments later, the captain was at his command console.

"Damage report," he demanded.

"Prelim reports indicate the hangar bay doors have been wrecked," replied Peters. "We've lost one Falcon and the SAR tug has been damaged."

"Navigation! Execute RAND alpha zero zero one! Sub-lightss on maximum," shouted the captain.

"Weapons! Return fire. All cannons."

"Already on it, Captain! Cycling through cannons one, two and three. Direct hits scored on the Structure."

The *Nemean* lurched again, as another missile exploded a few meters off her port bow.

"Sir! We're now far enough to launch our own missiles," said Peters from the tactical console.

"Do it! Standard volley. Yield level one."

A standard volley consisted of six missiles, with yield levels ranging from one to three. Yield level one was the lowest setting while three was the highest. Yield values were not linear but logarithmic, meaning that a warhead with a yield level of three was vastly more powerful than a warhead set at yield level one.

Commander Peters sent coordinates to Lieutenant Marker's station, where he instantly validated them and unleashed the volley.

Two of the missiles were intercepted by turrets rising out from the surface of the Structure, while a third collided with a missile intended for the *Nemean*.

The rest of the volley made it through and exploded one after the other on the Structure's surface. Large balls of atomic fire expanded outwards, engulfing the two laser turrets in fire and knocking out another three missiles just launched from somewhere on the Structure's surface.

"Sensors. Tactical. Can you locate the source of their missile launchers?"

"Searching," said the commander. "There could be hundreds of sites on that thing."

"Let's start by finding the ones pointing at us right now. We'll worry about the others later."

"Might have something, sir," said the commander.

A second later, a holographic image of the Structure hung in front of the captain's console, large enough for the entire bridge crew to see from their respective stations.

Red lines outlined a belt that ran across the Structure's center, like a line drawn across a planet's equator, while another set of lines framed a separate belt in the north-south direction.

"Looks like there are missile silos ringing the thing, along its equator and prime meridian," said Marker.

"Navigation! Amend RAND alpha zero zero one to minimize the number of times we cross a direct line with one of those silos."

"Sir!"

That was Lieutenant Marker.

"I'm picking up a flight of birds coming in off that nest. Dozens of them and headed our way!"

"Sensors, confirm!"

"Confirmed, sir. They look like tactical fighter craft."

"All weapons hot. Cannons to knock out individual craft and to assist with point defense. Missiles to destroy clusters. And keep pounding those missile sites."

"How long before their fighters are within weapons range?"

"Twelve minutes" replied Marker.

In that time, the captain poured over reports coming in from around the ship.

Fifteen hangar deck crew were cut off from the rest of the ship and might be dead…the captain couldn't be sure, as all communications with that section of the ship were cut off, fires and secondary explosions set off by the missiles having damaged internal comms.

Twelve minutes later, eight fighter craft came within firing range of the *Nemean*'s cannon. Lieutenant Marker deftly managed all three cannons from his console, obliterating the leading three fighters with direct hits and taking another two out of the fight with glancing blows to their fuselage.

The three remaining fighters banked to starboard and momentarily exited the *Nemean*'s cannon range, before turning back and unleashing a barrage of nine small tactical missiles.

The ship's automated point defense systems destroyed five of the missiles while cannon fire destroyed two more. However, two slammed into the port sub-light drive, causing the *Nemean* to rotate to starboard.

"Port sub-light's been hit! Our speed has just dropped fifty percent," said Lieutenant Harris.

The captain cursed under his breath. Standing from his console, he ordered engineering to put all available resources on repairing the port drive. Getting propulsion back to nominal was their number one priority and key to surviving the battle.

Suddenly, another flight of twelve tactical fighters entered weapons range, instantly unleashing their tactical missiles —one hundred and twenty in all.

The *Nemean*'s point defense system managed to defeat fifty-three of them, while Marker's cannon destroyed another thirty-four before two of the three cannons were overwhelmed by the incoming fire.

All told, thirty-three of the tac missiles slammed into two of the *Nemean*'s cannon and turret mounts and auxiliary areas, destroying them in the process.

"Sir," said Marker. "We can't take much more of this. They are overwhelming us with numbers. Individually those tactical missiles wouldn't hurt us much but when deployed in swarms like this our systems can't cope."

"Another squad of their tac fighters are entering firing range. Twenty-four in two close formations," said Peters.

The captain touched a control on his console and the formation of tactical fighters appeared to hover in space, the *Nemean* displayed on the left and the tac fighters on the right. In the distance, the display also showed the Structure as an enormous half sphere.

Red arcs traced from a point on the Structure's surface to the flight of tactical fighters headed their way.

"Commander, I had the computer analyze their flight path. I believe they are launching those fighters from a very small area, right near where the Falcons first landed." Gregory fed the coordinates to Peters.

"The coordinates match the reports of the first expedition team. That's about where they reported seeing those domes on the surface. Recommend we target that site," said Peters.

"Mr. Marker," said the captain. "I'm sending you a set of coordinates. Hit it with a volley of missiles — yield two."

"Aye sir!"

Ten minutes later an enormous fireball expanded from the surface of the Structure. It expanded out into space for several minutes before dissipating, dust and debris arcing up and away before falling into a gentle orbit around the Structure.

Five minutes passed with no further fighter-craft sightings.

"I think that worked, sir!" said Marker, a look of relief on his face. "Our point defense is getting low on ammo, and with one cannon left I don't know how many I'd be able to hold off."

"We're not out of the woods yet, Lieutenant," said the captain. "There are at least a dozen fighters unaccounted for. They are still lurking out there, somewhere."

"Sensors read clear. No contacts"

"Keep scanning," said Gregory. "They could be hiding behind all the debris floating out there."

At comms, Paris said, "Sir, I'm reading a Marine IFF signal. It's Alcmene!"

The commander, looking at his tactical screen, said, "Confirmed. There's a small craft approaching. IFF signal indicates Alcmene. I know it's impossible, sir. But there it is."

"Open a channel," said the captain. "Unidentified vessel broadcasting IFF signal XJL-390-GFQ-11-2. This is the captain speaking. You are *not* authorized to approach this ship until further notice. Engage station-keeping mode. If you continue your approach, you will be destroyed."

Commander Peters looked at the captain. "Trick?"

"We can't be one hundred percent certain," replied the captain, "but if it's not a trick, *who*'s piloting that thing?"

"Maybe some of our missing Marines captured one of their ships and rigged a friendly IFF signal?" replied Peters. "It wouldn't be the first time, you know."

The captain thought for a second. "My gut tells me otherwise. If they are friendlies, they'll understand. They've waited a long time to get back aboard the *Nemean*, a little while longer won't make a difference to them."

As if the enemy had guessed his decision, the *Nemean* was rocked by multiple explosions, her deck jumping from the force and the entire vessel listing to starboard.

"Direct hit on our starboard side!" reported Peters. "Emergency teams moving to contain the damage."

"Commander, coordinate with the damage control teams," said the captain. "Priority number one is our propulsion."

A new alert appeared on the captain's command console as Peters shouted, "Captain, we just lost the starboard drive."

More explosions rocked the ship, with multiple detonations lighting up the *Nemean*'s dorsal spine.

"Both hyperlight pods have been damaged, sir. Attitude control is still operational."

"What just hit us?" asked Gregory.

"That last flight of tactical fighters. They launched almost two hundred tac missiles. Point defenses took out fifty percent, the forward cannon took out thirteen before being destroyed. The rest hit our missile batteries, the starboard drive and the two pods."

The captain looked at his tactical screen. Tracing his finger from their present location to a point about eight hundred thousand kilometers from their present location, he said, "If we can get the sub-light drives repaired, we should be able to engage the hyperlight pods in about sixty minutes. It's time we put some distance between us and that thing. We are close, people. I repeat, that is our priority now. Lieutenant Marker, we still have a good number of missiles left. Use the atomics, maximum yield, to engage anything else they throw at us."

"Lieutenant Harris, use the attitude thrusters to keep this vessel moving away from the Structure at best possible speed. We might not get far, but I want to give them the impression that we are moving off and not a threat.

"Commander, I want you overseeing the repair of the sub-light drives. I'm going to the pod room to coordinate with the hyperlight teams. We need to get propulsion back online ASAP!"

Commander Peters and the two Lieutenants saluted as the captain left the bridge.

Agamemnon

System: Virgil's star (VGL 191)

Location: Aboard the Alcmene naval vessel Nemean

It was midnight, ship's time, aboard the *Nemean*. Things had been quiet for a while now, and the captain was running low on energy. He'd been on stimulants for days, but they were taking their toll. Dr. Smith ordered him off the stims and into his bunk. Captain Gregory reluctantly agreed and ordered the rest of his command staff to get a full five hours of sleep.

They deserved at least that much. They had all been working sleepless shifts, the crew going round the clock for three days to repair the *Nemean* after the battle with the Structure's tactical fighter swarms.

After veering off and putting sufficient distance between the *Nemean* and the Structure, things had returned to normal. The Structure continued to emit the same noise it had upon their first arrival and remained peacefully enigmatic otherwise.

An analysis of the battle with the fighter swarms suggested that the aliens' intent had been to *disable*, rather than *destroy*, the *Nemean*. Interestingly and perhaps tellingly, the first strike had occurred on the *Nemean*'s starboard side hangar bay doors.

That had been the site of Felix's Falcon launch, which incidentally had also been destroyed during the attack.

Retribution for Perseus Force's "win" over the tripedal phalanx? A forceful message indicating that further EVA visits were *decidedly* no longer welcomed?

After some deliberation, the captain decided that while they were perhaps no longer welcome to board the Structure, they were still free to stay in the Virgil system and continue their mission of exploration.

Just because the aliens had no further desire to have armed Marines aboard didn't mean they were no longer open to peaceful dialogue.

After all, the captain reasoned, *they* had initiated contact first.

In any case, mistakes were bound to be made during any first contact mission. Better to make them out here than at home.

At this late hour, the bridge was being manned by Sub-Commander Shimatowa and other bridge staff.

Shimatowa had strict orders to wake the captain should the Structure do *anything* unusual, or if ship status changed while he slept.

The captain didn't often remember his dreams, but he would remember the one he was having tonight.

He saw himself standing on the edge of a high cliff as large, powerful waves broke at its foot, shaking the ground beneath him.

Peering into the distance, near the horizon, he saw a giant ship approaching. It was an ancient ship, the kind he had read about during his historical studies.

As the ship drifted closer to the cliff, he could make out a name: *HMS Agamemnon*.

The *Agamemnon* had been commissioned several hundred years ago on Earth, part of the fleet belonging to the British Royal Navy. The *Agamemnon* was a Lord Nelson-class pre-dreadnought battleship and was famous for its actions during World War One, especially the Dardanelles Campaign, where the ship bombarded Turkish fortifications in support of British troops.

The captain had studied ancient ships while at the academy and knew that the *Agamemnon* had been an impressive ship in her day. She was armed with four 45-caliber, twelve-inch naval guns, arranged in two twin gun turrets — one fore and one aft. The ship also featured ten 50-caliber high velocity naval guns, arranged in twin gun turrets, at the base of each corner of the ship's superstructure. She also had an array of other weapons, including two dozen three-inch-high velocity guns used to defend against torpedo boats, as well as five torpedo tubes. Thick, twelve-inch armor protected the ship and main gun batteries.

The captain could see all these specs in his mind while watching the ship slowly making its way from the horizon to the cliff's edge. He realized that the *Nemean* was just a little over twice as long as the *Agamemnon* and wondered how he and his ship would fare in a naval against Lord Nelson commanding the British battleship.

As the *Agamemnon* drifted closer to the cliff's edge, a deafening roar thundered across the open ocean and slammed him in the chest…waking him up from his sleep. He quickly looked at this command console. All indicators were green. There was nothing going on, but he decided to check with the bridge anyway.

"Mr. Shimatowa. How are things going up there?"

"Fine, Captain. All quiet."

"Very well. Carry on, Commander. I'll see you in a couple of hours."

"Thank you, sir. Bridge out."

Unable to go back to sleep, the captain connected his console to the ship's library and searched for *Agamemnon*. Why had he dreamed of the *HMS Agamemnon*? Was his subconscious trying to tell him something?

He scanned through the results of his search.

Agamemnon was an ancient Mycenaean king who appeared in the epic poem known as the *Odyssey*. Since ancient times, scholars had debated which parts of the *Odyssey* were real and which were myth, but Gregory was sure it had to have some basis in reality.

According to the ship's library, *Agamemnon* led a Greek military campaign against the fabled city of Troy. While preparing to leave Greece, Agamemnon's army incurred the wrath of a goddess known as Artemis.

Who was Artemis? The captain filed that line of inquiry for later. In any event, the *Nemean's* library didn't give a conclusive answer as to why the goddess was angry with Agamemnon. According to one story, he had killed an animal that the goddess held as sacred, and later bragged that he was as good a hunter as Artemis.

Artemis must be a goddess of the hunt. I'll check that later, he thought.

In any case, things didn't go well for the ancient Greek king. After his return from Troy, he was killed by Aegisthus, lover of his wife Clytemnestra. Here again the ship's library could not give conclusive details — in some versions of the story, all of the king's followers are killed too. In others, it's not clear what happens to them. Sometimes, his wife kills him herself, in other versions his wife and her lover do it together.

Whatever the details, the captain knew he didn't want to be Agamemnon.

What was his dream trying to tell him?

Had this mission been cursed by some modern-day equivalent of Artemis? Was there someone out to get him? Was he somehow embarking on a foolhardy military campaign that would end in tragedy?

He didn't know.

What he did know was that he was a captain in the Alcmene Navy. He commanded a state-of-the-art ship run by the finest crew he had ever served with.

He was here, light years from home, on a mission of exploration. He didn't know who built the Structure floating out there. He didn't know if they were friend or foe. He didn't know what they knew about his ship, Alcmene, the Union or humanity.

He hoped he could answer some of these questions. That was his mission. That was what he had been tasked to do and would do his best to accomplish it.

Having had enough sleep for one night, and having spent enough time looking through the ship's historical libraries, he decided it was time to get back to the bridge.

No doubt, Dr. Smith would disapprove of his decision. He'd ordered the captain to get more sleep. He'd gotten about three and a half good hours of sleep and was only short one and a half from the proscribed amount.

He would lay off the stimulants for now. Except for a cup of coffee or two when he needed a pickup.

This mission was too important to spend it sleeping in his stateroom.

He opened the comm to the bridge. "Sub-Commander. I'll be there in ten minutes. I'd like you to stay on as my XO until Commander Peters returns to duty. I want to make sure he gets some sleep. This will also give you an opportunity to get more experience on the bridge."

"Thank you, sir," said the sub-commander.

"You are welcome," replied the captain and turned off the comm.

With that, he got up and started putting on a fresh uniform and began brewing a pot of coffee.

Gregory looked at himself in the mirror. He had kept himself trim and in shape, and his uniform fit smartly around his athletic physique. Although he was just a few years shy of being eligible for longevity nanos, he hardly looked it and was frankly not quite ready to admit that to himself. Being out here, in space, exploring and learning more about the universe is what kept him going. Except for the stresses of command, this was an ideal life.

It felt good to be going back to work.

Chapter 5

Distant visitor

System: Virgil's star (VGL 191)

Location: Aboard the Alcmene naval vessel Nemean

Three hours after ADAM should have completed its trip to the alien moon, a large blip appeared on Lieutenant Paris' sensor screen. From this distance, the Nemean's sensors couldn't discern too many details. And the constant barrage of neutrino interference put out by the Structure didn't help their attempt at clearly identifying the blip.

Lieutenant Paris transferred his display to the bridge's main viewer.

"Captain, we have a new contact. It's coming into view now, just over the Structure's horizon. It appears to be in a slow orbit around the alien moon, but from this distance we can't make out too many details. However, based on its gravitic displacement and its doppler-scatter pattern, my guess is that we are looking at an alien ship."

"Interesting. Heat signature? Weapons?" asked the captain.

"Negative, sir. It's cold. I'm not reading anything."

"Suggestions?", asked the Captain.

"Let's go in for a closer look," said Peters.

Marker concurred. "We should investigate. There are two main possibilities to consider. One, it could be a threat to us, in which case, we ought to find out as soon as possible. Two, it could be long dormant and contain weapons systems or other technologies that we would want to have a look at. Investigating seems to be our best option."

Collins, who had been studying the sensor readings, said, "There is a third option. It could be a live ship with advanced weapons systems that can blow us to pieces. I suggest watchful vigilance until we have more information."

"All good ideas," Gregory said. "I prefer the middle road here. Helm, take us in closer. Let's go slow and make our intentions clear. Plot a steady, visible course. Weapons, keep the cannons online but don't paint that ship with any firing solutions."

Keying his comm, the captain said, "Mr. Felix, I have a new mission for you. I want you, Agent Waverly and six other Marines on standby for a potential EVA mission. Mission planning session begins in ten minutes. Report to the bridge meeting room. Captain out." Turning to the ISAT field agent, he added, "Mr. Collins, inform Waverly of his new assignment and have him present for the planning session."

Collins nodded and used his console to send a text message to Waverly. A few moments later, Waverly acknowledged.

"Agent Waverly will report to the bridge in ten minutes, Captain."

"Thank you. Helm, you have the bridge. XO, Tactical, Agent Collins, I want you in on the mission briefing."

Ten minutes later the bridge officers, Waverly and Felix were seated around the meeting table waiting for the captain to begin.

Pressing a few buttons on the console before him, the captain said, "Our sensors made contact with a new object in orbit around the alien moon. As far as we can tell, it's an alien ship of some kind. It may be an active vessel with a full crew compliment, or it may be long dormant. We have no way of knowing from here.

"I've instructed the helm to take us in for a closer look. Once we get close enough for our sensors to paint a clearer picture, we'll decide whether or not to proceed with the EVA mission.

"Mr. Felix, Mr. Waverly. If conditions warrant it, I want you each to lead a team of three Marines on a boarding mission. You can handpick your respective teams. Your mission will be to find the bridge and learn everything you can about that ship. If you can, download the ship's logs, memory banks and anything else that will tell us something about who built it, where it's from and what its mission was. Any questions?"

Felix and Waverly shook their heads.

"Good. Now the floor is open for comments, ideas, suggestions, concerns…"

Collins was the first to speak. "I believe I've made my concerns about this mission clear. Since you have already decided to proceed, I advise extreme caution and patience."

"Agreed," said Commander Peters. "We haven't had the best of luck with any of the EVA missions we've conducted so far."

"Third time's the charm, or so the saying goes," said the captain. "Tactical, the decision to launch the EVA will rest on your shoulders. I won't order a *go* until you are a hundred percent satisfied the alien vessel doesn't pose a threat. Any signs of life or activity, and we back off."

The tactical officer nodded. "Understood, sir."

--

Felix went back to his quarters and keyed the comm key on his console. Three side-by-side images populated the screen.

"Josephine, CC, Layton — guys — the captain has a new mission for us. They've detected an alien ship in orbit around the moon out there. They want us on Ready Level One. If the TO signals all clear, we're gonna take a hop over there and have a look around. If we don't get the all clear, we stay home."

"Perseus Force rides again!" Josephine Nakamura exclaimed. "I'll stock up on the frag grenades, just in case."

"And I'll bring my PIG along for the ride," said Layton Nichols. "Who's gonna bring the big gun? CC?"

While medical had cleared Smalls for duty, he wasn't looking forward to another run in with any hostiles just yet.

"Guys, I really could use a vacation right about now. But seeing as our fearless leader here needs me to cover his back, I'll be there with a really *big* gun."

They all laughed.

"Great! Perseus Force — meet me at barracks prep area one. We'll gear up there and then head to the Falcon to await instructions."

"OORAH!" shouted the three Marines on the screen before Felix saluted and keyed the comm key off.

He trusted those three with his life, and if he were going to explore another alien vessel, it might as well be with his friends.

--

About thirty minutes later, Felix, Nakamura, Smalls and Nichols were at barracks prep area one, putting on their EVA suits, checking weapons and stocking ammunition.

Waverly walked in and saluted, before heading to the gear locker to prepare for the mission.

Waverly and the members of Perseus Force made some small talk before Felix finally asked, "So, who are you bringing along?"

"You probably know them," answered Waverly. "The Marauders."

As if on cue, Corporal Starkley strutted into the Marine prep area with his Marauders in tow.

"Someone call?" he asked with a hint of exaggerated drama and humor in his voice.

"Ladies and gentlemen, I present to you the famous Marauders," said Waverly.

"Actually," said "Tubbs, "we go by *Starkley's* Marauders and we are not famous, just *infamous.*"

They laughed and shook hands with the officers.

After introductions were over, Felix said, "Let's finish gearing up and get to Falcon One. The captain wants us on standby in ten minutes."

"Final prep, Marauders!" shouted Starkley, "On the double. The captain is waiting!"

Five minutes later both teams had completed their EVA suit system checks, slung their weapons, stocked ammo and done a final comm check.

"Overall command of both teams rests with me," said Felix. "HUD displays feed to mine as per standard protocols. Report acknowledgement via HUD for final systems check."

Seven green lights lit up in Felix's HUD display.

"Move out, Marines! Falcon One. On the double!"

--

"Captain, Felix's EVA team is ready and on standby aboard Falcon One," said Commander Peters.

The *Nemean* was one hundred thousand kilometers from the alien ship, and now her sensor package could make out quite a bit of detail.

The alien ship was three times the size of the Nemean and featured gray markings against a black hull, making the ship almost invisible against the blackness of space.

The hull was covered with small impact craters, suggesting it had been exposed to a micro meteor-rich environment sometime in the past. A fine layer of dust also coated much of its surface, which was smoothly contoured and lacked sharp corners.

An obvious cluster of antennas lined the forward nose of the ship, while what appeared to be gun turrets were mounted forward and aft along its belly.

Large twin exhaust nozzles were mounted aft while the bow featured a large ring-like structure that went all around the forward section of the ship.

"That looks like a ramjet setup," said Collins. "See the ring at the front and exhaust nozzles at the back?"

"Good observation, Mr. Collins," said the captain. "What level of technology does ram-jet usage suggest to you?"

"Socially speaking? Anywhere from a late Type 0 up to perhaps a mid Type I. It really depends on whether and when they developed hyperlight capabilities. In theory, in a long-lived civilization with sufficiently strong social forces driving continuity, it's possible to imagine even a late Type II civilization still using ram-jet technology."

"That leaves a pretty wide range of possible technological levels," said the captain.

"Yes. If we only use the ram jet as a criterion. Although I'm inclined to believe that unless that ship is native to this system or another nearby system, we are almost certainly looking at the product of a civilization that is at least in the early Type I stages."

"There's just one way to really find out," said Peters. "We need to see the rest of their tech."

"Tactical, are you detecting any activity from that ship?" asked the captain.

"Nothing, sir. It is completely cold. No life signs, no comms, no heat, no radiation beyond that coming from the surrounding area. I think that's an open invitation for us to go in and look around."

"Collins?"

"Captain, while I will always urge patience and caution on such matters, I think given the ship's apparent dormancy, its design and its apparent age, sending our boarding party seems to be worth the risk."

"Commander Peters, do you concur?"

"I do, sir. I think we have a chance to learn something here."

"As do I. Mr. Felix, your mission is a *go*. Get aboard and find out what you can. Remain in communication with the *Nemean* at all times. We'll monitor your progress from the bridge. Captain out."

"Aye sir! EVA mission is a *go*! Launching Falcon One in five...four.... three...two...one...Launch!"

The Daedalus

System: Virgil's star (VGL 191)

Location: Space

Falcon One was ordered to conduct several flybys of the alien vessel, her sensor recordings to be analyzed later. The alien vessel appeared to be heavily armored and showed signs of battle damage, with burn marks and metallic slag along her upper spine. Whoever had attacked her had concentrated their fire along the upper half of the ship, indicating that the area probably contained vital ship's functions — perhaps even the bridge.

The alien vessel's docking bay was severely damaged and completely unusable, so Felix's team decided to rendezvous with the craft and artificially dock by using the Falcon's powerful landing clamps to grasp onto one of the many hull protrusions along its starboard spine. Once the clamps were engaged, the team rigged a baffle to create an airtight seal between the alien hull and the Falcon's port hatch.

"*Nemean,* this is Falcon One. We've docked with the alien vessel. Preparing to use our HTCT to breach the hull and begin EVA."

"Acknowledged, Falcon One. Keep your comms and cams on. *Nemean* out."

"I'll crack this can in a minute, just stand clear, boys and girls," said Tubbs, who rated highest in metallurgicals and had the most experience using a high temperature cutting torch.

Felix and Waverly looked on from a safe distance as sparks flew around the enclosure they created, raising the ambient temperature by fifty degrees and causing their EVA suits' alarms to sound due to the rapid change in the environment.

The rest of the team re-checked their weapons and ammo stocks, and made sure their sensor packs were still properly calibrated while they waited for Tubbs to finish the job.

Three hours passed, not including Tubbs' four "coffee" breaks, rant storms and curse-filled tantrums, before a circular section of the alien craft's armored hull slowly slid away from view as it fell to the alien vessel's deck.

"*Nemean* this is Falcon One," said Felix. "We've breached the vessel's hull and are about to begin making our way in."

"Good luck, Falcon One. We'll be watching."

"What do you mean by '*we* breached the hull'?" Tubbs asked as he held his gloved palms up. "I've been slaving for hours over this hot pipe while you cats just sat back and played Jimmy the Donkey."

"Your hands will be fine," said Starkley. "Look alive, Marauders. Lance Corporal, permission to send my men in first."

Felix gave an exaggerated bow and said, "By all means. After you, my good sirs."

One by one, each member of the team stepped through the hole Tubbs had created.

The inside of the ship was pitch black, the only light being the team's headlamps. The walls were also covered with markings that looked similar to those on the outside. Here they seemed to flow in longer, continuous lines and brush strokes, whereas outside they tended to be short with abrupt endings.

The ship clearly had a functional gravity simulator, since all the Marine EVA suits registered a force of half a G pressing them towards the deck.

"Anyone else think the floor feels kind of squishy?" asked Waverly.

"Yeah, I feel it too," said Tubbs.

"Same here," said Billows.

"Feels like we are walking on a stiff sponge," said Felix.

The team walked several meters down the corridor before Waverly noticed what was going on. Or rather, what wasn't going on. "Team, look at your SITMAP recordings. Is it me, or do the map recordings look completely crazy?"

"Something's definitely not right," said Felix. "My SITMAP is recording the path I've been taking, but it looks jumbled when I scroll to a point beyond its immediate sensor range. It's as if the topology recorded by the STITMAP gets scrambled after we leave the immediate vicinity of the initial recording. "

"This is ISAT tech," said Starkley." SAS, what's going on?"

Waverly shook his head. "I have no idea. I've never seen this happen before. SITMAPs are supposed to record all vectors traversed by the user and create a real-time map of where they have been relative to their current location. In theory, you can't get lost if you have a functional SITMAP with you."

"Well…our SITMAPs aren't functioning," said Tubbs. "That means we're lost."

Billows smacked the back of Tubbs' helmet. "We're not lost. Not yet, anyway. The hole you made is just fifty meters that way," he said, pointing his thumb over his right shoulder.

"This ship is around three times the size of the *Nemean*," said Felix. "We should be able to find our way back here, with or without SITMAPs."

"This place could be a labyrinth," said Nichols. "We should find a better way to get back here besides dead reckoning."

"OK. Anyone seen Theseus?" mocked Nakamura. "Who's got a ball of string to lend us?"

"You know, that's not a bad idea," said Waverly. "Hold on. I'll be back."

"Famous last words…" said Tubbs before Billows gave him another knock across his helmet.

"While SAS is doing whatever he's doing, I vote we call this ship *Daedalus*, after the guy who actually built *the* labyrinth."

"I see someone's been studying history," said Billows.

"What? You thought I was all looks and no brains? Come on, man! Have a heart!"

"Stow it, you ugly runts!" ordered Starkley.

Felix keyed his private comm. "Waverly, what are you doing?"

"I'm in the Falcon. Remember the molecular twine stowed in the tool compartment? We've got several miles of the stuff."

"Don't tell me you've read *Theseus* too."

"The ISAT Academy at Io is pretty rigorous. Lots of assignments on the Classics."

"I hear you, man. Alcmene Naval isn't a joke either. I feel like I've read more Ancient Greek than the ancient Greeks did! By the way…where did you find these Marauders? Billows and Tubbs are like a bad comedy act, or like lovers who can't stand each other while professing their love for one another over chocolate-covered strawberries and cream."

Waverly laughed so hard he thought his respirator alarm would go off.

"That's just how they are. They're OK. You'll see. They'll have the team's back and Starkley keeps them in line if they start going off the edge."

"OK. Just get your ass back here ASAP with that twine. We've got a mission to complete and the bosses are watching."

Static crackled through the unit comm.

"Falcon One, this is the *Nemean*. We've got eyes and ears on you. Enjoying the show but don't get too comfortable. Engineering has been alerted of your SITMAP issues and will radio in a solution once they have one. Until then, you are a go for Mr. Waverly's Theseus solution."

"Understood, *Nemean*. Waverly is headed our way now."

"Very good. *Nemean* out."

A few moments later, Waverly fastened a line of molecular twine to a nearby bulkhead and mounted the rest of the spool on his back with his suit's retractable carrying straps.

"All right. If we get lost, we'll be able to find our way back here by following the twine."

"Great job, Waverly! Billows take point. Tubbs, cover our six. The rest of you, form up, two columns wide, behind Billows. Stay together. Let's move out."

The team slowly began making its way deeper into the ship.

--

"Nemean. This is Falcon One. Are you reading this?"

"We're reading, Falcon. But the visual is grainy. What are we looking at?"

Felix and the rest of the team had been walking through the *Daedalus'* corridors and climbed up several decks before they came upon a door that *looked* like it protected something important.

The team first tried the panel to the right of the door, but there was no power going to the interface and the markings made no sense anyway.

They tried prying the door open with no luck. The door was too heavy and too massive to be forced open.

After trying for several minutes, Felix ordered Tubbs to use the HTCT to cut through the bulkhead. It wasn't as tough as the outer hull, but a good forty-five minutes passed before Tubbs cut the last bits of material and the circular section of metal fell to the floor.

Inside, they found a towering cylinder with coils running its length. It hummed gently, and the temperature in this compartment was noticeably hotter than in the other sections of the ship.

"Captain, I think we've found the engine room. Or at least machinery that is necessary for this ship's powerplant to function."

"Is it operational?"

"It's humming and generating heat. It could be in some sort of standby mode," replied Felix.

"Record everything you can. Stills, sound, video, environmentals. Is there anything that you can definitively make out in terms of its function?"

"Negative," said Felix. "The ship's interior appears to be covered in writing of some sort, but we can't make out any of it."

"This is Waverly, sir. We've recorded a lot of the alien script — if that's what it is. We've also recorded it in context. We probably don't have enough to translate anything yet, but if all of the ship's interior looks like what we've seen so far, we'll eventually figure out some of this stuff."

"Noted, Waverly," replied the captain. "Any luck in locating the bridge?"

"Negative, sir," said Felix. "We're still looking for the bridge. We think it should be a couple of decks above our present location."

"Make it a priority, Lance Corporal."

"Understood, sir. Falcon Team out." Felix looked around at his team. "I'm betting the bridge is up that way," he said, pointing up at the ceiling. "Let's see what we find in the upper decks."

The Marauders nodded while Felix's team just shrugged.

Waverly said, "Anyone else think it's strange that we haven't found any crew quarters?"

"Could be below decks. Or above," said Nakamura. "This ship is a lot bigger than the *Nemean* and was designed by aliens. No telling how they deal with crew matters."

"We'll worry about that later," said Felix. "Let's make our way up to the next deck."

The team made it two decks above the engine room before they noticed that the gravity gradient there was a lot heavier than it was at their point of entry.

"My suite registers 0.8 G. I've never known a ship to have variable gravity," said Smalls.

"The gravity simulator may be malfunctioning," said Felix.

"Or," said Waverly, "the gravity gradient could be by design. They may have had a need for heavier gravity in the upper decks."

"What sort of need?" asked Nakamura.

Waverly shrugged. "Could be a million reasons. Maybe some equipment runs better at lower G environments, or vice versa."

"Or maybe this was a mixed crew," said Starkley.

"What do you mean?" asked Felix.

"Maybe this ship didn't belong to one group of aliens. It may have been crewed by different species that required different environmental conditions. The heavy-gravity guys lived in the upper decks and the light-G guys lived down below."

"A possibility," said Felix. "The fact is, we don't know right now. Let's keep an eye on our grav meters. If things get too heavy, our suits start to fail. I'm in no mood to get crushed by my own EVA."

After walking a few hundred meters, rounding several corners and forcing open three tightly secured hatches, the team stepped into a large chamber with a circular window looking out into space. In the distance they could see the *Nemean*, and further out beyond their ship hung the large alien Structure. From here the Structure, the *Nemean,* and the space beyond looked breathtakingly beautiful.

Situated about twenty meters away from the window area was what appeared to be a long, curved bench, large enough to accommodate perhaps fifty seated Marines. It appeared to be a viewing area for crew, the first sign that the ship did, indeed, once have crew aboard.

Further back beyond the bench were three pillars with protrusions facing the window.

"Look," said Nakamura, pointing to the protrusions. "Those look like light projectors."

"Like an old-style movie," said Waverly. "They used to use projectors to throw light up onto a screen, where the audience could view a movie that played on a reel."

"If those are projectors and this *is* some type of 'theater,' we could learn a lot about the crew, their appearance, culture…. among other things," said Felix. "I'll report this in to the *Nemean*. Billows, drop a radio marker here, just in case the twine gets lost."

Each EVA suit was equipped with one small detachable radio beacon. The beacons were standard issue accessories in their EVA tool kits and could be used to mark important locations during a mission. Between the team they had eight beacons in total.

The team could drop a beacon at strategic locations, making them easier to find later, as long as the beacon locator came within fifty feet of the device.

They couldn't use these to map their way from their ingress point, as there were too few beacons and only worked when the locator was line of sight with the beacon, but they did come in handy for "painting" important locations, like the engine room and now the viewing chamber.

"Over there," said Tubbs, indicating a bank of floor-mounted screens along a wall adjacent to the bench area.

Waverly made his way to the first screen and passed his recorder over it. "This *does* look like some kind of user interface. The markings here look pretty much the same as all the others, except these have shorter lines and look more tightly wound."

"Shorthand?" asked Billows.

"That, or their version of letters," said Waverly. "Hard to say."

"I'm guessing that's how you turn on the overhead projectors," said Tubbs.

"That's *if* those are projectors and *if* we can figure out what these symbols mean."

"SAS man, you are way too cautious," said Tubbs. "Press something and see what it does. What's the worst that could happen?"

"Temping as that may be," replied Waverly, "we are decidedly *NOT* doing that!"

Waverly continued examining the different floor-mounted devices while the team explored the rest of the chamber. It was a lot larger than it looked, with dozens of recessed alcoves and areas only visible when approached directly. What's more, in addition to the bank of floor-mounted screens Tubbs had noticed, the team found hundreds of smaller stations, consoles and other interfaces scattered throughout the chamber. All of them featured the same flowing, tightly wound markings.

"This is what I call an 'information-rich environment'", said Waverly. "This place might even tell us more about this ship's builders than the bridge. Lance Corporal, I think we need to get the *Nemean*'s computers working on translating this stuff ASAP, so that when we do find the bridge we'll have an idea what we're looking at."

"Can you transmit from here?" asked Felix.

"No. There's too much data to send over for my suit's comm system. It's not powerful enough to overcome the interference from the ship's hull and the jamming storm being put out by the Structure. I'll need to get back to the Falcon and try from there. The good news is this chamber has provided us with a lot of new data points with unique contextual reference points that we *know* were used by this ship's crew."

"*Nemean*, this is Felix. Agent Waverly believes we have enough data for the ship's computers to begin translating this text for us. Waverly?"

"*Nemean,* this is Waverly. The Lance Corporal is right. I'm fairly positive about that. I think the *Nemean*'s computers should be able to tease out some information from what we've recorded here. At least enough for some very rudimentary, approximate translations. The chamber we're currently in is a very information-rich environment with great contextual reference points — and as I explained to Mr. Felix, we *know* that the interfaces in this area were at one point *used* by the ship's crew. A cryptanalysis of the script overlaid with contextual data overlaid with object function sensor readings should shed a lot of light on things."

"Very good," said the captain over comm. "Begin transmitting as soon as you can."

"Will do, sir," replied Waverly and closed the comm.

"Felix, I'm going to try this from the Falcon. Here, take the twine," he said as he removed the spool strapped to his back and handed it to Felix. "I'll come back here as soon as I'm done. If you've moved on to another part of the ship, I'll follow the twine to find you."

"Sounds like a plan. Good luck, Waverly."

"Thank you." Waverly saluted Felix and followed the molecular twine trail he originally laid back towards their point of ingress and the waiting Falcon.

--

Agent Waverly worked over the Falcon's comm controls, establishing a heavy data feed link with the *Nemean*. Removing the data recorder from its slot on his left shoulder, he inserted the interface into an empty slot on the Falcon's comm console.

A light blinked green indicating a connection between the device and the Falcon had been established.

A second later, a blast of static burst through his helmet comm and out came a garbled voice. "Waverly! Reply."

It sounded like Lance Corporal Felix, his voice agitated and impatient.

"Waverly here. What's going on?"

"Something's happening. There's a klaxon sounding throughout the ship."

"Not registering here. I'm on the Falcon. Hold on, let me check—.... Shit! Felix, you have to get back here right now. Radiation and magnetic fields building up fast."

A moment passed before Felix replied, "Our EVAs read clear. No radiation warnings. Magnetic fields are nominal."

"Then it's building up out here, near the surface of the hull. Felix, I've got to put some distance between the Falcon and the ship's hull, otherwise it'll fry the electronics and my data recordings — not to mention me."

"Do it, Waverly! Get your ass clear."

"Sealing port hatch. Disengaging docking clamp. Falcon is free of alien craft. Maneuvering away on low thrusters."

"Felix. What are your EVA readings now?"

"Still all clear."

"Things are getting hot out here."

The *Nemean*, keeping station twenty thousand kilometers away, had a clear view of what was going on.

"Captain, I'm reading rising levels of radiation and magnetic activity around that ship's hull," said Lieutenant Paris. "Looks like the ramjet has been activated."

"That is a classic ramjet activation sequence," said Collins. "The team will be safe as long as they stay within the hull. Things won't be so pleasant for anything, or anyone, on the Falcon.

"Falcon Team. SITREP. Who activated the ramjet?", demanded Gregory.

"Unknown, sir," replied Felix. "We have no idea. Ship's alarms went off and then Waverly reported radiation and magnetic buildup outside, along the hull of the ship. He's moved the Falcon off to a safe distance until things cool down."

"Understood. Carry on and find that bridge. Agent Collins assures us that you'll be safe as long as you stay *inside* the hull. We'll collect Waverly and get started on those translations. With any luck we'll be able to print you up a fresh copy of that ship's manual so you can shut off the ramjet. Captain out."

Felix closed the comm and looked around at the rest of the team. "Well, you heard the captain. We're gonna be here a while. We've got our orders. The bridge is our priority. Let's go!"

--

Agent Waverly sat in the Falcon's pilot nest, two thousand five hundred kilometers away from the alien vessel, and watched as purple, yellow, blue and green magnetic field lines danced, twisted and arced across hundreds of kilometers as the ramjet continued its ignition sequence. It was a mesmerizing and beautiful sight, and Waverly felt like he could stay here and watch it forever. He had read about ramjet technology while at the academy and had seen simulations, but never anything like this.

He wondered what kind of people had built this ship, and if they could appreciate how beautiful it was. He suspected that the builders *would* certainly appreciate this sight. Perhaps that's what the viewing chamber was for.

Why else would they build a ship with a giant window looking out into space, if not for their ability to appreciate beauty — whether it was the beauty of the stars they traveled or the beauty of the drive that took them there.

For a second, Waverly felt a tinge of kinship for the unknown aliens and an even stronger desire to translate their language so that he could truly get to know them. He allowed his mind a few more moments to wander among alien vistas before shaking his head and directing his focus to the here and now.

"*Nemean,* Waverly aboard Falcon One. Beginning data transmission sequence now. Please acknowledge once the data stream link has been securely established."

A few moments went by.

"Agent Waverly, this is Lieutenant Paris. Link confirmed. Please rendezvous with the *Nemean.* You are clear for docking port two. We're monitoring the alien craft from here. Science teams have been assigned to sift through your data recordings with the immediate goal of establishing a translation matrix. That should help us figure out how to shut down the ramjet. Meanwhile, engineering has a plan to enhance the Falcon's shielding. If we can't turn off the ramjet, at least we'll be able to go back and pick up our guys using the Falcon."

"Roger that. Setting course for the *Nemean*, docking port two. See you in a few. Waverly out."

--

An hour later the ramjet's intensity had reached the point where communication with the EVA team was spotty at best, and the *Nemean*'s science teams had yet to establish a translation matrix to decipher the alien language.

That was when things got complicated.

"Captain, the ramjet seems to have reached peak power — and its thrusters just came online. It appears to be breaking orbit and on course for this system's primary."

"That explains a lot," said Collins. "I thought this design looked familiar."

"Explain, Mr. Collins," ordered Captain Gregory.

"ISAT has quite an extensive history exploring ramjet technology. What we're looking at is what ISAT terms a *plow* design and it *is* as unimaginative a term as it sounds. Basically, the ramjet is activated and brought to full strength, upon which time-primary propulsion engines accelerate the vessel to a significant fraction of the speed of light — preferably through an environment rich in solar wind byproducts like electrons and protons from hydrogen, atomic nuclei…basically an alpha-particle bath. Barreling through that at a high enough speed is enough to ignite the ramjet's propulsion section and off it goes. I'm oversimplifying, of course, but that's the gist of things."

"We need to stop that ship now," said the captain. "Mr. Marker, can you target the ram-scoop assembly?"

"I'd advise against that, Captain," said Collins. "These designs are delicate dances of fuel, energy, radiation and magnetic fields crisscrossing along each other's paths. A stray shot or an errant explosion could very well destroy the entire ship."

The captain pressed his comm key. "Engineering, ETA on the Falcon's shield upgrades?"

"Uncertain, sir," said the voice answering his comm. "We're still working out the metallurgical and radiation shield-power curves. The ramjet is putting out an awful lot of radiation that could very quickly kill our crew and destroy the Falcon's electronics. Also, sir, we're low on raw materials. We used much of our initial stocks to repair the *Nemean* after the last battle."

"Understood. Keep working on the problem. I want another update in an hour."

The captain closed the comm and turned to his bridge officers. "Ideas?"

"Let's keep pace with the vessel," said Commander Peters. "Stay in comm range until the translation matrix is complete or we figure out how to safely rendezvous and recover the EVA team."

"Just what I was thinking, Commander," replied the Captain. "Helm, maintain safe range with the alien vessel. Match course and speed as needed."

"Aye sir. Maintaining fixed range. Matching course and speed."

Looking at his XO, the captain asked, "Things can't get any worse, can they?"

The executive officer shrugged. "Always room for improvement."

"Indeed."

Felix relayed the news to the rest of the EVA team. The *Daedalus* was on the move and accelerating, apparently in-system towards the fuel-rich environment surrounding the local star. According to the last report, the *Daedalus* was traveling at zero point zero five percent the speed of light. *Nemean*'s science department expected it to have accelerated to perhaps 0.15c by the time it made its closest approach to the system's primary.

"Let's hope we're back aboard the *Nemean* well before then," Felix told his team. With the Falcons' ion drive topping out at a velocity of about zero point one percent light in real space, they wouldn't have too many chances after that if the *Daedalus* kept accelerating. Using the Falcon's hybrid jump-propulsion drive was also likely out of the question, more so at higher velocities approaching significant fractions of the speed of light.

A Falcon would have to be sent within the next few hours or else the EVA team would have to disable the *Daedalus'* drive on their own. And if they couldn't do that…

"We're pretty much screwed," said Nakamura. "Two ISAT agents and a whole slew of science heads on that ship and they can't coordinate an EVA for us? What are we paying them for again?"

"Space is complicated," said Felix. "Traveling through it is even more complicated. I'm sure the captain and crew are doing everything they can to figure this out. But we don't have to wait around hoping we get EVAC out of here. We can still find the bridge and turn this boat off ourselves."

"Lead the way, Your Majesty," said Tubbs.

"Marine," growled Starkley, "button your lips before I button them for you!"

"Thank you, Corporal," said Felix, waving for Starkley to stand down. "Despite our circumstances, we are still on a mission. We are to find the bridge and learn everything we can about this ship and her builders. We have time on our hands, people. Let's use it productively instead of complaining about our circumstances. You grunts signed up for this mission knowing the risks, now prove to me that you are worthy of being called a Marine!"

"OORAH!" shouted the team — including Tubbs, who opened a private channel to Felix and apologized for his earlier comments.

"It's fine, Marine," said Felix. "I can take a lot more damage than that. Now keep on your toes and look sharp, else next time I won't stop Starkley from biting your head off."

Since finding the windowed observation chamber, the EVA team had explored another four upper decks but had yet to locate the bridge. The *Daedalus* was curiously sterile, especially in terms of creature comforts. Much of the ship had been built for function and function alone. In fact, a lot of it appeared to be automated, with little need for an active crew. However, the halls, corridors and rooms all continued to feature different types of slashes, arcs, curves and other lines that were incomprehensible to the team but that, nevertheless, gave off a sense of *belonging* exactly where they were found.

The upper decks continued with the pattern of heavier gravity, with deck gravity on OD+4 (Marine shorthand for observation deck plus four — meaning four decks above the observation chamber) coming in at 0.85 G.

Beyond the gravity gradient, the ship seemed to feature an illumination gradient as well, with decks OD+3 and above having slightly more lighting than those below. In fact, while lighting was still dim by human standards, the lighting on OD+4 was sufficient to allow for well-adjusted eyes to navigate without bumping into walls. If they went up a few more decks, the EVA team could at least turn off their headlamps and conserve power.

While all the decks were so far devoid of atmosphere, Felix wondered if they'd find breathable environs if they went up enough decks. That would make any extended stay on the *Daedalus* much more comfortable.

OD+4 turned out to be another dud, with no signs of the bridge or anything else of interest to the team. Felix keyed open the command channel and tried to raise the *Nemean*. Static filled his mic, with a few words interspersed between the sound of crackling air. "Text…Forward…"

Felix understood the meaning of "Text." Audio and visual comms were no longer practical, and so from now on the *Nemean* would be communicating via tight-beam text messages. Not the most efficient way to communicate, but the only way given the amount of interference building up around the *Daedalus*. He quickly dictated a report that his suit's computer converted into a short text message and beamed it back to the *Nemean*. A few moments later a reply was received, which his suit displayed on his HUD.

An image of a circle with an arc anchored to one end appeared first, followed by an equal sign below that, followed by the words "command/control" under that.

They had cracked the code! Or at least one symbol. But what an important symbol it was!

He flashed the information to the other Marines and said, "That circle shape with the attached arc…they think that means 'command' or 'control.' I'm pretty sure I saw that in the engine room at least once, but not since. Be on the lookout for that symbol. Now let's move out and see what OD+5 has in store for us."

"Can't wait," said Nakamura.

"Don't worry, I brought my big gun" said Smalls.

"Let's hope we don't need it, Smalls. Stay alert, people. We now have an idea of what to look for," said Felix, taking point as they entered a sloped corridor that led to OD+5.

Several hours later, the *Nemean*'s engineering team worked out a plausible design to strengthen the Falcon's shielding enough to attempt another docking with the *Daedalus*.

However, it was not foolproof and would not last for long.

By the time it was brought to the captain for approval, it was already too late. The *Daedalus* had accelerated to 0.20c, well beyond the maximum velocity of the Falcons. The crew considered taking the *Nemean* directly alongside the *Daedalus'* hull, burning through and rescuing the EVA team.

However, there was no way to protect the crew during transit between vessels, where they would be exposed to open space, and besides the ships were too large for such maneuvers to be carried out safely; the energy flux between two vessels traveling at such a significant fraction of the speed of light in close proximity to a star would create havoc for sensors, navigation and other vital systems.

The captain instructed comm to send a text message to Lance Corporal Felix: FALCON TEAM. NO EVAC POSSIBLE. WORKING TO SHUT DOWN RAMJET.

While shutting down the ramjet would ultimately be the best solution, Gregory worried that even if his science team did manage to create a sufficiently robust translation matrix, it would be impossible to deliver it to the Falcon team to implement. At best, they might be able to beam a few vital translation key snippets to the Falcon Team, and that would have to be enough. Now more than ever, the captain had to rely on the smarts and ingenuity of the people he selected to lead field operations.

Felix was smart, capable and a good Marine. He'd come up through the ranks with grit, determination and hard work. His was a true success story and the captain had selected him to lead this mission for a reason.

--

The Falcon team had just exited the ramp, opened a hatch and stepped onto OD+5. Felix gave the "all stop" command as he examined his EVA's sensor readings. He noticed a green light gently flashing in his HUD.

His hunch had been right.

Felix's environmental gauge came to life here, registering an atmosphere consisting of ninety-two percent carbon dioxide, three percent nitrogen and two percent argon, with trace levels of water vapor, carbon monoxide, hydrogen and oxygen. Atmospheric pressure came in at seven millibars.

Next to the environmental gauge readings was another alert. CLOSEST UNION COMPARISON: MARS.

According to Felix's EVA computer, the atmospheric readings on this deck most closely resembled the natural conditions found on Mars, outside of the designated habitable zones.

"Check your environmental gauges, everyone — we've arrived on Mars," said Felix.

"I've always wanted to visit," said Smalls. "I hear Martian chocolate is great. Where can I get some?"

"Food always on your mind, Smalls," said Nakamura. "Or should we start calling you 'Bigs?'" She chuckled at her own joke.

Looking over his shoulder, Starkley hesitated for a second and then pointed out beyond the hatchway.

The deck stretching out before them was literally a maze, with corridors going this way and that, winding turns and u-turns in plain sight, doors and multiple paths to choose from, turning the exploration of that space into a gamble.

Since the discovery of the viewing chamber, it had become apparent that the *Daedalus'* designers had intended for each deck to be at least a little different from the one below it, but they had gone all out on this one.

"If I were trying to hide the bridge," said Felix," I'd probably steer clear from the very top and very bottom decks. I'd place it on one of the middle decks. And I would make sure that whatever middle deck I selected would be a pain in the ass to navigate for anyone not part of the crew. Ladies and gentlemen, I bet you one month's salary that the bridge is on *this* deck, right here."

No one took Felix's bet. Instead, Starkley said, "There are five entrances to this deck and seven of us. If we are going to find the bridge anytime soon, we are going to have to split up. We can't afford to stay together anymore. And besides, we haven't run into any hostiles yet. This ship is probably empty."

"I agree that splitting up is going to allow us to cover more ground. However, I'm not so convinced that the ship is completely empty," said Felix. "The lower decks were vacuum and less hospitable. The higher we've come, the more they begin to have conditions that mimic planetary environments — even if only on a minute scale. Maybe the crewed quarters are here in the upper decks."

"No one has challenged us yet," countered Starkley. "If this ship were crewed, wouldn't someone have tried to stop us by now?"

"Possibly," replied Felix. "We have no idea how a hypothetical alien here even thinks. No telling how they might react to us or view our arrival, nor can we say anything about their intentions. That being said, I do think splitting up is our best bet in finding the bridge quickly. Starkley, you and Billows take the first entrance over to the left. Nakamura, Smalls, Nichols, you take the next three corridors. Tubbs, you're with me. We'll take the one on the right."

Nakamura pointed to the spool of molecular twine on Felix's back and said, "We'll each need a length of that. How much do you have left?"

Felix looked at the readout attached to the spool. "We started with seven miles and now have five point three miles left. You'll each get a mile. Tubbs and I will take the extra third. Hopefully that will be enough. If it's not, we meet back here and regroup. If we thought we needed this twine for the other decks, we're definitely going to need it now."

Felix used the automatic spooler on his back to measure out five new, mile-long spools of the twine. Each spool weight one and a half pounds and could fit comfortably around a removable holder the Marines could mount on the outer thigh of their EVA suits. Felix kept his spool mounted on his backpack.

"OK, let's move out. Good luck, everybody!"

Green acknowledgements lit up in Felix's HUD.

And then they entered the labyrinth.

Chapter 6

A jump in space

System: Virgil's star (VGL 191)

Location: Aboard the Alcmene naval vessel Nemean

The *Daedalus* had continued accelerating in-system for the last several hours. The *Nemean*'s science team had added several more pieces to the translation matrix but it was a slow-going process. Methods for communicating with aliens had been discussed, theoretically, for hundreds of years. However, no one had any real experience with how to *actually do it* in the real world. It was a hard problem to crack. Truly *understanding* an alien mind was almost impossibly difficult.

You could, in theory, assign motives to observed behaviors based on known, or assumed, essentials — in humans such things would be the need for nourishment, the need for sleep, the need to reproduce, the need for companionship, the need to explore. How many of such elemental human needs would be shared by aliens was a difficult question to answer, especially since they had never been observed in daily life.

However, one could assume certain things in a more general way; for example, the need for nourishment could be generalized into the need for energy, which as far as the captain was concerned, was the only truly elemental need that all organisms would share. All the others were currently unknown.

Despite the depth of this problem, Felix's team had gathered good information that helped contextualize the observed symbols, and a picture was slowly developing.

But the captain didn't have time to consider it in detail, as the *Daedalus* continued to accelerate across Virgil's system, in time reaching seventy percent of the speed of light, then eighty percent, then ninety percent, then ninety-five and finally ninety-nine before...

"Sir, the *Daedalus* just vanished!" gasped Lieutenant Paris.

"Vanished? How?"

"Unknown, sir."

Commander Peters cycled through several of the computer's analytical readouts. "Captain, my guess is that the *Daedalus* just engaged some type of FTL drive. Just before it vanished from our sensors, the computer recorded an unusual distortion in the space around the vessel. Then the local gravity gradient surrounding it went to nil and there was an enormous release energy — about twenty times the output of our engines at maximum and about seven times the energy output of the ramjet."

Collins had also been studying the data streaming in.

"I concur with the commander," he said. "While the technology is unknown to ISAT, the implied science is not. That ship is very likely now traveling at the equivalent of some multiple of the speed of light."

"And there's no way our sensors can track it," said the captain. "Lieutenant Paris, are you reading anything at all that could enable us to guess its course?"

"No sir. The space it previously occupied is showing a lot of chaotic activity — gravity eddies, exotic particles and fluctuations in the local energy matrix — but nothing that would enable us to extrapolate a course."

"Collins. Do you concur?" asked the captain. "Has the *Daedalus'* jump to FTL left behind any energy or space-time topographical clues as to where it might be heading?"

Collins took a few moments before answering. "If you will, allow me some time to further analyze the data. I will require Lieutenant Paris' assistance. However, my first impression is that it's unlikely we'll be able to determine that ship's course."

The captain nodded. "Do what you can. Lieutenant Paris, provide whatever assistance Mr. Collins needs. Helm, full stop all engines. Ease us into orbit around the primary. Commander, keep collecting data from the *Daedalus'* FTL transition point and make sure Mr. Collins and Lieutenant Paris receive a live feed, pre and post computer analysis."

Turning to Collins and Paris, Gregory added, "I want you looking at the data from every possible angle."

They nodded in acknowledgement.

Turning his attention back to Commander Peters, the captain said, "And I want to keep monitoring the Structure for any signs of activity. Continue all sensor probes. Don't be shy about it — probe it with everything we have. I am particularly interested in determining whether or not it had been in any form of communication with the *Daedalus.*"

"I can answer that already, Captain," replied the commander. "Our sensors didn't record any comm between the Structure and the *Daedalus* at any time."

The captain looked skeptical. "Keep looking. They may have used a means of communication we are not familiar with."

"Or communicated in a way we don't normally consider a form of communication," interjected Collins. "Captain, Lieutenant Paris and I will augment the commander's analysis for alien communications as well. With your permission, of course."

"Permission granted. Commander, you have the bridge."

"Aye sir. I have the bridge."

Gregory looked around the bridge one more time, walked down the ramp and exited.

--

The captain entered the sick bay through the private entry way leading directly to Dr. Smith's office. He had known Doc Smith for over ten years and had come to consider him a friend. Not the type of friend he'd accompany on a night out on the town or at the types of dive bars he used to frequent when he first made the rank of captain, when he'd use his newly minted stars to impress any woman who would even casually glance his way.

Those days were behind him now, and as he grew older, he recognized the need for friends like Dr. Smith. The kind of friend that remained the same despite how much time went by before you saw them again. A deep kinship that didn't diminish through physical absence.

The doctor was sitting with his back to the door, busy peering at a star map displayed on his console.

"Harry, how many times have I warned you against sitting with your back to an open door?"

Dr. Smith slowly turned in his chair and said, "More times than I care to remember. I just can't seem to get my paranoia up to your standards."

"Practice makes perfect," replied the captain with a smile. "May I come in?"

"Please, Captain. My door is always open to you...so long as I'm not busy with a patient."

"Thank you." Nodding to the star map on the doctor's console, Gregory said, "That's not your typical reading."

"This? Oh, this is a star map centered on this system. I'm rather intrigued by the fact that they selected *this* point in space to make their presence known."

"You mean our friends out there, aboard that giant moon?" asked the captain.

"Exactly them. And I'm not sure they are our friends."

"Neither am I, Doctor. Although I've been basically operating on the assumption that they either *are* our friends but don't know it yet or *will eventually* become our friends...some day."

"That is an optimistic view of things."

"I'm not sure there is a better way to look at it."

"With caution, Captain."

Gregory smiled. "You sound like Field Agent Collins. He wants us to leave the system and go back home."

The Doctor raised his eyebrows. "Well, I'm not sure *that* is the right course of action either."

"Glad to hear that, my friend. I can't say I liked the idea of leaving now...although I do admit that I've considered it several times."

"That's the sign of a good captain," said Dr. Smith as he reached for a cold cup of coffee sitting on his desk. "A good captain carefully considers all options — gives them all a fair hearing, even the ideas he doesn't agree with."

The captain shook his head. "The thing is, Doc, I'm not sure what I'm *supposed* to do."

"Use the facts on hand to make the best decision you can possibly make, balanced against known risks and mission objectives."

"Nice!" said the captain. "That's straight out of the academy's handbook."

The doctor placed his hand on the captain's shoulder and said, "That's why it's called a *handbook*. It's the cumulative wisdom of all the captains that have come before you summarized in a few pages."

"Good one, Doc. I've always enjoyed your sarcasm."

"No offense intended. I'm just trying to provide a bit of comedic relief to an overworked captain. And as your doctor, I can see how stressed you actually are — despite your uncanny ability to keep it hidden from the rest of the crew."

"I've launched three expeditions and all three have been failures."

"That's not a fair characterization. And by '*not fair,*' I mean not fair to you and not fair to the teams that went on those missions. They gathered massive amounts of data which will take time to sift through and properly analyze. They were not failures by any means."

"I guess what's bothering me is that each mission, except for Perseus Force's attempt to retrieve Duffy's team, has led to an unacceptable number of MIAs. It seems every time I sent a team out there, at least some part of it ends up MIA. We've now lost Felix's team and the *Daedalus*."

The doctor thought about that for a moment. "Have you considered that has been happening by design?"

"By design?" asked the captain. "What do you mean?"

"Maybe our friends out there are making it a point to keep some of our people behind."

"To study them? Yes, I've considered that."

"Not just to study them…but to study us. Our response to the loss of our people."

The captain nodded. "That is a very real possibility. I had a fleeting thought about that as well, although I've been more preoccupied about getting our people back than thinking about *why* our people keep going MIA. But that makes a lot of sense. Aside from one person who may or may not be KIA, Marine Private Martinez, there have been no confirmed deaths on this mission. And we have yet to positively confirm that Private Martinez is actually KIA."

"Think about what you've been tasked to do here," said Doc Smith. "Diplomacy, threat assessment, first contact, research and exploration on your own, over a hundred light years away from home, with no external support, drifting a few thousand kilometers away from a giant alien moon inhabited by at least two sentient races — that's a tall order for any captain and crew."

The captain smiled. "Thank you, Doctor, for your perspective. If they are using the MIAs to test our resolve, then I won't disappoint them. I intend to stay the course and see this mission through, and that includes getting back all our missing crewman. If they want to see how humans behave, they will at least know that we don't leave people behind."

The doctor nodded. "I'm glad I could help. I think you're making the right decision. Showing them that we don't consider our fellow humans expendable is a wise course of action."

Glancing at the time, the captain said, "I'm needed back on the bridge. Thank you, Doctor. Next time, I want to hear your thoughts on why you think they selected this system to make their presence known."

"Don't hurry back on that one, Captain. I don't have the slightest idea. But maybe you can get someone from the astrophysics department to chime in."

"I'll do that. Thanks again."

The doctor waved and turned his back to the door again, closely eyeing the star map. Gregory gently closed the door behind him. He paused for a moment to make sure it was locked from the outside before calling out, "Locked it for you, Doc!"

He heard a muffled "thank you" through the door and smiled. The doctor would take his advice someday, but he didn't have time to persuade him now. He had to get back on the bridge and discuss his next course of action with the commander.

--

Back on the bridge, the captain sat in his command console and looked at the reports waiting for him.

Paris and Collins had completed their preliminary analysis of the *Daedalus'* pre-FTL jump spatial data. The data contained a lot of interesting information for the analysts to review at length, but nothing immediately suggesting any way to reconstruct the ship's likely course or destination.

The report from Peters also came back negative, with nothing suggesting that communication between the *Daedalus* and the Structure had taken place before the ship's jump into FTL flight.

"Mr. Collins, Lieutenant Paris — I've read your report. Create a summary of all key environmental conditions when the *Daedalus* disappeared into FTL flight. Commander, meet me in the conference room in five minutes. Ms. Harris, you have the bridge."

"Aye sir. I have the bridge."

Five minutes later, Peters entered the captain's conference room. Gregory projected a display of several camera views of the *Daedalus'* jump, along with key metrics along the left side of the screen.

"Commander, I think following the *Daedalus* is the most important thing we can do right now. If Paris and Collins can't find a way to plot the *Daedalus'* course from the data we have, then I want to see if recreating the exact spatial conditions and activating our hyperlight pods will allow us to follow the *Daedalus*."

"Sir, we don't know exactly how their FTL drives work. We use different technologies."

"I know that, Commander. But the basic principles are the same. FTL depends heavily on our ability to manipulate the space around the ship. Our ship's inertial coefficient has to drop to zero, along with the local gravity gradient. How that's accomplished are details, but the results on the surrounding space are the same. I have a hunch that if we can recreate the *exact* environmental conditions surrounding that ship down to the sub-atomic, sub-space level, we'll be able to follow them through an exact copy of the jump point the *Daedalus* created and arrive at the same destination."

"That almost sounds plausible, Captain, but I'm doubtful. What does the science department have to say about your theory?"

"Well, Ron. Let's look at it this way: Ships like the *Nemean* have hyperlight pods that allow us to travel to the same destination over and over again. Most likely, the *Daedalus*, regardless of the details of its technology, has the same capability. It ought to be able to travel to and from a given destination over and over again. If it didn't, it would make for a pretty limited FTL capability. Still valuable to a space-faring civilization, but limiting. I have to assume that they've got FTL drives that can replicate destinations at will."

"Let's assume that works," replied Peters. "Are you sure that following the *Daedalus* is our best course of action? What about the Structure? And our people still inside that thing?"

"We're not giving up on our people or the Structure or the aliens. I just think following the *Daedalus* has become our immediate priority. Not only because we have people aboard, but because so far it's provided us with the most tangible information on an alien race. It's also a chance to potentially seize — or at least study — alien technology, alien libraries, alien star charts. It's an easier win for us right now. I fully intend to return to the Structure on a priority basis, whether we are successful in finding the *Daedalus* or not."

Commander Peters carefully weighed the captain's words. He tended to agree with Gregory on most command decisions, and while he didn't disagree with the logic being presented to him this time, he was also not entirely convinced that following the *Daedalus* was the best course of action.

"To be honest with you, sir, I can't say I'm a hundred percent behind this decision. I do agree with all your points. But frankly, I don't know if that's the best thing for us to do."

"How long have we been friends now," asked Gregory? "What has it been...twenty plus years?"

Peters nodded. "*Plus* is right. Our first mission together was on the patrol boat *Elliot*, when we were handed orders to put down some second rate pirate raiders."

The captain laughed. "We did that how again? I distinctly remember calling for weapons only to be told that we had none."

"Exactly," said Peters. "You turned the water cannon on them and froze their airlock solid. They couldn't get back inside and they were caught outside with the stolen goods."

"Yes, I remember now," said Gregory. "Then we put on our EVA suits, pointed Z-7 pistols at them and told them to give up. That put an end to that. Was that reckless Ron?"

Peters shrugged. "Probably. But it worked."

"And now? Are you worried that this is another reckless decision?"

"I just can't see through this one," replied Peters. "Logically, I have no problem with it. But there's a part of me that's doubtful if this is our best course of action."

"I understand, Commander. I also have my doubts. I have doubts every time I issue an order that may potentially get someone killed. I have doubts all the time. I know this is a risky decision. But all things considered, I do feel it's the best one at the moment. My gut tells me the Structure is going to be right here when we get back — and if things go well with the *Daedalus*, hopefully we'll be in a better position to understand who we are dealing with out there, and maybe even open a friendly dialogue."

"Consider me an optimist, Captain!" said Peters. "I'll talk to Lieutenant Paris and Agent Collins and brief them on what we've discussed here. Perhaps we can begin with small-scale experiments before attempting a full-scale test with the *Nemean.*"

"Very good, Commander. I've got a few things to take care of. You have the bridge."

The commander saluted and left the captain's meeting room.

Captain Gregory touched his console and projected a star map centered on this system's primary star, Virgil, also known as VGL 191.

Why *had* the aliens selected this system to make their presence known? The captain had an idea.

The rest of the day had been quiet, with no further activity from the alien Structure and the *Daedalus'* course remained undetermined. Collins and Paris had continued working on the problem into the evening with little further success, and the captain told them to take a break and look at it with fresh eyes in the morning.

Gregory handed the night watch to Sub-Commander Shimatowa and left the bridge. After stopping at docking bay lounge east for a quick meal, he took a walk to the doctor's quarters. He pressed the comm panel next to the door and a few moments later Smith greeted the captain, a cup of coffee in his hand.

"Harry," said the captain, "are you busy?"

"I was getting ready for bed. What's on your mind?"

"May I come in?" asked Gregory.

"By all means. Please, have a seat."

"Thank you."

"Coffee?"

"No, thank you. Look, I took some time this afternoon to study the star chart you were looking at. Have you made any progress with it?"

"To tell the truth, I gave up about an hour after you left. It's just not in my makeup to make sense of such things."

"Nonsense. You're the one who opened my eyes to it. I think I know why they selected this particular star system to beam their message from."

The doctor looked interested. "Go on."

"I don't know how much of this you know, but the signal was first picked up by the North Brunswick Observatory in New Fountain, on Alcmene. The astronomers were impressed by the energy behind the message — it was enormous and clearly designed to remain coherent for long interstellar distances. At first they thought it was just a pulsar, but it repeated in a sequence of 4....9....5...13...18...9."

"Yes, I do remember that," said Smith. "It was in the first briefing report handed to me before we left the shipyards."

"The astrophysicists tore that sequence apart, and all sorts of theories rose up around it. Some sound, some silly. But the important thing at the time, at least to the President and Naval Command, was to investigate the source of the signal. So they sent the *Nemean*."

"Lucky us," laughed Smith.

"Now, getting to the star chart you were looking at. If you center the chart on Virgil's star, you'll note that Alcmene is one hundred thirty-nine light years away from here."

The captain paused and brought up a display of the star chart using the console on the doctor's desk.

"And you see, there's another system three hundred nineteen light years away over here, about sixty degrees in that direction. And up here, there's another system around three hundred ninety-one light years away."

"Interesting, Captain. I'm following you so far, but I still don't see the significance."

"Bear with me, Harry. We have three systems centered on Virgil's star, at one hundred thirty-nine, three hundred nineteen, and three hundred ninety-one light years away. And the message the aliens beamed contained the numerical sequence 4 – 9 – 5 – 13 – 18 –9."

"OK," said the Doctor. "Those numbers suggest *something* to me, on an intuitive level, but I have no idea what you are getting at."

"Kaprekar's operation Harry," replied the Captain. "Take any three-digit number and move the digits around so that you find the largest number and the smallest number the digits can possibly make. Then, subtract the smallest number from the largest number to get a new number and carry this operation on for each new number that it generates. In time, you'll end up with a constant result — in this case 495."

The doctor nodded. "I see. And the sequence begins with 4 – 9 – 5 ..."

"Not just that, Harry. If you add 4 and 9 you get 13. Then add 13 to 5, you get 18, then add 1 to 8 and you get 9. The alien's signal is clearly making a reference to the number 495, a known kernel in Kaprekar's operation. That in itself is interesting, in that they are using a very specific mathematical property of three-digit numbers to announce themselves to other sentient races. Knowledge of Kaprekar's operation requires a certain level of mathematical sophistication. Perhaps not a whole not — but definitely beyond that of civilizations just beginning to delve deeper into the mathematical sciences."

"Is there some significance to the number 495," asked Smith, "beyond this particular number trick?"

"I don't know. It could be an incidental result with no deeper significance than the fact that it happens to be so. The other important piece of this puzzle is found in your star chart — specifically the distances to the other star systems."

"I'm keeping up, Captain, but haven't made the leap yet. What have you found?"

"I think they are trying to draw our attention to a system not shown in our star charts, that happens to be nine hundred thirty-one light years away from Virgil."

"Where?" asked the doctor. "Where is this system?"

Pointing to a blank space in the upper edges of the star chart, the captain said, "My guess is that it's somewhere around here."

"And exactly how are you making that leap?"

"Consider: First, we've already established that they are communicating in terms of Kaprekar's operation and we know for three-digit numbers the kernel is 495. That's their exact signal. We also know from the star chart that we are dealing with three-digit arrangements consisting of 139, 319 and 391. If 139 is the lowest value, 931 must be the largest — and that's the only point in our star chart that is blank."

Pointing again to the blank space on the map, he said, "It's my guess they are drawing our attention to something nine hundred thirty-one light years away…right here."

"Interesting," said Smith. "Brilliant, actually. But how do we know they are not drawing our attention to the other systems on the map? The systems that are three hundred nineteen and three hundred ninety-one light years away. Or for that matter, the other three-digit number missing here, which is nine hundred thirteen?"

"That's a good point, Harry. They may very well be doing that as well. I was thinking they were trying to show us something that we are not currently aware of — but you're right, they could be drawing our attention to any one of those systems, or all of them."

"Or none of them," said Smith. "Maybe they are using these numerical properties just to make sure that whoever receives their message has some level of mathematical knowledge."

"That's true too."

"In any event, you have clearly uncovered something. You've made a convincing case that they used Kaprekar's operation in their initial communication burst, and have positioned themselves in space to further reinforce the fact that they are very much aware of that mathematical property."

"Exactly. I think at the very least we have been pointed to several new locations in space that require investigation."

The doctor nodded. "Have you told the commander yet, or any of the other staff?"

"Not yet. I wanted to share this with you. You were the one who asked the question in the first place. I was too preoccupied to even think of asking the question."

"Thank you, Captain. Are you still planning on following the *Daedalus*, or are you now setting your sights on these new points in space?"

Gregory shook his head. "The *Daedalus* remains my top priority. We're in no position to explore those other systems. Those will have to be part of a follow up mission, if Naval Command authorizes it."

"I doubt you'll have any trouble getting them to authorize expeditions to those other star systems. Navigating Union politics is going to be the tricky part. I'm sure there are going to be many five-star admirals wanting to keep this under wraps."

"Yes. This mission is already close to skirting the Union treaty on encounters with non-human sentient life. In any case, that's a discussion for another time."

"I'll be here if and when you want to have that talk, my friend."

"Thank you, Harry. Have a good night."

Smith held the door for the captain as he exited his quarters and wished him a good night. He wasn't sure if the captain was making the right decision in pursuing the *Daedalus*, but he couldn't disagree with the captain's logic.

Saying a small prayer for the captain and crew, Doc Smith turned out the light and went to bed.

--

The captain had had a good night's sleep, free of strange dreams or unwanted interruptions.

Sub-Commander Shimatowa's report was already on the captain's console. The night watch had reported no unusual activity. Systems were operating at nominal levels — or as well as could be expected under the circumstances — and there were no major personnel issues to address.

Pouring himself a cup of coffee, Gregory had high hopes for the day.

If things went well, the crew would be starting trial runs today to test the feasibility of following the *Daedalus* based on the data collected.

However, a short alert from Peters put a damper on that.

"Agent Collins is throwing a tantrum. Officially advises against following Daedalus. *Has removed himself from research team and Alcmene naval service."*

The captain keyed the comm on his console. A moment later an image of Commander Peters appeared on screen.

"Good morning, Commander," said Gregory. "I hope your sleep was as restful as mine."

"It was adequate, sir," said Peters. "Glad to hear you slept well. You've been running on too many stims lately, if you don't mind me making the observations."

"That's what Doc Smith told me as well." Taking a sip from his coffee cup, the captain continued, "I read your message about Collins. He's removed himself from the *Daedalus* research team and naval service? Is he serious?"

"He is, sir," replied Peters. "He said that by formerly removing himself from naval service, he is under no legal obligation to follow our orders, since he doesn't fall under our formal command nor jurisdiction anymore. He cited the exact passage from the Union / ISAT treaty granting him that right. I had it checked with legal. He can do it, sir."

"I don't doubt it, Commander," the captain replied. "But, like it or not, we *need* his expertise. He is, by default, our chief science and technology officer."

Peters shook his head. "Collins has sequestered himself in his stateroom. There is nothing we can legally do."

"Very well," replied the captain. "As naval officers, it is our duty to uphold the law and ensure that everyone on this ship is treated with dignity. I won't force anyone to do something they don't want to do."

"Agreed, Captain."

"Ron, one of the reasons I didn't abandon this mission when Collins first advised we leave the system are the Marines aboard that Structure out there." The commander nodded while the captain paused to sip from his coffee cup. "It's not only our military ethos about not leaving fellow soldiers behind. It's not just our duty to those soldiers' families to do everything we can to take them back home. It's all those things and *more*. We don't know who we are dealing with yet. We have no idea who, or what, those aliens are, or what they want. I want to make it plainly clear to them how much we value human lives and what we are willing to do to protect those lives. I was hoping Collins would understand that."

"You tried to convey that to him, sir," replied Peters. "Multiple times."

"You say he's in his stateroom?"

"Yes sir."

"OK, then. I'm going to conference him in on this call. Let's see what he has to say for himself."

A moment later the captain's console displayed an image of Agent Collins alongside Commander Peters.

"Agent Collins, the commander has told me about your 'resignation,' for lack of a better term."

Collins nodded. "I strongly advise you, captain, to abandon your pursuit of the *Daedalus* and return to base at once. We are dealing with things here that are very much beyond our capabilities."

"Then why did you agree to work with Lieutenant Paris when I asked you to analyze the *Daedalus'* FTL jump data and the feasibility of following it?"

"Curiosity, Captain. I am, after all, an ISAT agent. It was a chance to study new technology and gather rather fascinating data."

"And you'd have that same opportunity if we caught up to the *Daedalus* and recovered the EVA team."

"That is true. But I am very patient," said Collins. "Now is not the time to follow that ship. You have no idea where it could lead us — what pandora's box we could be opening up. What if it led us to another star system filled with aliens vastly beyond our comprehension? What if it's a distraction, or trap, set by the Structure aliens? There are too many unknowns attached to following that ship. And as I've advised you before, staying *here* is also foolhardy. Both EVA teams have been attacked by hostile aliens. We have heard nothing from ADAM and the Rosetta message went unanswered. If they had wanted to talk to us — on friendly terms — they would have done so by now. My guess, Captain, is that they randomly beamed out that message and waited to see who responds. They are clearly not impressed with us. We've overstayed our welcome. It's time to go home and let the many highly capable minds on Alcmene, Io and the rest of the Union mull over the problems we've already created here. And remember, Captain, the longer we stay here, the more likely it is that they will eventually determine the coordinates of the Union worlds. You do not want *that* on your record, I am sure."

Before the captain could respond, Collins closed the connection.

"I don't think he is open to persuasion, Captain," said Peters.

"No, he's not. I will send you a few crew reassignments. Our science department is full of very smart people. If this can be done, our own crew will figure it out. I'll see you on the bridge in ten minutes."

"Aye sir."

The captain ended the conference session and his console screen returned to black.

Finishing his coffee, he made a few notes regarding which personnel he wanted assigned to the *Daedalus* project and sent them off to Peters. As he walked towards the bridge, he smiled as he thought about how delicately fickle humans could be when dealing with those they didn't agree with.

--

The emergency klaxon rudely woke Waverly from a deep slumber. Despite the wailing sounds of the ship's emergency systems blasting his ears, his eyelids still felt heavy and a part of him wanted to remain in the comforting embrace of his bed sheets. Cursing, he shook his head and managed to push himself out of bed and out of his quarters.

He found the halls filled with ship personnel running to and from duty stations. Marine rapid reaction forces were on the move and fire suppression teams raced through the corridors.

The ship must be under attack! he thought.

But why hadn't he been summoned by Collins?

Standard ISAT protocol under such conditions called for two courses of action:

One, if the field agents had been assigned to pre-determined battle stations, they were to proceed to their stations.

Two, if no such orders had been pre-issued, then ISAT agents were to gather together at a designated location and present themselves for service to the ship's command staff.

The second protocol was to be done under the leadership of the senior ISAT officer on board.

Waverly keyed his comm frequency to Collins' and opened the channel "Agent Collins? Are you there? This is Waverly."

No reply.

Waverly then used the buzz feature that alerted the other party that a call was coming through.

No reply.

Careful not to knock anyone down, Waverly ran down the hall, took a lift up one deck and ran down two more sections before coming to a halt in front of Collins' stateroom door. He rang the bell and then started beating his fist against the door.

No response.

Either Collins was incapacitated, or he was…

The deck lurched under Waverly's feet, causing him to fall to the ground. An explosion somewhere below decks rocked the ship.

Waverly fought to get on his feet, the deck below him lurching side to side.

He had one foot planted squarely on the deck and the other still knee down when he felt an armored hand tighten around his bicep and yank him hard to his feet.

"What are you doing down on your knees, man?"

Parker!

"No time for prayer," shouted Parker over the klaxon. "It's time to kick some ass!"

"What's going on?" shouted Waverly.

"Don't know. Last I heard we were being boarded."

"By who?"

"The Cetos man! Who else?" replied Parker. "Look, I've gotta go. You better cover our six!"

Parker waved and ran down the hall and out of sight, melting into a detail of Marines turning the far corner of the hall.

None of this made sense.

Why would the inhabitants of the Structure try to board the *Nemean*? It's true they were hostile when the Marines boarded their ship — if that's what it was — and they did launch an attack on the *Nemean* after their battle with Felix's team….but they had been quiet ever since. They didn't seem to pose a threat when the *Nemean* and her crew kept at a safe distance.

Waverly frowned and shook his head. Hoping he was wrong, he looked around to get his bearings and headed for the bridge.

--

As the ship's nerve center, the bridge was a jumble of activity. Everyone on the command staff looked grim and were busy evaluating reports, issuing orders or examining their data displays.

Gregory stood near his command console, listening to a report from the captain of the *Nemean*'s rapid-reaction Marine force.

"No sign of hostiles on this deck. Bulkheads all look secure. If they breached, they didn't do it here."

"Understood," said Gregory. "Internal sensors still show a breach in that section. Sweep the rest of the decks and report back immediately if contact is made."

"Yes sir," replied the Marine.

Gregory closed the channel. Marker looked up towards the captain.

"Sir, I don't know what happened, but that ship is gone. Disappeared completely from our sensor array just as quickly as it appeared. I can't explain it, sir."

A few moments later the Marine lieutenant called the bridge again.

"Sir, all teams have reported in. No breaches on any of the decks. No hostiles sited. All decks report clear."

"Very well. Conduct another sweep of the entire ship. Keep eyes on cleared areas as you go, deck by deck. I want to be one thousand percent sure."

"Understood sir. Over and out."

Once the captain finished speaking to the Marine, Peters said, "Fire suppression teams report that they have things under control. Primary fires are out. A few secondaries are still burning but will be out shortly."

"Damage report," said the captain.

"Non-lethal damage to an extensive list of primary systems. Life support. Sensors. Propulsion. A significant job for the engineering teams, but they can do it. However, damage is extensive enough that they are advising a full retrofit will be in order once we get back to space dock. They don't have the material on hand to complete all repairs on everything that's been damaged. We'll be running at seventy-five percent capacity until we get back."

The captain shook his head. "How did their ship evade our sensors long enough to insert their force right under our noses? How did they board the ship and not leave any traces of their entry? How did they cause so much damage without a trace of them ever being here?"

"Sir!"

Both Gregory and Peters turned and saw Waverly running up the ramp to the command observation deck, where the captain's command console was located.

"Field Agent Waverly," said the captain. "Good timing. Where is your commanding officer? ISAT may have what we need to get this ship back to full strength without the need for a visit to the space dock. I also want you to join one of the Marine details to see if any of your ISAT devices can assist in locating any hostiles that may be hiding aboard my ship."

"Sir, the ship hasn't been boarded. We're not under attack."

Both commanding officers looked at him sharply.

"Explain," said the captain.

"Sir, I think it's Field Agent Collins. I think he's sabotaged the ship."

"What makes you say that?" asked Peters.

"For starters, he hasn't followed ISAT protocol. When a ship is under attack, ISAT agents are to either attend to their pre-assigned battle stations or assemble and present themselves to the command staff for orders. I haven't been able to raise him by any means."

"Maybe he's injured or ill," said Peters. "There are other possibilities."

"No sir. I don't think so."

"Give us details, Waverly," said Captain Gregory. "You've made a serious charge against your superior officer."

"Sir, he's confided in me that he thinks this mission should have ended a long time ago. He thinks we ought to have left and headed for home after the MC1 came back from our first encounter with the aliens."

Captain Gregory nodded. "Yes, he's shared that opinion with me as well."

"And with me," added Peters. "He's told everyone who would listen."

"That's the thing, sirs. No one took his advice. He told me that when a revolution is necessary and no one listens to you, then you must force their hand. He said that you must 'provide a driving force for change from the top.'"

The captain's eyes widened. "He's trying to force our hand. Cause enough damage to the ship's vital systems that I'm forced to order the *Nemean* back to space dock."

"Exactly, sir."

The captain keyed his comm to the rapid-reaction force's frequency.

"Yes, captain," the voice on the other side answered.

"Lieutenant, let me spare you an update on your sweep for hostiles. You haven't found any, right?"

"No sir. We have one section to go, but none spotted so far."

"Complete that final section. Then I have a new assignment for you. On a priority basis, locate ISAT Field Agent Romanov Collins and escort him to my bridge."

"Understood, sir."

The captain closed the channel. Turning to Waverly, he said, "Thank you, Field Agent. You are dismissed until further notice. Please remain nearby should I require your assistance or further information."

"Yes sir," replied Waverly. Saluting, he turned, went down the command ramp and left the bridge.

The captain watched him go.

"It's a shame, Ron," he said to his XO. "It's a shame that someone as talented as Waverly has to be under the command of someone as repulsive as Collins."

"The kid did the right thing," said Peters.

"He did. I just don't know how much he realizes that right now. He probably feels guilty for turning in his superior."

"He probably also feels some guilt by association," said Peters. "I'll see to it that it's clear in our reports and for the gossips among the enlisted."

The captain smiled. "The ship's rumor mill is a delicate beast, isn't it? Keep it happy with rumors to chew on but don't let it get its fangs too deeply into anything. Then you've got real damage."

"In the case of Waverly," said Peters, "the rumor mill could also lead to a few broken bones for the young man. A few drunk Marines hear that Waverly was a saboteur and he'd be in big trouble."

"Let's not let it come to that."

Peters nodded. "Leave that to me. What about Collins?"

"Brig or airlock?"

Peters smiled.

"I'm not sure I'm joking," Gregory said.

"That probably won't go over well, sir," said Peters.

The captain shrugged. "Probably not."

Peters continued, "Let's try to get a full confession from him and build a case. Military court martial would provide swift justice. I'm sure ISAT would also pile it on. He's disgraced the entire ISAT-Union world's cooperative program. They aren't going to stand for that."

"Hope you are right, Commander. It would be a scary thought if ISAT had a lot of people like Collins among its ranks."

"You've never really trusted ISAT agents, have you?' asked Peters.

The captain shook his head. "Why? Have you?"

"No sir," answered Peters. "But they are useful to have around. And there are good ones, like Agent Waverly."

"You are right, Commander. Thank you for reminding me why you are my XO. Now about those repairs. See to it that the teams are given every resource we have aboard to get the ship in tip top shape."

"Aye sir! Will do!"

The commander saluted, turned and left the bridge.

--

Collins stood with his back against a bulkhead, holding his breath lest any movement disturb the optical distortion field he was using to conceal his whereabouts.

It was obvious from the comments made by the Marines patrolling the ship's halls that they their mission objective had changed. They were no longer preoccupied with their search for hostile boarding parties. Instead, they were now very focused on finding him.

Clearly, the captain suspected him, but Collins wasn't sure how much the captain had already figured out.

It didn't matter now anyway. Collins would try to evade the patrols for as long as he could. Ideally, he'd evade them all the way back to space dock, where he'd slip off the ship and report to headquarters.

He had already tried to get back into his stateroom, but it was guarded by Marine sentries.

His original plan, to spoof the sensors into thinking the ship was under attack and being boarded by hostile aliens while he sabotaged the ship's vitals, almost went off without a hitch.

The only snag was that the ruse didn't last as long as Collins had calculated. He had been almost certain that it would take at least two hours for the command staff to declare the ship alien-free and confirm that the sensors were being spoofed. However, they did it in less than half that time, and simultaneously blocked access to his stateroom by posting sentries.

Collins wondered if he had underestimated the captain's abilities. Gregory was a cautious but reckless man. He would take his time confirming that nothing had entered the ship from the outside, ordering his troops to check and re-check every nook and cranny, every compartment, before declaring it clear.

He'd also order his staff to run multiple diagnostics on the ship's sensors before he could trust them again. He knew the captain was methodical and would follow regulations on such matters to the letter.

The psychological profile in Captain Gregory's dossier was plainly clear on this.

What made him a bad choice for this mission was his recklessness. Collins believed that the captain was simply out of his depth there. Such missions required nuanced reasoning, a polymath's range of knowledge and an artist's sensitivity.

The captain is none of those things, Collins thought to himself.

Then the answer to Collins's question presented itself to him, face to invisible face.

He saw Field Agent Waverly walking with a detail of Marines. The Marines were armed with assault rifles, while Waverly was clearly holding a distortion field detector.

Waverly had turned him in.

With Waverly assisting in the search, it was only a matter of time before he was found.

Rather than prolong the chase, Collins turned off the optical distortion field and put his hands up in the air.

The Marines quickly spotted him standing against the far bulkhead and rushed towards him, their weapons drawn and aimed squarely at his chest.

Waverly didn't bother going any closer. He just watched as the Marines quickly searched Collins and bound his hands with a length of VRC — a variable-resistance cord. VRCs were designed to increase binding tension in direct proportion to the force being exerted on the cord. If someone tried to pull the cord apart, it would respond by tightening its grip around the prisoner's hands, effectively negating their desire to remove the VRC.

The Marines quickly secured Collins and hustled him away towards the bridge.

Waverly wasn't sure how he felt. On the one hand he was glad to have stopped Collins from further damaging the ship or the mission, while on the other he felt dejected and confused.

His loyalties were with ISAT first, and with Alcmene Naval Command second. But his true, primary loyalty was to himself and his sense of right and wrong.

He knew Collins would probably feel vindicated in his actions, especially when the ship arrived at space dock.

Waverly wondered how Collins would feel once he found out the captain had no intention of going back to space dock and had ample resources to make necessary repairs right there in open space.

--

The Marine detail manhandled Collins up the ramp and onto the command deck. First Lieutenant Andrews saluted the captain and said, "Prisoner has been secured."

Gregory got out of his command console. "Very well, First Lieutenant."

Looking at the other officers on the bridge, he turned to Peters and said, "You have the bridge. Agent Collins and I are going to be in a meeting for the next thirty minutes."

"Aye sir. I have the bridge."

The captain walked towards his private meeting room without looking at Collins. His bearing signaled that he *expected* Collins to follow without being asked or ordered to accompany him.

Collins took the cue. With arms still bound, he followed the captain into the meeting room.

When Collins walked in, Gregory was already seated at the head of the table. He motioned for Collins to shut the door and take a seat. Collins closed the door with his leg and found a seat opposite the captain.

"Mr. Collins, we have some things to discuss."

"Of course, Captain. What is it you'd like to talk about?"

"First, you are going to be confined to the brig for the remainder of this mission."

"I assumed as much. Go on, Captain, what else have you got to say to me?"

"I'm a reasonable man, Field Agent. I want to give you a fair hearing. Why did you sabotage this ship?"

When Collins remained quiet, the captain said, "I hope those binds aren't too tight for you. You look a bit uncomfortable."

"I'm fine, Captain," answered Collins. "As I've told you repeatedly, it is time to end this mission. You are in over your head and it's time to get this ship and her crew back home, before it's too late."

"And by attempting to disrupt the ship's key systems, you assumed I'd order us back to space dock for repairs, effectively ending this mission."

"That is correct. Frankly, you are not well suited for this mission. Even commander Poznyk would have been a better choice, despite his low scores on creative thinking and diplomacy. Alas, he's not as well connected as you, so that was a non-starter." Collins looked intently at the captain. Nodding, he added, "Yes, I know about Poznyk's scores. I know about your scores. I know you are unfit for this command. You were much better off in the Intelligence Directorate, where your responsibilities were more mundane."

"I will make a note to include spying to the list of charges my staff is preparing against you."

"How interesting, Captain," said Collins, a smile on his face. "I'm especially intrigued by your spying charge. Coming from a former spy, that tells me a lot."

"Former spy?" asked Gregory

"Come now. Tell me that you didn't work for the President's Special Projects Intelligence Directorate?"

The captain cleared his throat. "We've known for some time that ISAT agents also double as spies. Not incidental spies who happen to overhear things in the course of their normal shipboard duties, but as actual spies reporting back to their handlers. Tell me, Mr. Collins, what was your real mission aboard the *Nemean*?"

"My mission, Captain, was exactly the same as yours. To learn more about that object out there. To determine whether it's a threat to us or not."

"And by 'us,' who do you mean, Mr. Collins?"

"I mean all of us! ISAT, Alcmene, and the rest of the Union. I am a loyalist, Captain. Are you?"

"That's good to hear. But aboard my ship, I expect all my crew to be loyal to me first."

"That I've been…"

"No! You have not been loyal to me, this crew or this ship. Let alone the Alcmene Navy."

"And was the Alcmene government loyal to the Union when it began secretly building up its naval forces, in direct violation of Article 7 of the Unity Compact, which states all planets will have parity in arms, with special consideration to their needs and means?"

The captain looked flustered. "Mr. Collins, I don't know what you are referring to."

Collins cut him off. "The hell you don't! You were the director of Naval Intelligence when the buildup began, and you were one of the key figures who recommended building out the fleet to the President."

"I won't sit here and debate you, Collins! What I need from you is technology to penetrate the hull of that object out there or anything that will help stop that other ship. If you've got technology that will assist us in finding our missing crewman, then I demand you turn it over now. If you don't do it, I will have my Marines take it by force."

"First, I should warn you that my stateroom is protected by a variety of self-destruct mechanisms. If anyone I have not personally authorized attempts to enter my stateroom, I can have it all destroyed in a matter of seconds. Second, why should ISAT share technology with you, when you have withheld the same from other Union members?" Collins allowed himself a smug smile. "Yes, Captain, ISAT is aware of Alcmene's clandestine military buildup, as well as its illegal research into new technologies. We are also aware you oversaw the development of both projects. It's therefore no surprise to us that your government selected you to captain the *Nemean*, the most advanced ship in your fleet, and tasked you to investigate the Structure."

When the captain remained silent, Collins added, "There are no real coincidences, are there, Captain Gregory?"

Gregory stood and walked out of the meeting room. Entering the bridge, he said, "First Lieutenant, escort Mr. Collins to the brig. He is to remain there for the duration of this mission."

"Aye sir!" said the Marine.

Giving a hand signal to the other Marines in his detail, First Lieutenant Andrews and his unit shoved Collins down the command ramp, into a lift and towards the brig.

Chapter 7

System: Virgil's star (VGL 191)

Location: Aboard the Alcmene naval vessel Nemean

The *Nemean* had suffered heavily under the Structure's swarm attack, and while the damage to the hyperlight pods and sub-light drives had been mostly repaired, the systems were still fragile and needed full retrofits. Collins' sabotage had destabilized navigational control and mostly undid the crew's repairs, causing both the light and sub-light drives to fail. With material to repair the ship running low, Lieutenant Harris parked the *Nemean* in a long, slow orbit around the system's primary until navigational control could be reliably repaired again.

The captain considered using the remaining attitude thrusters to keep station with the Structure, but decided against it, happy to let his ship drift as far away from it as possible.

Engineering believed they could repair one of the hyperlight pods, but it would take another week, while fixing the drives would take sixteen additional hours of concerted efforts. Most of the ship's duty sections had at least a few personnel that had been injured during the battle, but thankfully none critically so.

Given the damage that the senior ISAT agent aboard the *Nemean* had been responsible for, the captain decided it was time to forcefully extract as much assistance from Collins as possible.

"Commander, you have the bridge. I'm going to have another chat with Collins."

"Aye sir. I think I know what you have in mind."

The captain grinned. "Nothing that would violate any *wartime* regulations."

The brig

All able-bodied members of the MC1 were assisting the ship's crew in clean-up and repair activities. Except for the medical team and their patients, everyone who could be doing *something* to help get the ship underway again was doing something. Everyone except Collins, who sat on a bunk in the brig.

Presently, Collins heard the outer door of the brig unlock and a shadow appear at his cell's window. Thinking his guard had come back to check on him, he said, "You can report back to your superiors that I'm not causing any trouble."

"That's good to hear, Collins," said Gregory as he walked into the cell, the Z10 pistol in his hand aimed squarely at Collins' chest.

The agent looked at the pistol for a moment before turning his attention to the captain.

"Stand up," said Gregory, motioning with his pistol.

Slowly standing, Collins dusted himself off and adjusted his shirt collar. "Lead the way," he said, performing a slight bow and gesturing with his hand.

The captain grabbed Collins by the collar and shoved him towards the door. "Start walking. We're going to inventory your stateroom."

Collins stepped through the brig's door with the captain following close behind. When they got into the main hallway, Collins immediately crinkled his nose at the smell of burning material, as electrical fires were still burning behind control consoles throughout that section of the ship.

"You don't have to answer me, Captain. I can see exactly how well your efforts to repair the ship are going. No wonder you need my help now. But what you really need are the space docks orbiting your world."

"Collins, we've always needed your help. That's why ISAT posted you on this ship. However, you have willfully disregarded your duties, attempted to subvert my command and sabotaged this ship. You have earned your time in the brig along with the court martial that I intend to recommend when we get back to Alcmene."

Collins stopped walking and turned to face the captain. Looking at the pistol, Collins asked, "If I help you, will you drop all charges against me?"

"Let's see what you come up with," replied the captain. "Now keep moving."

A few minutes later, Collins and the captain arrived at the ISAT agent's stateroom. The captain stood a few feet behind the agent, the pistol still pointed at his back.

Collins punched a few keys on a control pad hanging to the left of the stateroom door, and it slid open. Looking over his shoulder, he stepped inside, with the captain following closely on his heels.

"Welcome to my stateroom. As you know, this is sovereign ISAT territory. Your Naval Command has no authority over me while I am here. You are here as my guest. However, I cannot allow you to keep brandishing that pistol. Either put it away or I will ask you to leave."

The captain holstered the pistol, keeping his hand on the butt. "What have you got in here, Collins?"

"What do you need?"

"I want a full inventory of items and their capabilities."

"That's classified. I can't allow the Alcmene government or its Naval Command or especially its intelligence services to gain access to any of the technology ISAT has placed under my care. Even worse, I can't let those aliens out there get their hands on it."

"You are stalling, Collins," said the captain. "You have sixty seconds to produce the inventory I've asked."

"And if I don't?" asked Collins.

"We will create it ourselves," said the captain. "And you are in no position to destroy this stateroom — not unless you plan on killing yourself in the process."

Collins lowered his gaze. "You win. Fine. While this won't be an inventory in the traditional sense, I have just the thing for you, Captain," said Collins, before turning around and rummaging through a container sitting by a wall.

After a few moments, Collins stood holding a six-inch diameter sphere in his hands. "This should take care of all your needs," he said, before tossing it towards Gregory.

The captain had no doubts about Collins' intentions and side-stepped to the right to avoid the sphere. However, the device rapidly expanded in midflight, reaching a diameter of three feet. The extra size neutralized the distance the captain's sidestep had created, instead striking Gregory's head with a glancing blow and knocking him to the floor unconscious.

With the captain knocked out cold, Collins removed the pistol from the his holster and lightly touched the sphere with the palm of his hand, causing it to revert to its original size.

Picking up the sphere, he walked to the stateroom's comm console and keyed the bridge.

"Bridge, this is Field Agent Collins. I am calling you from my stateroom. Don't bother sending anyone after me. You won't be able to stop me. I intend to detach my quarters from your ship. You will find your captain on deck 3, outside my stateroom door. Collins out."

Led by Sergeant Stevens, three Marines were immediately dispatched to retrieve the captain. Their secondary orders were to burn through the stateroom's door and stop Collins.

"Bridge, this is Stevens! We have the captain. He's unconscious but vitals read normal."

"Acknowledged, Stevens. Medical team is on the way. Any luck gaining access to the stateroom?"

"Negative. My men are attempting to cut the locks with torches, but it's slow going."

The medical team arrived a few moments later and took the captain to sick bay.

The Marines continued their attempts to burn through the bulkhead, but it would not yield to their torches. The stateroom was heavily reinforced, by design, to protect ISAT secrets.

A few moments later, Sergeant Stevens' comm buzzed. "Sergeant, stop your burn now. The stateroom has just separated from the ship. If you cut through, you'll be exposing that section of the ship to vacuum."

The Marines immediately stopped what they were doing. A tech team was called to the site to ensure that they had not done anything to compromise the integrity of the ship in that location. Luckily, everything checked out fine and the bulkhead was not compromised.

However, the stateroom, and Collins, were now somewhere out in space.

"Sensors! Any sign of the stateroom?" asked Commander Peters on the bridge.

"Negative, sir. It's small, and with all the debris floating around out there, it's hard to spot."

Soon after the captain walked onto the bridge and said, "And it's probably protected by stealth technology too. Going to be hard to find in the mess out there."

The commander saluted. "Glad to see you on your feet again captain."

"That bastard got the drop on me. I was careless. Should have shot him and busted down that door myself."

"Sir, ISAT staterooms have failsafe mechanisms. Had you done that, it would have probably self-destructed and taken a chunk out of the *Nemean*'s flank. You did the right thing."

"Thanks Ron. We'll deal with Collins later, if he survives out there. How are the repairs coming along?"

"Reasonably well, sir. There was extensive damage to various critical parts of the ship. Sub-light drives and hyperlight pods should be operational in fifty-five minutes and one hundred nineteen minutes, respectively.

"Very well. How about that thing out there? Has it been behaving?"

"All quiet sir. I guess they don't see us as a threat anymore."

"We'll see, Commander. The captain nodded to Peters. "Keep the bridge. I'm going to walk around the ship and show the crew their captain is still with them — see where I can help. I'm no mechanic, but it boosts morale."

Peters saluted, "Yes sir!"

The commander thought about that for a moment. Gregory was the only captain in the fleet who had ever shown such personal involvement and engagement with the enlisted crew. Sure, most other captains were concerned about the wellbeing of their crew and did their best to keep them out of harm's way. But none had ever shown such a personal touch as Captain Gregory. He was well loved by his crew and staff, and that love was deserved. The crew would follow him anywhere — even to this place. And that was both a comforting and a somewhat frightening thought.

The reality was, Peters would follow his captain anywhere too. And he wasn't sure how he felt about that.

Alexander Lotte

System: Virgil's star (VGL 191)
Location: Somewhere on the Structure

He couldn't exactly say what his dream had been about, but the feeling it left him with was frightening. Now awake, he kept his eyes closed, his eyelids feeling heavy as if weighed down by the dream. Part of him was afraid to open his eyes. At least when he was asleep, he felt no pain. But the cold air stinging his face was hard to ignore, like the strange rumbling he felt beneath him.

Taking a deep breath, he sat up, opened his eyes and looked around.

He wasn't in the cube chamber anymore, and he wasn't in any type of suspended or immobile, semi-conscious state either. He was now wide awake and dressed in his full EVA suit, except for the helmet lying on the ground a few feet to his right. His rifle was propped on a boulder behind him, and the rest of his gear was strewn randomly about his feet.

Slowly, he stood up.

It was hard to see, but there was light — dim blue light — emanating from the walls and ceiling. The walls looked rough, rocky and old, while the ground was hard and covered in a gravel-like substance.

Alexander surveyed his surroundings for any clues as to where he was and which way he should go. After around ten minutes, he decided there were no clues to be had here…other than the direction he was facing when he first sat up.

Gathering the gear and shoving it into his pack, he fastened it to his back, slung the rifle strap over his shoulder and put on his helmet. The HUD enhanced his vision, and he could see a hundred meters further than before. However, it didn't matter much because both ends of the tunnel stretched out far beyond his enhanced vision — and neither direction appeared more appealing than the other.

He checked his SITMAP. It contained data from when MC1 first entered the Structure, but details were limited to when he, Major Lewis and Private Martinez were retreating to the shuttles. There were no contacts on his motion sensor, and atmospheric readings appeared nominal — if a bit on the cold side.

Taking one last look around, he scratched an "X" on a nearby boulder and set off into the tunnel.

--

The hike had so far been uneventful. The terrain was moderately challenging, with hills and slopes leading into shallow gullies, interspersed with relatively flat ground. After walking a few clicks, Alexander's hike was stopped by a massive door.

Alexander tried pushing and pulling the door from different angles, but it was completely solid and unyielding. He guessed that it had to weigh several tons. He considered using his grenades to blow it open, but such an explosion could potentially cause a cave in, given the relatively tight confines of the tunnel. Plus, there was a part of him that didn't want to cause damage to the door, given its unique appearance and the encounters he had had with the Structure's inhabitants. Somehow, he knew they wouldn't take kindly to him blowing up their door.

The door was covered in strange markings: lines and swirls and abstract-looking objects. It was dotted with small rocky protrusions in a random pattern, and the center contained a familiar looking design — a spiral shape he'd seen decorating many of the yoga classes he had attended over the years. Below the spiral was a ledge that contained slots, the first three of which were filled with small objects that looked like the protrusions from the door.

Upon closer inspection, the protrusions were small pebbles lightly fastened to the door. Alexander took one off the wall and held it in his hand. It was light, small and looked just like the ones in the slots along the ledge.

He placed the pebble in the fourth slot. It *felt* like the right thing to do, even though nothing happened.

Unsure what to do, he sat down on the floor to rest and mediate. Alexander had never done yoga wearing an EVA suit (it wasn't exactly designed for such activities), but he did manage to sit cross legged and achieve a passable lotus pose.

He closed his eyes inside his helmet and softly chanted to himself. He slowed his breathing and in time achieved a sense of stillness. He let his thoughts wander on their own, not engaging them but observing as they paraded in full view of his detached awareness.

Alexander saw an image of a sunflower, bright and yellow, facing the sun, small moist droplets glistening in the light. His awareness focused in on the sunflower's center and slowly he recognized the similarity between the sunflower and the design on the door.

Bringing his awareness back to the tunnel, he wondered how the aliens could possibly know about a plant native to Earth. In fact, sunflowers were not even found on Alcmene, having been banned from importation because they were considered an invasive species, poisonous to certain native fauna.

He thought perhaps they could have extracted the image from his mind, as it was an image he'd meditated upon hundreds of times in his yoga practice. But the door before him looked, and *felt*, ancient. No, this door predated Alexander and probably the entire practice of yoga on Earth by millennia.

Again, his attention was drawn to the spiral and the slots on the ledge.

He looked more closely at the pebbles in the first three slots.

The first slot contained one pebble, as did the second. The third slot contained two pebbles, while the fourth contained the single pebble he had placed in it.

Something didn't look right to him.

He got up and looked at the pebbles more closely, noticing they were all different sizes. He removed three of smaller ones from the door and held them in his hand. When held together like that, they seemed to occupy the same volume as the pebbles in the first two slots.

He removed the pebble he had placed in the fourth slot and replaced it with the three smaller pebbles.

And then he knew why this all looked and felt so familiar.

He plucked five more pebbles from the door and placed them all into the fifth slot, and continued in this fashion, plucking increasingly smaller pebbles from the door and placing them in each of the slots…eight pebbles in the sixth slot, thirteen in the seventh slot and twenty-one in the eighth slot.

The door, Alexander guessed, was protected by a Fibonacci lock and completing the sequence should unlock it. However, after filling the eighth slot with twenty-one pebbles, nothing happened.

There were no more slots on the ledge and no more pebbles mounted on the door.

Alexander took a few steps back to get a better view of the door and surrounding area.

There it was!

The central spiral shape contained a subtle depression that was optically masked by the dots making up the design. He looked around for anything that might fit the slot, but he had exhausted the door's pebble supply, and despite the ground being strewn with rocks of different shapes and sizes, none of them looked like they would fit as snuggly into the slot as the others had.

Frustrated, he sat down, closed his eyes and assumed the lotus pose again.

Letting his hands drop to his sides, he pressed his fingers into the ground beside him and had the answer.

Sand!

Brushing away a layer of coarse gravel with his armored hand, he dug deep into the ground and scooped up a handful of silky, fine sand.

Careful not to let the sand spill out of his hand, he stood up, walked to the center of the door and poured the sand into the depression at the center of the spiral.

Nothing happened.

Damn!

"Come on, open!" Alexander shouted, as he pressed both hands against the door, his heels digging into the ground as he pushed with all his strength.

Slowly, millimeter by millimeter, the door began to lift slowly, until Alexander could get his armored fingers just underneath its bottom edge, fighting to re-position his legs and straining against its weight — his arms, legs and back burning with the effort.

An alarm went off in his HUD, indicating his vitals were entering the danger zone, but he couldn't stop now. Feeling as if he was about to pass out, he lifted with all his strength until the clearing under the door was just enough for him to slip under.

Realizing there was no way for him to roll under the door before it slammed back into the ground, he squatted and thrust his lower legs below its bottom ledge, the door now resting on the column that went from the top of his armored knees to the bottom of his EVA boots. Hoping the weight of the door was less than the compressive load his EVA was designed for, he worked to disengage the two blast protectors fastened to the front of his shins.

Alcmene Marines had been taught to use their armored shins as blast shields for decades, but this time Alexander would be using those armored reinforcements as structural supports.

Having removed the heavy shin guards, he jammed them between the bottom of the door and the hard ground below. Taking just a moment to test their ability to support the door's weight, he dove and rolled under it, clearing the threshold, but not before his left foot knocked one of the supports out of position. A moment later, the heavy door overcame the remaining support's structural integrity and came crashing into the floor.

That was close!

Alexander checked the suit's environmental readout — the air was breathable on this side of the door. He removed his helmet and inhaled deeply, filling his lungs and belly before letting it all out with a satisfying sigh.

The effort to lift that door had exhausted him, and he needed to rest. Crawling to one side of the new section of the tunnel, he propped his back on the wall and stretched out his legs, his muscles grateful to be free of the massive load they had been straining against.

--

There was a moment, in that space between wakefulness and the dreamworld, when Alexander thought he heard a sound worth investigating. But the sleep tasted so sweet and the rest was so satisfying that he couldn't bring himself to end it yet.

Just a few more moments like this and then I'll get up.

A few more sweet moments of blissful rest elapsed gracefully before *it* slammed into him like an atomic blast, cratering the center of his EVA suite and sinking Alexander half a foot into the rock wall behind him. Dazed, confused and unable to hear, he opened his eyes and saw it standing there…enormous, monstrous and angry.

It roared, a blast of hot air blistering the skin on Alexander's face, momentarily creating a cloud of droplets that rose in the resulting updraft, as the cavern's cold air mixed with the beast's hot breath.

Unable to reach his rifle, which had been knocked several feet out of his reach, he palmed the sidearm strapped to his thigh and fired three rounds into the beast's chest.

The beast took a few steps back, wincing from the impact of the rounds, then steadied itself before dropping two of its four arms to the floor, snorting like a bull about to charge.

Alexander managed to free himself from the depression in the caved-in rock wall, rolled for his rifle and picked it up with his right hand before spinning around and leveling its muzzle straight at the crouching beast.

Long, silent moments passed, as Alexander and the beast stared each other down, watching for any motion, any sign of weakness, before the creature charged and Alexander unloaded round after round into the top of the its head.

Metallic sparks ignited wherever the rifle rounds landed, as the beast's head was covered with heavy armor, deflecting the rounds and only slowing the charge long enough for Alexander to pick up his helmet and run.

He ran for half a kilometer, up inclines and steep hills and down gullies and deep valleys, before finally stopping to catch his breath and look behind him.

No sign of the beast anywhere. All was quiet.

He took the opportunity to reload his rifle and side arm, and fastened his helmet to his EVA suit. Once secured, he turned on his night vision and used his SCOPE to look for any signs of the beast.

Nothing.

Since much of the terrain he had covered was hilly, it was possible that it was just behind the nearest hill or valley and out of his line of sight.

However, even his motion sensor returned a negative reading, which meant that the beast was somewhere out there, either completely motionless, out of range, or using other ways to evade the EVA's sensor suite.

The most probable option, Alexander thought, was that it was out of range. The more distance he could put between him and that thing, the more likely he was to survive. It wasn't all that common to come up against something that could take direct rifle rounds to the head and survive.

Taking one final look behind him, he continued onward, double timing it through the cavern, navigating the tight twists and turns as best he could, always mindful that the beast could be behind him at any moment.

Until he knew exactly where the beast was, Alexander wasn't confident relying on his EVA's sensor suite and with no other options, asked for divine intervention. He didn't ask for much. He didn't ask to be teleported back home. He didn't ask for the beast to be kept at bay. He didn't ask for superhuman strength. He simply asked for a warning. If the beast were to step out of the shadows and bypass his sensors, then at least *give me a warning.*

Another half a klick down and the tunnel led into a large chamber-like opening, stalactites dotting the upper dome and stalagmites rising up from the floor.

Navigating around and over the stalagmites crisscrossing his path, Alexander came to a fork in the road.

He had a choice. He could continue along the main tunnel's path directly ahead of him, or he could try the path on the left, which appeared to further branch out into additional tunnels through the rocky landscape.

He checked his SITMAP for any clues; there were none. The SITMAP was still malfunctioning and offered nothing in the way of insight. The suit's other sensors were also silent, with readings from both openings indicating identical atmospheric and thermal variables.

According to the EVA suit, both were equally compelling paths to follow.

However, strategically, Alexander reasoned that the main path he was on made the most sense, as there would only be two ways to approach him, from the front and back; while the path on the left, integrated as it was into a larger system of tunnels branching off in all directions, represented multiple avenues through which he could be attacked.

On the other hand, it also offered him multiple avenues of retreat.

Alexander stood a few meters back from the fork in the road, eyeing each side equally, trying to make the decision that made the most sense.

As he was about to make up his mind, a red light winked on in his HUD display, the motion sensor having picked up activity somewhere nearby. Quickly spinning around on his heel, Alexander swept his rifle counterclockwise as he scanned for a target.

With no target in sight, but with the red light remaining on, he wondered if the motion detector was malfunctioning. After all, his suit had taken a lot of damage and was due for a heavy retrofit.

Unfortunately, Alexander's suit was working fine, a fact that his semi-conscious mind dwelled upon as he struggled to regain his bearings after a massive blow cracked open the armor covering his right shoulder and sent him rolling twenty meters, his momentum slowed as his exposed shoulder was pierced by the ragged, yet sharp, tip of a black stalagmite.

The pain of the initial blow was brushed aside by the lancing pain that danced through is body, as the stalagmite bit deep into his shoulder muscle and the sodium compounds in the rock literally rubbed salt into his wound.

In a rush to bring his weapon to bear, he twisted his shoulder down towards the ground, causing the rock to dig deeper into his shoulder before he managed to level the weapon in the general direction of the beast.

He opened fire.

The sounds of automatic fire ricochet off the cave walls, amplifying the angry sound of the weapon.

Alexander didn't know how many rounds actually found their target, as he struggled to get back on his feet, blood coating his armor in streaks of red. Using his good hand, he reached into his med kit and plugged the hole in his arm with emergency medical foam designed to stop heavy bleeding and clean wounds in the battlefield.

At this point, Alexander no longer cared about which path to take. He just wanted to put more distance between himself and the beast, and ran for the nearest exit.

Behind him, the beast roared so loudly that Alexander thought the vibration from the sound would cause the cave's roof to collapse. That gave him an idea. He stopped his run, turned around and slowly made his way back towards the cave opening. The beast roared again, a deafening, angry sound that made his skin crawl, so primal that it made him feel like helpless prey. Unable to pinpoint the exact source due to the strong echoes, Alexander reached for a frag grenade, primed it and tossed it towards the general direction of the roar and dove for cover.

The roaring grew louder as the grenade exploded, causing the ceiling to rumble. A stalactite cracked and fell to the ground, followed by another and another. Alexander tossed another grenade into the chaos and ran full speed down the tunnel, sliding around tight turns, clawing up steep inclines and roughly sliding down sharp declines until his heart was pounding so loudly in his ears that his HUD display lit up with overexertion warnings.

--

It was hard to say how long he had been lying there, deep in the shadow of the rock formation he had found along the way. It had been a perfect place to rest, as it afforded him with an elevated view of the tunnel in both directions. Since he was still alive, Alexander reasoned that the beast had either not followed him this far or had come this way and not noticed him hiding among the rocks.

He'd been out cold, so exhausted that even the stims his suit had pumped him with were insufficient to keep his eyes open for more than the few minutes it took him to set up "camp" among the rocks.

Now he felt rested but weary, and in better physical condition although his muscles still ached, and his shoulder was a knot of pain.

Peeking over the nearest rock, he turned on his SCOPE and looked for signs of the beast. There were no footprints in the area, not even his own; the ground was so hard it was nearly impossible to leave any behind. The motion sensor also registered all clear, and the air was still, calm and quiet.

If the beast was somewhere nearby, it was once again either completely motionless or somehow able to evade all his sensors.

In any case, he had to keep moving. He had no idea where he was going, but he knew that he was free to go, although what free truly meant in this situation wasn't so clear.

They had told him, repeatedly, that he was not a prisoner. That he was free to go. At any time, of his own choosing. However, if that were really true, then why had there been times when he literally couldn't move? Why had there been so many times when he was rendered unconscious, only vaguely aware of what was going on through the strange dreams that unfolded in his mind.

He didn't hate *them*. He didn't even know who *they* were. He just knew that this time he really was free to go. Although no one told him where to go or how to leave, he *felt* that if he kept moving, he'd eventually find a way back home.

However, that beast, whatever it was, seemed to have other plans, as it stalked him in a cunning and unnerving way, appearing out of nowhere whenever Alexander thought he had long left it behind.

That meant that it was probably closer than he thought.

Most likely it was here, right now, waiting for him to leave the cover of the rocks.

Alexander checked his rifle and pistol. They had full magazines. He also had three frag grenades left and a blast disc in the compartment in his upper back. He reached his left arm behind him and pressed a knuckle into a curve on the lower back of his EVA suit, which opened the compartment holding the blast disc.

He set the explosive yield to maximum, two thousand five hundred kilo joules, which was the equivalent of ten standard grenades.

With all his weapons now primed and ready to go, he started climbing down the rock formation.

--

Back on the ground, he took a look around and started off at a moderate jog.

Each footfall registered in his ears as a loud crunching sound, but there was nothing he could do about it. He could either move very slowly and hope to evade the beast through stealth, or he could move purposefully and deal with whatever came his way.

Alexander jogged another klick and a half without any incident.

The tunnel's distinct blueish hue now transitioned to a lighter green. Besides the lighting, his EVA's sensors didn't register any other changes; temperature and air composition remained constant.

Not sure what to make of the new lighting, he unslung his rifle and slowed his pace to a fast walk.

This section of the tunnel also featured strange shapes, long arcs covering entire sections of wall, interspersed with sections that were featureless.

An alert flashed in his HUD: ENERGY SOURCE

The EVA's sensors had detected an energy source emitting heat well above ambient temperature somewhere a hundred meters into the green section.

The energy source was behind a smooth, metallic-looking hatchway.

Alexander tried to open it, but it wouldn't budge. It was either locked or extremely heavy — or both.

This hatchway didn't give him the same impression as the door with the Fibonacci lock. It didn't have the same ancient feel, nor did it appear to be a puzzle of any sort. It was just a door standing in his way.

He tried poking and prodding all along the hatchway's surface, looking for anything that might open it.

There weren't latches, buttons or pressure sensors anywhere that he could see.

Alexander took a quick personal mental inventory. All EVA suits were equipped with tool kits but didn't contain anything that could open this door. Besides the tools, he had a rifle, sidearm, three frag grenades and a blast disc.

The blast disc was the only thing he had that stood a chance of forcing open the hatchway. He'd originally planned on using the blast disc against the beast stalking him; he had planned to pin the disc on the beast during their next encounter and setting it off from a safe distance.

With no other choice, he placed the blast disc against the hatchway, set the fuse for thirty seconds and ran the way he had come. He found cover behind a large boulder several hundred meters away seconds before the blast disc went off.

A furious plume of smoke and hot air rushed through the tunnel, over and around the boulder, pelting his armor with rock and other debris.

After a few moments, Alexander walked back to where the hatchway had been and found the metallic substance it was made from had twisted inward, with a jagged hole cut right in the center.

Giving thanks to whoever invented blast discs, he stepped through the hole, looked around and gasped.

The hatchway opened into an enormous cavern-like enclosure. It contained row after row of what looked like space fighter craft.

The fighter craft featured a five-wing design, with two wings each located on the port and starboard side, situated thirty degrees apart, while the fifth wing jutted straight up from what could only be the pilot's nest.

A laser cannon was mounted on each of the port and starboard wings, while the fifth wing was bisected by a long tube-like structure that looked like a missile launcher.

Two large exhaust nozzles were positioned aft of the fighter. The front was blunt and open but the inner space crowded by what appeared to be a sensor array consisting of small dishes and other exotic-looking devices.

An atmospheric heat shield was mounted on the underside of the craft, likely for rapid atmospheric descent during planetary combat runs.

Overall, it was a sleek and aggressive design, devoid of any markings other than something that looked like a stylized triangular shape encircled by an ovoid ring.

Alexander wasn't sure if any of his EVA cameras were still working, as their connections to his HUD had been severed during his first encounter with the beast. However, he made an effort to carefully move his suit's camera mounts around the nearest fighter craft, for later retrieval and analysis by the *Nemean*'s crew.

He spent forty-five minutes recording as many details of the craft as he could, and then tried to access the pilot's nest by climbing up the side of the craft and manipulating what appeared to be a series of latches around the transparent canopy.

After a few unsuccessful attempts, a certain combination of latch positions unlocked the canopy.

He spent several more minutes moving his camera mounts all along the pilot's nest surfaces, getting close-up views of the controls, instruments and seat contours.

Alexander had no idea if he would be able to pilot the craft — at this point, he didn't even know how to turn on the engines.

The pilot's nest was about ten feet off the ground. An armored Marine could easily fall from such a height and not feel the slightest bit of discomfort. However, even while armored, a Marine violently pulled down by both legs and slammed into the ground would daze even the toughest soldier.

Alexander's head and back and legs ached. He knew immediately he'd been found the instant his left foot began to slide off the fighter's wing. It had all happened too fast for him to react.

Once again, the beast had evaded his sensor suite and was now pummeling Alexander with savage blows that dented, caved in and cracked his armor.

The beast stood to its full height, raised all four of its thick, powerful arms overhead and roared, a sound that was now terrifying, as Alexander laid helpless on the ground, his suit so damaged that it almost immobilized him.

Unable to reach his rifle, he looked at the side arm still attached to his thigh, palmed it and emptied the entire magazine into the beast — twenty-four rounds in total.

The beast dropped two arms to its chest, frantically swatting at the wounds, while it used two other arms to pick up and heave random debris at Alexander.

The Marine did his best to block and dodge the volley, although most of the debris consisted of rocks weighing around fifty pounds, as well as an assortment of devices lying about that were likely used to repair and maintain the fighter craft.

Running out of things to throw at Alexander, the beast staggered around, still clutching its chest, in search for a larger weapon.

As it turned its back to him, Alexander reloaded his sidearm and fired round after round at the beast, hitting it in the spine, legs, shoulders and head.

The beast roared angrily, found what it was looking for and bent to dislodge a large boulder from the ground. Using all four of its arms to lift it overhead, it staggered under the boulder's weight as it slowly walked back towards Alexander, who was still lying on his back, immobilized by the damage to his suit.

When it got to within five meters, the beast threw the boulder at Alexander's lower body, shattering his feet and legs and breaking his pelvis in three places.

Alexander screamed, his agony a private affair thanks to the helmet still on his head.

He was in too much pain to pay attention to all the warning lights that populated the inside of his HUD, or to notice the medical nanos his onboard computer was frantically injecting into his system, with the immediate goal of staving off shock, sepsis and catastrophic blood loss. If he could get to a hospital in time, such measures could save his life.

None of that mattered, however, as the beast now stood over his supine body and leveled blow after angry blow at his chest, neck and head.

Alexander had a moment to consider the imminence of his demise, as his grip on consciousness faded fast. He had done nothing to deserve this. He was simply trying to go home. He never meant to harm the beast. He'd shot it in self-defense.

A sideways blow to his helmet knocked it free and brought Alexander face-to-face with his attacker.

He looked into its eyes as it roared once more, its victory over the alien intruder secured.

With his final conscious thought, Alexander pressed the detonator on each of the three frag grenades strung across his right arm.

They were set with three-second fuses.

Three seconds.

Alexander closed his eyes.

Two seconds.

The beast tore at Alexander's right arm, trying to detach it from its socket.

One second.

Searing white heat.

And then darkness.

--

The sensation was not entirely unfamiliar.

Floating in an invisible sea, Alexander couldn't see or feel his body, nor could he place himself in space relative to any external reference points. Thoughts began to surface, giving purpose to his existence in the featureless sea.

Human beings are worthy simply because they exist. Loving another means that the lover finds intrinsic worth in the loved. Such worth is immeasurable. That worth simply exists because it does.

According to the sage, for God so loved the world, that he gave his only begotten Son, that whosoever believeth in Him should not perish, but have everlasting life.

A perfect example.

Those traits were not displayed in the recent struggle.

Let them merge in congruence.

Alexander was aware of the thoughts speaking in his mind. They were his thoughts, surfacing from a deep well he could barely glimpse when he was in this place. Presently, a new mind floated in the sea with him.

"Intruder! Why have you come here? You have invaded my place. Disturbed my tranquility. The lock was meant for sages. Not your kind. Now you've brought me here."

"This was not my intention," thought Alexander, speaking to the other mind. "You left me no choice. I just want to go home."

Probe now the depths of truth, are all beings worthy simply because they exist? Is this only true for humans? How far will you thus extend your idea?

Who is worthy of love?

The sea began to churn, and Alexander felt a rising sense of remorse.

"I don't have the capacity to love the beast. I'm sorry. I don't."

Chapter 8

The missile

System: Virgil's star (VGL 191)

Location: Aboard the Alcmene naval vessel Nemean

Captain Gregory sat at his command station, reviewing status reports, when a chime from Lieutenant Paris' station rang in his ears.

"What have you got, Paris?" asked Gregory.

"Sir, we've just detected a missile launch from the Structure. It's big and it's headed our way."

"Range?"

"Just over one point two million kilometers and closing, sir. The doppler array clocks its speed at over two hundred fifty-five thousand kilometers per hour. At that rate it will be here in four hours, forty-eight minutes and thirty-three seconds, sir."

"Is it on a collision course with the *Nemean*?"

"Aye sir, it is."

"Ms. Harris, can our remaining attitude controls nudge the ship out of its path? "

Harris looked down at her control console. "I will try sir, but with attitude controls, we won't have meaningful tactical maneuvering capability once that thing gets close."

"Do what you can," said the captain. "Mr. Marker. Status on all weapons."

"We have one operational plasma cannon, but the ship's targeting system has been fried. The techs are working on it. Right now we can fire the cannon manually and hope for a good result."

The *Nemean* used a sophisticated computer-controlled fire control system. The operator fed general parameters into the system and the ship could calculate dynamic firing solutions in milliseconds, taking the operator out of the equation. Humans simply didn't have the speed or steadiness to fire such big guns accurately without computer assistance.

"Missiles?"

"We have fifteen missiles left but are unable to fire any of them. All four missile battery systems were destroyed by the fighter swarms. However, we can still fire the missiles in KE mode using the magnetic rail. But that's at five percent strength right now, and we still have the problem of programming dynamically updating firing solutions without the ship's targeting system online. I can try for a manual shot, but we are very far off..."

The captain shook his head. "Won't do any good. A retaliatory strike using at five percent launch strength would take much too long for our KEs to reach the Structure, and if we used them to intercept the missile it would just cause a larger explosion closer in, as they wouldn't get far enough away from the ship to make a difference."

Peters thought for a moment. "What if we create a mine field with the missiles in atomic mode? We can use the Falcon to deploy them as a barrier between the ship and the incoming boogie. The Falcons can move faster than the rail system can fire them now, and we can be much more precise on how we lay them out."

"Good," said the captain. "Work with Mr. Marker and Lieutenant Paris to determine the optimal layout pattern. We want to maximize our chances of intercepting that missile while minimizing blast damage to the ship. If that missile gets through and hits us dead on, we're finished. But a residual blast from the atomic missiles at a good range we can survive. Report back to me in thirty minutes. "

With that, the captain stood from his command console, motioned to Ms. Harris and said. "Navigation, you have the bridge. I've got some prep work to attend to."

"Aye sir," said Ms. Harris, as the captain quickly strode off the bridge.

--

Half an hour later the captain returned to the bridge.

Nodding to Harris, "anything to report?"

"Negative captain. No further launches or activity from the Structure. The missile is still on course for the Nemean, now 4 hours, 18 minutes away.

Lt. Paris and Commander Peters were hunched over Mr. Marker's control console. Satisfied that they had optimized the topography of Peter's proposed mine field, the Commander stood first and reported that they were ready with the minefield coordinates.

"Very good, Commander. Have the topography loaded onto my memory matrix."

"Yes sir. Uploading the topography now."

Looking around at his bridge officers, he asked, "Is there anything else to report?"

"One thing, sir," that was Paris. "The missile seems to have been launched from the same area where we detected that explosion earlier. Could be related."

"Keep tracking everything. Commander, you have the bridge."

"Aye sir." Taking a few steps toward his captain and speaking in a low voice so no one else would hear, Peters asked, "Where are you going, sir? I notice you have your pilot's belt on and the extra respirator."

"As captain, this ship and this crew are my responsibility. And every good officer knows that he should not order his men on any mission he himself would not undertake. I'm taking one of the Falcons out to lay the minefield."

"Sir, that's too dangerous. You're needed here on the ship. I can lay the minefield just as well as you can, sir."

"No doubt about that, Commander. But while you were calculating the mine's ideal topology, I went down to the weapons bay and spoke to the duty officer on hand. He said that the warhead shielding had been partially compromised, and that they are emitting low level radiation. Prolonged exposure could kill a crewman. His team was coming up with a plan to either contain the radiation or jettison the warheads safely. I came just in time and offered him a third solution. The warheads are being loaded onto the Falcons now."

Peters opened his mouth to say something, but Gregory raised his hand and continued.

"I will be piloting the Falcon, with the mini shuttle slaved to mine. I'll use both birds to lay the field and then position them as two additional mines to up our odds that the missile will hit a mine, the Falcon or the mini rather than the *Nemean*. "

"But, sir," Peters protested. "Harris is an excellent pilot. If anyone can maneuver this ship out of harm's way, it's her."

"And she readily admitted she may not be able to do it. It's too close anyway. We need to put space between that missile and the ship. This is the only way. "

Peters' face flushed. He didn't like what he was hearing. The captain's plan was suicidal.

"Sir, Marker can handle the cannon. I'm sure of that. He doesn't need automated weapons control systems. That man is a genius when it comes to firing a gun."

"Those guns require more than a genius to fire them accurately, Ron," said the captain, using the commander's first name. "They need hand-eye-machine coordination that's faster than possible with what we have available. And besides, those guns barely have the range to detonate that missile at a safe enough distance. I ran the numbers already, Ron. The landmine barrier is the only way. And the only way to set up the barrier is with the Falcons. I won't risk another person on this mission. I've made my decision."

Peters nodded and saluted his captain.

"Understood, sir. We'll keep the lights on for you. Godspeed."

"Thank you," and with that Gregory strode off towards the hangar bay and the waiting Falcon.

--

Three hours later, Captain Gregory was at the leading edge of the minefield, positioning the final two nuclear warheads at their proscribed coordinates. The minefield's closest approach to the *Nemean* was thirty light minutes away, far enough to ensure that even if multiple missiles detonated at the same time, the blast would not incinerate the ship.

From edge to edge, the minefield occupied an expanse of two light minutes by one light minute.

After positioning the final warheads, the captain loaded the Falcon's navigation computer with coordinates that would position it two miles behind the minefield, in the space between the minefield and the *Nemean*.

"When I was in the academy," said the captain over the Falcon's comm link to the *Nemean*, "I loved soccer and was always best at the goalie position. If that missile gets through those warheads, I'm going to goalie it with the Falcons. Ms. Harris, I think you have as much lateral velocity as you're going to get at this point. Use the remaining attitude fuel to put as much space between the *Nemean* and the minefield. Every little bit counts."

"Aye sir," said Harris.

Switching to the general channel because she wanted the rest of the bridge crew to hear, Harris said, "Sir, what you are doing for us is amazing. I know captains are supposed to go down with the ship. But you are taking that one step further. I know the rest of the crew feels the same way. We want you back aboard, sir, as soon as possible. And in one piece."

The bridge crew erupted in applause, and Commander Peters played Harris' remarks through the ships intercom system.

Even from the bridge, Peters could hear applause, shouts and hoots coming from the ship. "The rest of the ship's crew seconds Ms. Harris' sentiment, sir. Good luck and for goodness' sake, don't miss that shot man!"

"I'll do my best, Commander. Captain out."

--

The missile inbound for the *Nemean* was still traveling over two hundred fifty-five thousand kilometers per hour when it entered the leading edge of the minefield.

"Missile entering the minefield. We'll know in a little under twenty-three minutes if any of the warheads take it out." Twenty-two point four nine minutes, to be precise, was how long it would take the missile to traverse the minefield's expanse.

According to the topology's coordinates, the captain estimated that the missile should be meeting its first opposition in about thirty seconds. When thirty seconds came and went and nothing happened, he called the *Nemean*.

"Mr. Marker, according to the minefield's topology and the missile's trajectory, we should have seen at least one detonation by now. Do you agree?"

"Yes sir. But our sensors didn't detect any. The next warhead is coming up in one minute and forty-eight seconds. At its current trajectory, the missile should set off the warhead's proximity fuse. Countdown will commence at T-minus sixty seconds to proximity fuse detonation."

"Sixty seconds. Mark!" called out the weapons officer. "T-minus fifty-nine, fifty-eight, fifty-seven…"

"Helm. Sensors. Communications. Turn all your sensor arrays towards that missile. I want to see what it does as it gets close to our warhead," ordered Peters.

When moving so close to the speed of light, getting a good look at the missile at this range was a tall order for the *Nemean*'s sensor arrays. The damage the systems had sustained during the previous battle as well as Collins' attempt to sabotage the ship only made the situation worse. The constant barrage of interference emanating from the Structure didn't help either.

Despite that, when Marker called out, "Now!" as the missile entered the warhead's proximity detonation envelope and noting happened, the sensors told an interesting tale.

"Sir!" called Peters into his comm. "That thing is maneuvering around the warheads and is evidently smart enough to know how far away to stay so as to avoid detection by the proximity fuses."

"Navigation," called the Captain. "Based on the warheads' scatter pattern across the minefield and the missile's current trajectory, and factoring in the minimum required adjustments the missile has to make to avoid all the warheads and their proximity detonation fields, give me the missile's three likeliest minefield exit points. I am assuming they will all be pretty close to one another."

Harris' fingers moved quickly across her console.

"Uploading now, sir. Yes, you are correct. All three probable exit points are within one hundred kilometers of each other, sir."

"Very good."

"What are you planning?" asked Peters.

"I'm going to position Falcon Two midway between the second and third likeliest exit points and set the Falcon to autodestruct if the missile exits from either point."

"And what are you going to be doing while Falcon Two waits for its prey, sir?" Peters knew the answer already, but he was hoping the captain had something else up his sleeve.

"I'm going to be waiting for it at the third and most probable exit point."

"And then?"

"I'm going to shoot at it for about half a second. If that doesn't work, I'm going to detonate the warhead in the Falcon's storage bay. I kept one aboard as a reserve."

Commander Peters remained silent. There wasn't much he could say. Watching the missile's flight path from his console and knowing that they were down to just a few minutes before the missile exited the minefield, so far unscathed, he opened the channel and said, "Thank you, sir. Good luck."

"Whatever happens to me Ron, make sure you get my crew back home. They deserve at least that."

"Will do, sir."

Peters called down to the *Nemean*'s intelligence officer. "Major Lamathi, prep the reconnaissance flyer. Ultra-stealth mode. Load it with all the ship's logs, all the Marine reports, the interviews, the analyses and launch it ASAP. Get it as far away from the *Nemean* as possible. Preferably in orbit around one of the bigger rocks in this system's asteroid belt. Window for launch closes in about five minutes. Get that done in three."

"Already prepped, sir. We had it on standby. Logs and reports loaded. Ready for launch in one minute."

"Excellent. Launch when ready. Give my regards to your team, Major."

If the *Nemean* didn't survive this, at least the recon flyer would. And any ship Naval Command sent after them could potentially retrieve the flyer and the logs it carried aboard. Too much had gone on out here that Naval Command had to be warned about.

Peters was Christian by birth. Saying a small prayer, he made the sign of the cross and bowed his head, asking for heavenly guidance. Satisfied that he had done all he could, he stood with his bridge crew, waiting to see what the missile would do next.

--

Gregory anxiously watched the instruments aboard the Falcon. If the missile was to exit from this location, it would be doing so in the next twenty seconds. Ten seconds later the Falcon's instruments were overwhelmed by electromagnetic radiation, and the video screens flared white and then went black, as the Falcon's cameras were burned out by a massive blast of photons.

Aboard the *Nemean*, thirty light minutes away, the bridge crew saw a massive ball of light originating from the missile's likeliest exit point which completely enveloped the Falcon and severed all communications with the craft. Long seconds passed before the *Nemean*'s crew could reliably use their sensors again as the photo bath dissipated.

It was Paris who saw it first.

The Falcon had survived the explosion, and evidently so had the missile. In fact, the two craft were floating in space just ten meters apart from each other.

"Captain!" called Peters. "This is the *Nemean*. What is your status?"

"*Nemean*, Falcon One here. The Falcon has been damaged but is operational. Life support is nominal. Propulsion is down. And the ship bay doors are no longer under my control. The missile is flying into the cargo hold, under its own power!"

"Captain! What's going on out there? Repeat your status!"

The captain got up from the Falcon's pilot's station, took a side arm and exited the flight deck. Taking the stairs one deck down past the passenger compartment and into the cargo bay area, he saw a long silvery cylinder lying on the deck. The missile was glowing with a strange, pale blue light, but according to his sensor pack was not emitting any type of radiation.

As he approached the cylinder for a closer look, he noticed that the top part of the cylinder was transparent.

There was something inside.

Stepping closer, he looked inside and gasped.

"Commander, have the space tug come and retrieve this ship on the double! You won't believe this."

"SAR Team One!" called Peters into his comm. "Execute immediate retrieval protocol Alpha dash two. Get that Falcon and the captain back here ASAP!"

Search and Rescue Brigade One, known as SAR One, set out immediately on the space tug to retrieve the Falcon and the captain. En route, the captain issued strict orders to the SAR team that what they saw was to be kept under wraps until told otherwise. The captain didn't want any rumors spreading among the crew until they knew exactly what was going on here.

The Package

It had taken five hours for the SAR team to fly out and retrieve the captain, but he was finally back aboard the *Nemean*. The tired crew cheered him as he came aboard, and the captain returned the honor, congratulating them on their bravery, dedication and hard work in keeping the ship together.

After a few minutes of congratulatory hoorahs from the crew, they disbursed and went back to work repairing the damaged ship, while the captain ordered Commander Peters to take a detail of Marines and escort the cylinder to Dr. Smith's sick bay.

"Sick bay? What have you got in that Falcon, Captain?" asked the commander.

Gregory ordered the remaining hangar bay crew to clear the area and motioned for Peters to follow him into the Falcon's cargo hold.

Gesturing towards the clear end of the cylinder, the captain said, "See for yourself."

The commander looked and then looked again, bending down to get his face close to the transparency that covered one end of the missile.

"What's he doing in there?"

"No idea. But we're going to need the doctor to revive him. Let's cover this end with that tarp over there and get this thing to sick bay. I'll meet you there in ten minutes."

"Aye sir."

The captain waited the few moments it took for Peters to round up four Marines, who helped lug the tarp-covered cylinder onto a utility cart. The Marines double timed it down the Falcon's cargo ramp, onto the *Nemean*'s hangar deck and into the hall toward sick bay.

Following them out, he saw that many compartments were running on emergency lights, and the smell of flamed out electronics still hung in the air. It would take a lot of work to get the *Nemean* space-faring again, but he was sure the crew could do it.

Despite the setbacks, the work ahead of them and the possibility the ship would be attacked once more, being back aboard his ship had never felt as good as it did right now.

--

Ten minutes later the captain, Commander Peters and Dr. Smith stood in a semicircle around the clear end of the cylinder. The doctor had run spectral checks on the internal environment of the cylinder and its occupant and was sure that it was OK to pop the lid.

Technical Master Jason Landau had been summoned to the sick bay to do the honors of removing the transparency from the cylinder without damaging its cargo.

He crouched low around the cylinder, inspecting the seam mating the transparency to the metallic surface of the cylinder body. After running a few tests with his field kit, the technician was confident he could simply heat it loose by using a portable torch.

That made no sense to the captain, as the heat that cylinder must have already endured traveling at relativistic speed must have been enormous; but that didn't matter, as a lot of things didn't make sense on this mission.

What was one more oddity in a mission full of them?

"All ready here, sirs," said Landau, as he offered visors to the two command officers and the doctor, before donning one himself and lighting up the torch.

He pressed the flame against the base of the transparent material, causing it to change from blue to green to yellow. After a few moments on one spot, he moved it further along the seam, and then again and again, until it finally fell off on its own.

Marine Private Alexander Lotte immediately sat up, eyes wide open, gasping for air.

His face was pale and pasty, and he looked like he'd been asleep for years. Except for the absence of a helmet, he was fully clad in his EVA suit, which was dirty and damaged but still apparently functional.

His gasps turned to shallow breathing, and then relaxed into deep inhalations, which the captain and commander both recognized as a form of combat breathing. All Marines had to learn it as a coping mechanism for times of great stress.

Gregory was about to say something, but Smith motioned for him to remain quiet as he monitored Lotte' vitals using remote probes. Blood pressure came in at 120/80 mm Hg, his respiratory rate was fifteen breaths per minute, his pulse was eighty beats per minute and his temperature came in at a 98.6 F.

Textbook-perfect stats.

Lotte was still staring straight ahead and hadn't seem to notice the other people in the room. The doctor moved to Lotte' side, put a hand on his shoulder and asked, "Do you know where you are, son?"

The Marine turned his head and looked at the doctor. It took a few moments, but recognition grew in his eyes and he finally said, "I'm aboard the *Nemean*. In the sick bay. And you're Dr. Smith." Glancing over the doctor's shoulder, he saw his two commanding officers, fixed his slouched posture and saluted. "Sirs!"

"At ease, soldier," the captain said. "We're glad you to have you back, in one piece and alive."

"Sir, I need to speak with you. Right away."

"We will definitely talk. But first I want to make sure you are all right. That's most important. Doctor, please run a thorough medical check on this brave Marine. If there is anything you need to make his stay in your sick bay any better, all our resources are at your disposal."

The doctor nodded.

"Good. Let us know when you are through here," said Gregory, turning to the soldier again. "Mr. Lotte, we are looking forward to talking with you once the doc clears you, OK?"

Lotte nodded.

Not wanting to distract the doctor or Lotte, the captain motioned to Peters and they exited the sick bay, leaving the doctor and his team to assess and treat the Marine.

Outside in the main corridor linking the sick bay with the common area, Peters turned to Gregory and asked, "What do you think happened to him?"

The captain shook his head. "I can only speculate, and I'd rather just get the story from him. Let's plan to convene an easy, unofficial debrief once the doctor gives the all clear. Just the two of us for now."

"Sounds good, sir. I'll be on standby until we hear from the doctor."

"Very good. Take the bridge Ron. I'm going to have a walk around the ship and see if there is anything I can do to help take the load off the men and women running this ship. God knows they need *something* — they've been working so hard."

"That's good of you, sir. That's why your team always remains loyal to you."

"Is that what it is? I was hoping you'd say it's because I win battles all the time."

The captain tried to keep a straight face but failed, laughing out loud at his own irony.

"Aye! It's that too, Captain! You'll make a fine general someday!"

"Ha! See you on the bridge, Ron. Let me know if that Structure out there does anything else."

"Will do, sir. Although honestly I have a feeling that we've just seen the last act of this play — for now, at least."

The captain nodded at that, placed his hand on the commander's shoulder and walked off towards the repair team down the hall. Peters, still smiling, headed off towards the bridge.

--

Dr. Smith kept Lotte in the sick bay's isolation ward. After forty-eight hours of tests, checks and observation, the doctor and his team had conducted every study they could think of on Marine Private Lotte and concluded that he was perfectly fit for duty. Physically at least.

Psychologically, they couldn't be so certain. The fact was that Lotte didn't exhibit any of the markers of a psychological disturbance or any of the symptoms of post-traumatic stress disorder.

For the Doctor to make a PTSD diagnosis, Lotte would have had to exhibit at least some of the typical symptoms, like difficulty sleeping or concentrating, or feeling irritable or easily angered, or being on edge as if something were about to happen. The doctor probed for possible triggers, but nothing seemed to cause an issue. Nor was Lotte experiencing any flashbacks or other dissociative reactions.

Rather, Lotte was relaxed, calm and talkative, eager to share his experiences and, for all intents and purposes, seemed perfectly normal.

The doctor had no verifiable medical reason to hold Lotte back from active duty, although PTSD symptoms might appear at a later time — months or years later. However, since time was the one thing they didn't have, he decided to issue a clean bill of health with ongoing periodic checkups to monitor Lotte' psychological and physiological state.

Sitting at his desk, Smith pulsed the captain's personal frequency.

"Yes, Doctor," answered Gregory. "How's our patient?"

"He's fine, Captain. I'm ready to release him. We've found nothing wrong with him. He's sustained some injuries, some very significant. I can see where organs were probably crushed, bones shattered, and skin and tissues punctured and torn off, but he's fine now. All his injuries seem to have been successfully treated and he's technically fit for duty."

"I didn't think the medical nanos could repair injuries that severe so quickly or completely," said the captain. "I thought the nanos could be used as a stop-gap measure in the field and could, in time, heal a range of injuries, but not without the environmental protection and resources available in our med tanks. Can the nanos heal the injuries you found outside of a med-tank environment?"

"To be honest, I'm not sure if the nanos could heal some of the things I saw even if a patient spent a year in a med tank," said Smith. "The nanos work great and have been a godsend to us in the medical field — and to our patients — but they can only do so much. For example, at some point over the last several weeks, Lotte suffered a broken back. It would have paralyzed him from the waist down. I saw that clearly in our scans. Now, while the nanos would have definitely been able to heal that kind of break, he would have never healed that well, if at all, without a med tank. And certainly not so quickly. Even planetside at one of our premier medical facilities, he'd still need about three months linked to a med tank to heal this well."

The captain was silent for a moment before asking, "And what about his mental state?"

"He seems fine, Captain. No sign of any mental disturbance. No PTSD symptoms. I recommend putting him on a monitoring program — physical and psychological — but otherwise he is technically ready for duty. Now, that's not to say, given the circumstances, that he ought to be put back on duty. But I do think he is ready to talk to you. In fact, he's been practically begging me to discharge him so he can see you."

"Thank you, Doctor. Discharge him. I'll have Commander Peters pick him up and we'll begin debriefing."

"Very well, Captain. I'll let him know."

--

Peters and Lotte made small talk as they walked from sick bay to the staff meeting room. Lotte was interested in what had happened since he left the ship, asked about the ship's condition and the status of his commanding officer, Major Lewis, and about Private Martinez and the rest of his squad.

Peters told him they would be filling him in shortly as he led Lotte to the meeting room, held the door open and motioned for him to find a seat.

The captain stood and greeted Lotte with a handshake, which Lotte heartily accepted, and added in a salute for good measure.

Gregory and Peters remained standing while Lotte took his seat, and then they sat down, facing Lotte across the meeting table.

"Let me begin," said the captain, "by once again welcoming you back to the *Nemean*. We are glad you made it off that thing alive and in one piece. No doubt you have a lot to tell us about your stay there, and I can assure you we are eager to hear what happened. You have our full attention."

Lotte smiled and nodded at both officers, looked up towards the ceiling and asked no one in particular, "Where do I even begin….?"

"Up to you, Private," said Peters. "Our reports last place you with Major Lewis and Private Martinez during Marine Force One's retreat from the Structure. That was the last time anyone saw you. Maybe you can start from there."

Lotte instinctively reached around and absentmindedly rubbed the small of his back.

"Right. OK. We were under heavy fire from forces protecting the Structure. They came out of nowhere. They were fast and precise in their assault. I remember thinking they had to be machines, they were so exact in their shots. Major Lewis ordered a general retreat back to the Falcons, and Martinez and I were ordered to provide cover for Waverly. Waverly slowed those things down using gravity grenades."

"So far that tracks with what we've already been told," said Peters. "What happened next?"

"It's kind of a blur, sir. The major ordered both Martinez and me to bug out, and we began a staggered retreat. There was an explosion, and I remember my EVA getting so hot it was burning my skin. I remember feeling like I was falling but nothing too clearly comes to mind here. The explosion must have knocked me out. Clearly, I survived that, though."

"Yes, clearly" replied the captain.

"Mr. Lotte, we have a good idea of what happened during the combat portions of MC1's time on the Structure. I can tell you that Major Lewis, Sergeant Wessler and his squad are all MIA. Until a few days ago, your status was also MIA. We believe Private Martinez is KIA, although we are not completely certain about that. What we'd like to know, is what happened *after* the battle. You clearly survived and were rather eager to share your experiences with us. That's what I'd like to get to, Private."

Lotte nodded. Clearing his throat, he said, "Captain, that thing out there, what we've been calling the Structure since the first mission briefing, is a space habitat, a ship, a troop transport, a zoo, a proving grounds, an arena, a testing facility and a fortress."

That got both officer's complete attention.

Lotte continued.

"Sirs, we are in trouble."

"Hold on for a second there, Private," said Peters. "Are you saying we are under imminent threat of attack?"

"No sir! They will not be attacking this ship again. We are free to go as soon as we can. I understand from talking to the medical staff that the *Nemean* has sustained a lot of damage and is in no condition to fly yet. Don't worry about that. They won't bother us. They want us to get back home."

"Who is the 'they' you keep referring to?" asked the captain.

"The aliens, sir. The ones who built that thing out there."

"What can you tell us about these aliens?" asked the captain, leaning forward. "Where are they from? What do they call themselves? What do they want?"

"I don't know where they're from and they never told me their name. As for what they want, they want us, sir. They want our help."

Peters looked at the captain for a second, before saying "and what could we possibly help them with? They clearly have us beat. And there's nothing much we can do to help them at this point. If they wanted our help, they should have thought of that before they wrecked the *Nemean*."

"They don't need our help right now, sir. I don't understand everything, so I'm sorry if this all sounds crazy. But basically, they are looking at us — at all humans — as potentially useful in their Grand Plan."

"Have they told you what their 'Grand Plan' is?" asked Peters.

"Not exactly, sir. Sirs, what you must understand is that the Structure out there is a test. They are testing us. They are observing us. They are evaluating us. Our tactics. Our technology. Our responses. Our ability to cope with what they throw at us. Those Marines who are MIA…Major Lewis, Wessler's squad…if they are still alive, they are representing us, all of humanity, in the alien's court. If they perform well, we look good. If they perform poorly, we look bad. If we look good, they will seek our help."

"And if we look bad?" asked Gregory. "What happens to us if we look bad in their eyes?"

Lotte began to hyperventilate, sweat forming on his brow as he trembled. Peters hit the comm button on the table, ordering a medical team to the meeting room.

"Wait. Sir. Before you call the doctor…I'll be fine. I just want to tell you…if we don't perform well…I think, sir, we had better perform well."

He started to mumble something further but became incoherent and blacked out.

Both Gregory and Peters rushed to his side, checked his pulse and held him in place so he wouldn't fall to the ground. A few moments later the medical team rushed in, placed medical devices all along one of Lotte's arm, chest and around his neck before laying him on a gurney and taking him back to sick bay.

"So?" Gregory said to Peters after the medical team had left the meeting room. "What do you think?"

"I don't know, sir. He sounds delusional. But I don't know. We need to continue his debrief as soon as possible."

"Agreed. In the meantime, I'm going to have a chat with Waverly."

"Waverly, sir? What are you thinking?

"Waverly is ISAT. And he's cooperative. I want to find out what ISAT has to say about aliens."

"Their position on alien life is clear, sir," said Peters. "They believe it's a complete certainty. And I think this mission proves that hypothesis conclusively."

"Indeed," replied Gregory. "What I want to know, is what they say *unofficially*. ISAT keeps a lot of secrets to itself. And for a long time, the Union worlds have accepted the status quo on that. I've already broken with tradition by confining Collins to the brig. And I'm the first captain in the history of the Union to have provoked an ISAT Field Agent to the point where he felt compelled to jettison his stateroom from a planetary naval vessel. What's the worst that could happen with me skirting a few more regs and finding out what Waverly knows?"

Peters smiled wryly. "Careful. We don't want ISAT coming after us too."

The captain smiled and said, "Oh, I think they'll be coming after *me* soon enough. Sorry for getting *you* into this mess."

"Much obliged, Captain. Much obliged. Happy to help you get the good folks at ISAT riled up a bit."

--

With Collins off the *Nemean*, standard protocol called for the next ISAT officer in the chain of command to take over shipboard ISAT responsibilities as well as the ISAT stateroom. However, given the fact that the Nemean no longer had an ISAT stateroom, the captain had instructed the barracks master to prepare new, special berthing for Waverly.

Typically only Naval Command and executive officers had their own staterooms, but in this case the captain felt that forcing Waverly to share a bunk with another officer would be pushing things too far with ISAT conventions. He got the agent a small one-person stateroom squarely in the middle of officer country, separate from the enlisted berthing. Beyond trying to play nice with ISAT and rewarding Waverly for his exemplary conduct, it also made it easier to keep trusted eyes on him and maintain easy access as well.

Unannounced, the captain made his way down to Waverly's stateroom and knocked on the door. After a few moments, the agent opened the door, looking like he had just been woken.

Quickly shaking the sleep from his eyes, he saluted. "Captain! How may I help you?"

"May I come in Waverly?" asked the captain.

Waverly stepped away from the door and stretched out his arm towards the interior of the room, welcoming Gregory.

The barracks master had prepared a nice set up for Waverly. It was small and efficient looking, with a fold-down desk, a small cabinet for personal belongings, a safe for valuables, and next to the bunk, a small wash basin. Waverly had to use a common head down the hall, as there simply wasn't enough space for his own private bathroom.

All in all, the captain thought it looked comfortable and perfectly designed for Waverly.

The young man sat down on his bunk, and the captain took a chair across from him.

So, what's on your mind, Captain?" asked Waverly.

Gregory had the impression that Waverly was like a small boy who knows he is in trouble but is not quite sure what he is in trouble for. Was Waverly nervous about something?

"I've got some questions about ISAT's thinking on a few things. And you are the ranking ISAT representative on this mission? "

"With respect, sir," Waverly replied, "Field Agent Collins is my superior and thus the ranking ISAT agent."

"Collins is no longer aboard this ship, and until such time as he can be retrieved, you will remain the ranking ISAT agent. What's more, when he is retrieved, I intend to confine him to the brig until I can hand him over to Alcmene Naval Police. If I have my way, he will stand trial for attempting to foster a mutiny and for sabotaging this ship. As far as I'm concerned, he will *never* again have any formal standing or rank on my ship. That leaves *you*."

Waverly looked burdened but nodded.

"I understand your position, Captain. I will try to assist to the best of my ability."

"I have no doubt about that Waverly. You've shown yourself to be a valuable asset on this mission, what with your performance in combat with our Marines, and your adherence to the higher values of honor and duty when you turned in Collins."

Waverly looked away. "I'm not sure if I'm proud of my actions against Field Agent Collins. He is my superior officer, and I disobeyed his direct orders."

"I wouldn't worry about it," said Captain Gregory. "If ISAT has a problem with what you did, I'll recommend you for a position in the Alcmene navy, under my command."

That seemed to make Waverly happy. The truth was, Waverly believed very strongly in what ISAT stood for and the work it did. His father and grandfather had been ISAT agents in combat roles, like he was. His grandfather had even become a planetary ISAT director. His father had also had a promising career, before he was killed during a training exercise.

But these days, Waverly felt ISAT was being steered down the wrong path. It had lost the old ISAT ethos that had been so very tangible in both his grandfather and father. They had believed in *something*. Something greater than themselves. They saw ISAT as the key to humanity's survival. But in recent years, ISAT had allowed people like Collins to rise through its ranks. People that would put their self-interest first and others that would pursue a radical ISAT agenda that was unrecognizable to people like Waverly's father. He wasn't the only one who believed that ISAT was on course to split into two opposing factions — one upholding ISAT's original founding principles and one that coveted power and influence. The former held an almost selfless belief in human progress that just needed some self-regulation, while the latter believed in power and control and didn't care how it got it.

Right now, with all that had happened with Collins on this mission, a break from the stress around that kind of life was a welcome call for Waverly. A commission in the Alcmene navy would be a ticket to a new life. That being said, he knew that the navy had its share of problems, and was certain that the captain, as likeable as he might be, had his own agenda too. Waverly was an idealist, but he wasn't naïve.

Focusing his attention back to the present conversation, he said, "Thank you, Captain. I would very much welcome such a commission."

The captain nodded. "Very good to hear. Now, as to my questions..."

"Yes sir. What would you like to ask?"

"Summarize for me ISAT's position on non-human intelligence in the universe."

"Aliens, sir?" asked Waverly.

"Yes."

"Well, ISAT has long held the view that we are not alone. We've always held the view that it is immensely unlikely that humanity is the only intelligent life form in the universe. Given that humanity can now be found on eight different planets across a bubble of space nearly fifty light years in diameter, the chances that others like us exist, and I use the term '*us*' in a very general sense, has for a long time seemed a near certainty. Now, as per this mission, I believe ISAT's position has been validated."

"Indeed it has, Waverly," said the captain. "One thing Collins and I agreed upon was that this mission, from the start, was really a first contact mission rather than a reconnaissance mission. We may have bungled that, I must admit."

"Sir, the shooting started before anyone could implement First Contact Protocols. I wouldn't blame you for that," said Waverly.

"In any case, what's done is done," replied Gregory. "In your opinion, what made ISAT so sure of itself when it asserted that other intelligence life forms existed in the universe? To be fair, ISAT is by no means the first organization to assert that that the existence of non-human sentient life is very probable. Scientists, writers and philosophers have been saying that for centuries, if not millennia. I think the main difference between all those others and ISAT is that the agency asserted that statement as an absolute truth. An actual certainty. Wouldn't you agree?"

"Captain, are you familiar with the ISAT training institute at Io?"

"Yes. I was a guest speaker there once, when visiting Earth. Isn't Io together with the immediate environs of Jupiter essentially ISAT's defacto headquarters?"

"Essentially, yes. ISAT is a decentralized organization, but even so, some centralization is necessary. Pretty much all ISAT officer training begins and ends at Io. The thinking is that if everyone's ultimate intellectual and philosophical roots stem from the institute at Io, most ISAT agents will adhere to our founding core principles. That hasn't always been the case, as Field Agent Collins well demonstrated."

The captain nodded.

"Every cadet studying at Io has, at one point or another in their career at the institute, heard the rumors," Waverly continued.

"What rumors?"

"The details tend to change according to who tells the story, but the basics are that fifty years ago, ISAT discovered intelligent life during a clandestine expedition which would theoretically have taken the explorers towards Orion."

"Are you talking about the constellation of Orion? They launched an expedition towards that region of space?"

"Yes sir. That's not to say they were headed to the stars making up the constellation itself — that's too far for our drives, even today. But in that general direction."

"If I recall my history, early Earth astronomers looked towards Orion as a potentially fertile hunting ground for extra-solar planets."

"Correct, Captain. Have you ever wondered why none of the Union planets have followed up on those early leads for habitable worlds?"

The captain thought for a moment before saying, "You know, I've never really thought about it. But you are right. It's a subject that hasn't really been brought up, even among Naval Command. Our explorations have always tended to look elsewhere." Gregory glanced around the room, as if trying to recall something. "Waverly, correct me if I'm wrong: As seen from Earth, the most prominent stars making up Orion's belt are Alnilam, Mintaka and Alnitak. Bellatrix makes Orion's left shoulder while Betelgeuse establishes the hunter's right shoulder...how am I doing so far?"

Waverly nodded. "Fine, sir."

The captain continued, "The tip of Orion's sword is made by Hatsya, and Meissa forms Orion's head. Rigel forms his left knee — and that's also the brightest star in the constellation. I forget what star forms the right knee."

"Saiph, sir. And the Orion Nebula forms the middle star in Orion's sword," said Waverly.

"OK, I've got my stellar bearings now. So, what are you saying Waverly? Why haven't any of the Union worlds launched expeditions towards Orion?"

"Because of the Meissans, sir."

"The Masons? What have they got to do with this?"

"I'm sorry, sir. Not the Masons but the Meissan, from Meissa — Orion's head."

"Meissa is nearly one thousand one hundred light years away from Earth."

"Exactly, sir. The story goes that when ISAT went out in that direction, they encountered people from the Meissa system, and for whatever reason we've never been out in that direction again."

The captain looked amused. "That's a great story. But doubtful too. If we were to believe *that*—"

"But it does accounts for the facts," interrupted Waverly. "You wanted to know what ISAT believes with regards to intelligent alien life forms. It believes they are real. In fact, ISAT has believed that to be an indisputable fact for a least half a century. And that belief is encapsulated in the story cadets hear within their first couple of days at the institute."

"What else can you tell me that's not based on rumors and speculation?" asked the captain "Does ISAT *officially* teach anything further on this topic?"

"About the Meissans, sir? No. They just allow the rumor to circulate."

The captain nodded. "What about your senior officers? Have any of them ever shared any information with you? Collins, for example — is there anything he shared with you that would provide me with more insight than I already have?"

"I'm afraid not, Captain. The belief is pretty well ingrained in ISAT personnel. We just take it for a given. As it turns out, we were right."

"That you were."

The captain stood, thanked Waverly for this time and left the junior officer's stateroom.

Back on the bridge, he called sick bay for a report on Lotte. Lotte was still unconscious but otherwise seemed healthy. Dr. Smith wanted to keep Lotte under observation for a while longer before attempting to revive him.

"Very well, doctor. I'll check in with you in a few hours."

--

Lieutenant Paris had spent much of the afternoon making repairs to the communications system and running diagnostics to ensure that it was working properly. Collins' enhancements were still operational and collecting vast amounts of data that Paris had yet to figure out what to do with. The Structure seemed to continuously emit neutrinos and other *noise* that made no sense to Paris or the *Nemean*'s computers.

Presently, Paris' board lit with an alarm indicating new activity from the Structure.

"Sir, something's happening. I've got an active broadcast coming from the Structure."

Gregory, Peters and Marker crowded around Paris' console.

"There it is," said Paris, pointing to a string of numbers repeating itself on his screen. "I'm running it through the analyzers. Nothing yet."

"At least they are talking to us now," said Peters.

Harris, at the helm, said, "Lieutenant Paris, can you put it up on the bridge viewer so we can all see?"

Paris pushed a button on his console and the incoming transmission scrolled across the bridge's main viewer screen.

Harris stared at the numbers scrolling across the screen. They somehow looked, or rather *felt,* familiar to her, but she didn't know why. After a few minutes, she began scribbling on her data pad. Slowly, a look of recognition gathered in her eyes.

"Captain, I think I know what that is," said Harris.

"Enlighten us, Lieutenant," said the captain.

"Lieutenant Paris, run that string through the sound converter and pipe it through the speakers," Harris requested.

A moment later the speakers crackled with static and then:
AAAAAAAAUUUUUUUUUUUUUUUMMMMMMMMMMMM
Followed by five seconds of silence and then:
AAAAAAAAUUUUUUUUUUUUUUUMMMMMMMMMMMM

"It's a chant," exclaimed Harris. "They are chanting AUM!"

Commander Peters looked puzzled. "A chant? *AUM?* What?"

The captain was back at his command console, his fingers quickly moving across its surface. He read: *"What world does he who meditates on AUM until the end of his life, win by that? If he meditates on the Supreme Being with the syllable AUM, he becomes one with the Light, he is led to the world of the Absolute Being, who is higher than the highest life, that which is tranquil, unaging, immortal, fearless, and supreme."*

The commander wheeled around on his heel. "Captain?"

"I just read that, Commander. It's from the Prashna Upanishads, an ancient Sanskrit text from India. According to other sources, meditation on the sacred mantra AUM, fixing one's mind on the sound of the mantra…AUM is the sacred symbol that symbolizes and embodies Brahman, the Absolute Reality. The purpose of chanting AUM is to free oneself from suffering and limitation. It was believed to be a universal symbol, the sound of the universe. It's all in the ship's library, Commander."

"What are they trying to tell us?" asked Paris.

No one spoke as the next *AAAAAAAAUUUUUUUUUUUUUUUUUMMMMMMMMMMMM* filled the bridge speakers.

"Turn it down, Mr. Paris, but don't turn it off," said the captain.

"Captain, I think they are trying to convey friendship," said Harris. "Chanting *AUM* is in no way a threatening gesture."

"No, it's not," agreed the captain.

Before he could continue, his comm buzzed. It was Dr. Smith.

"Yes, Doctor?"

"Captain, I think you ought to come down here. It's Lotte. I think you should see this yourself. "

"Let me guess, Doctor, he's chanting AUM."

"Yes, Captain! How did you know?"

"Because my bridge speakers are chanting AUM too. I'm on my way."

He closed the channel saying, "Commander, you're with me. Mr. Paris, keep recording everything they transmit. Ms. Harris, great job on figuring this out. Keep working with the techs to get our navigational system working again. Mr. Marker, keep a watchful eye on our friends out there. This is definitely a friendly gesture, but I don't trust them yet. Call me immediately if anything changes. If we are attacked, don't wait for authorization to engage. Engage as needed."

He and the commander walked down the ramp and out the bridge doors.

As they crossed the ship's main corridor, Peters asked "Captain, how much of what you read do you believe?"

"About chanting AUM?"

"Yes."

"I don't know. To be honest, I did enjoy listening to it over the speakers."

"Me too. It put me at ease, and I don't like that. Not here. Not now. I'd rather be on edge."

"Maybe this is a lesson for us," replied the captain.

"A lesson? About what? How to relax?"

"A lesson on life. A lesson on how we can do our best in any given situation, while remaining centered and mindful of the bigger picture."

The commander thought that over. "Maybe, Captain. Although, I must admit, I'm not entirely sure what the big picture is anymore."

"Don't worry, Commander. You're not alone. The important point, perhaps, is that we are aware that a bigger picture exists, even if we don't know *what* it is."

"Aye captain. That's a good way to look at things."

The captain nodded. "Now let's see if our friend Lotte can shed some light on this."

--

Lotte was laying down flat on his back, palms up and legs extended straight out. He looked like he was incredibly comfortable in his medical bunk, having assumed an intentionally restful pose.

The only thing that differentiated him from someone sleeping was his chanting.

AAAAAAAAUUUUUUUUUUUUUUUUMMMMMMMMMMMM

Which lasted for ten seconds, followed by five seconds of silence, and then again:

AAAAAAAAUUUUUUUUUUUUUUUUMMMMMMMMMMMM

"How long has he been doing this?" asked Commander Peters.

The doctor glanced at his data tablet. "Fifteen minutes ago."

"Which is when Lieutenant Paris first picked up the broadcast." Gregory keyed his comm. "Mr. Paris. Is the Structure still broadcasting?"

"Yes sir, no change."

"Send the audio to my data tablet — real time, no delays."

"Aye sir, will do."

A moment later

AAAAAAAAUUUUUUUUUUUUUUUUMMMMMMMMMMMM

played out of the captain's tablet.

He placed his tablet next to Lotte' bed and listened.

Both Lotte and the tablet chanted in unison, chanting AUM for the same ten-second interval with the same five seconds of silence in between.

"I've never seen anything like this," said Smith. "I've had patients who mumbled or talked or sung to themselves before, so chanting isn't necessarily that far off. But to have it sync with this broadcast…"

"They must have done something to him," said Peters. "Implanted this message into his mind. It could be a safeguard. Maybe they reasoned that if we missed their transmission there would at least be a chance that we'd get their message via Lotte."

"And what exactly is their message?" asked the doctor.

"That's what we're trying to figure out," said Gregory. "AUM can symbolize many things. Universal unity, for starters."

The captain turned off the tablet's speakers and keyed its surface.

"According to the ship's library, AUM is said at the beginning and end of prayers, and in chants to help clear away spiritual obstacles and to reaffirm one's spiritual intentions. Other texts say that the sound of AUM is an illustration of the unity between earth, heaven and atmosphere. These date back to the dawn of Hinduism, so we could translate them into modern analogs."

"Well," began Peters, "we could translate into our modern worldview by saying 'Earth' symbolizes planets and 'heaven' symbolizes space. Not sure what 'atmosphere' modernizes to."

"The stars," said the captain.

"OK, gentlemen. So what are you saying?" asked Smith. "My patient is trying to deliver a message of some kind. What is it?"

The captain shook his head. Reading from his tablet again, he said, "According to another text, AUM may also symbolize components of the mind. The waking mind, the mind in a state of deep sleep, the dreaming mind and an unknown state of consciousness. This last state is said to be so far removed from human experience that it cannot be known by ordinary humans."

"Those ideas are very old," said the doctor. "But that still doesn't explain what's happening to Lotte. Nor what this supposed message is actually saying."

Peters and Gregory shrugged in unison.

"Look here," said Smith, pointing to one of the medical monitors attached to Lotte. "This is a graph of our patient's brainwaves. Notice how steady they are. The medical community has long known that chanting AUM, among other things, has physiological benefits. Mainly, it helps bring calmness to the chanter. Without going into details, this can be attributed, at least in part, to the calming effects chanting has on the limbic system. Chanting AUM essentially deactivates, or turns down, the limbic system. The limbic system basically controls emotions, like fear and anger — and drives desire, like hunger or sex. So, turning that down would naturally have a calming effect."

"Thank you, Doctor. All good points," said the captain. "This brings up additional questions. Are the aliens merely trying to communicate with us, to send us a message, or are they deliberately trying to calm us down and put us at ease, figuring we'd transform their digital broadcast into sound?"

"The corollary question to that," added Peters, "is how do they know enough about human physiology and psychology to realize how this chant might affect us?

"They've had access to Lotte for days. And there are many other missing Marines. They potentially have plenty of subjects to study and experiment on. Doctor, have you seen any signs of experimentation on Lotte?"

"I think, Captain, that is a certainty," replied Smith. Gesturing at Lotte, who was still chanting, he said, "This man has been through a tremendous amount of stress. His body, as healthy as it is, bears all the telltale signs of repeated, widespread injury and invasive medical procedures."

"That could explain some things, but it still does not enlighten us as to how they even know about this specific chant. How *could* they know about AUM, as that is a very ancient, human development? Think about it, this developed in ancient India, on Earth, thousands of years ago and hundreds of light years away. Even on Earth it was not widely known across cultures until at least the twenty-first century. How can these aliens know? Dissecting our Marines wouldn't tell them that."

"Perhaps AUM is indeed a universal sound, as the ancients thought," said Smith.

"I can't believe that," said Peters. "And even if it is a universal sound, the type of *sound* we are talking about only has meaning to beings like us, with physiological systems like ours. What are the odds that this particular sound would have the same symbolic meaning, and physiological effects, on aliens from a different part of the universe? I just don't buy it. The odds are astronomically impossible."

"Those are good points, Commander," said Gregory. "The odds that an alien civilization would develop a system of belief from which grew mantras that have certain physiological effects on the chanter, identical in this very specific regard to a mantra stemming from a Dharmic religion of ancient Earth are next to impossible."

They all looked at each other and shrugged. "So, if all of that is impossible, what's left?" asked the doctor.

"*I* told them about it."

They all turned and looked at Lotte, who was now sitting up in his bed.

"You've stopped chanting," said the captain. Keying his comm, he said, "Mr. Paris, this is the captain. I take it the Structure has stopped broadcasting."

"Yes sir. The broadcast stopped a few moments ago."

"Thank you. Captain out."

"I think it's time we resumed our discussion, Private. Doctor, is he up to it?"

Smith panned over the various monitoring devices, checked vitals and found no abnormalities.

"Mr. Lotte is a pillar of health. He's clear, Captain."

--

Lotte sat across the conference table. It was an informal setting again, with just the captain and commander debriefing the Marine.

"What do you mean you *told them* about AUM?" asked Peters.

"I practice yoga, sir. I do it every day. I begin and end each session by chanting AUM. They learned that from me," said Lotte.

"Do you know why they chose this particular mantra to communicate with us?" asked Gregory.

"With respect, sir, my guess is that they were not trying to communicate with *you* or the *ship,* per se. I think they were just trying to calm me down."

"Calm *you* down?"

"Yes, Captain. I was trying to deliver their message before, but then I passed out."

"How would they know that?" asked the captain. "How are they monitoring your vitals? The doctor hasn't found anything anywhere on or within your body that could be used to track your health signs."

"I don't know," replied Lotte. "All I can say is that they made it clear that I was to deliver their message to you."

"And what is that message, Private?" asked Peters.

"In a nutshell, they are giving us time. Time to prove ourselves. Time to show them that we are worthy. Time to show them that we can earn a place in their Grand Plan."

Raising an eyebrow at Peters, the captain said, "Sounds all rather cryptic. What do you make of it, Commander?"

Peters shrugged. "I'd caution against reading too deeply into an alien message. No telling what they are really trying to say. I think the best we can extract from this is that whatever set of actions they are contemplating as 'next steps' in their first encounter with humanity are on hold pending the actions we take now. So, patience and deliberation are in order when planning our response to them."

"Agreed," said the captain. "We've got some more work to do before we can get the *Nemean* underway again. I think we should stop broadcasting the Rosetta Message now. No need to muddy the conversation with that now that Mr. Lotte has delivered his message. And besides, they still have ADAM and that may have tilted things a bit in our favor."

Turning his attention back to the Marine, Gregory said "Mr. Lotte, you've done a great job. Mr. Waverly credits you, Mr. Rodriguez and Major Lewis for saving his life. Beyond your combat role, you've proven instrumental in establishing some form of communication, and maybe even *understanding*, with the aliens. And I can only imagine what you had to endure before this dialogue could be had."

"With respect, sir, you *can't* imagine what I've been through," said Lotte. "*I* don't even know what I've been through. Not all of it. It's a jumble of crazy memories that don't even make sense. And that's just the part that didn't hurt."

The captain nodded. "You are off duty for the remainder of this mission. If you think of anything else, or you are able to make sense of any of those memories, put them on your recorder and let us know."

Lotte saluted. "I will, sir."

"Before we end this debrief," said Peters, "I just want to know something. Our teams encountered two different sets of aliens. The MC1 encountered mechanical soldiers, as you know. Another team, led by Lance Corporal Felix, encountered beings with three legs — we've been calling them tripedals. After you were separated from the rest of MC1, did you get a chance to see who your captors were?"

"No, I didn't. But my impression was that they were different. They didn't *feel* like the mechanical soldiers that attacked the MC1 and I doubt they were those tripedals you mentioned. I could tell they were *different* from anything like that. And sir, I never *felt* like a captive. They told me several times that I was free to go, only I didn't know how."

"Thank you, Private," said Gregory. "Now go get some rest."

"Thank you, sirs." Lotte stood, saluted the two officers and walked out of the briefing room.

"That was interesting," Gregory said. "And I think your take on 'next steps' is correct. Let's tread carefully here. Priority number one is to get the nav and engine systems back online."

Chapter 9

System: Virgil's star (VGL 191)

Location: Aboard the Alcmene naval vessel Nemean

Even without the assistance of Field Agent Collins and the secrets held in the ISAT stateroom, the focused efforts of the *Nemean*'s crew managed to repair most of the ship's damage, and despite having seen much better days, both her sub-light and hyperlight drives were now operational.

Though he had many doubts, the captain had made up his mind well before the final spit and polish was applied to the *Nemean*'s drives — they were going to follow the *Daedalus*.

The science team, with Lieutenant Paris' assistance, had managed to recreate every variable of the *Daedalus*' FTL jump in their simulations. Small scale live tests had taken a back seat to the simulations, as the enormous task of repairing the ship required every spare piece of equipment aboard the *Nemean*.

In ninety percent of the simulations, the *Nemean* followed a path that led it to a region of space within ten AU of the *Daedalus*. In seven percent of the simulations, the *Nemean*'s FTL jump led it to parts unknown, while in two percent nothing happened — the ship never left Virgil's star. However, in one percent of the simulations, the ship was destroyed by an overload in the hyperlight drives.

Reviewing the simulation reports with Commander Peters, the captain said, "Overall, the simulations suggest we have a ninety-two percent chance to either succeed or remain here."

Peters nodded. "And we have a one percent chance of blowing ourselves up."

"I won't order this, Ron, without your full agreement. As my XO, you know that I rely on you to tell me when I'm wrong, stupid or reckless."

"The simulations speak for themselves — the odds are in our favor. But there's a small chance we'll end up as a cloud of wreckage orbiting Virgil's star. On the other hand, if we are successful, we stand to gain an enormous amount of knowledge — *if* we can get the *Daedalus* under control."

"So you are in agreement?" asked the captain. "I want you to speak directly."

"You have my agreement, Captain," replied the commander. "The more I think about what Private Lotte told us, the more I believe this is exactly what we ought to be doing. If they really are observing us to see what we will do, going after the *Daedalus* makes the most sense."

"Exactly," said the captain. "We are not going on the offensive by attempting to land another armed party on their Structure — which they could view as belligerence. We are not turning tail and running for home — which they could see as cowardice. We are going after an alien ship carrying our crewman; that hopefully suggests to them we are inquisitive, curious and care about our fellow human beings. We'll reinforce that last point when we return here to retrieve our MIAs."

"Agreed, Captain. Although on your last point, I don't have any suggestions on how to do that just yet."

"We'll find a way, Commander. Lotte' report and his very *presence* back aboard the Neman gives me a lot of hope that we'll find a way."

"Next steps then?" asked Peters.

"Commander, for the record, I hereby officially order you to set conditions for the *Nemean* to follow the *Daedalus*, wherever she may have gone."

"Aye Aye sir. I'll begin preparations. See you on the bridge."

Peters stood, saluted and left the captain's meeting room.

--

Mission Log

It would be an hour before the crew set conditions for the *Nemean*'s *Daedalus* jump.

That's how much time the captain had to devote to his personal mission log, which he began:

This is the personal mission log of Captain John Benjamin Gregory, commander of the Alcmene Naval vessel Nemean, *ID verification number XNE-899-747-ATN-7797.*

We successfully traversed the one hundred thirty-nine light years between Alcmene and Virgil's Star, and located the Structure, arriving in system at 0100 local time.

Although the instruments in our home system could not resolve any details about the Structure, we have taken many scans and measurements, and I believe the data will prove very interesting. Full scan logs have been added as an addendum to this message.

We have been unable to provide you with periodic updates due to in-system interference. Virgil's Star is a very large and active star. We have kept our distance, as getting much closer would be perilous to the ship and crew. Compounding the communications issue is that fact that the alien Structure is also emitting a rather powerful neutrino-like field, which has detrimentally impacted our ability to conduct long range communications. We always knew that communicating across a gulf of one hundred thirty-nine light years would be difficult with or without additional environmental interference. My recommendation for any other such future missions is to equip Alcmene Naval vessels with multiple deployable message cannisters.

Our Marine EVA teams have personally encountered at least two types of alien sentients aboard the Structure. Each contact was hostile, and our Marines evacuated their respective contact areas. We have had one unconfirmed but likely KIA — Private Martinez — and several confirmed MIAs. A full roster list is included as an addendum to this message.

One of our MIAs, Marine Private Alexander Lotte, was returned to us by at least one of the sentients aboard the Structure. Full details of Lotte's debrief regarding his stay about the structure is included as an addendum to this message. A complete description of the sentients encountered by the other Marine units is also included as a separate addendum to this message.

At mission clock designate Alpha 2 we survived an attack launched by the Structure and made repairs to the ship. Details about the battle are enclosed in a separate addendum to his message.

At mission designate Alpha 7 the Nemean detected an apparently dormant alien vessel in orbit about the Structure. I ordered Lance Corporal Eugene Felix and a team of seven Marines, including ISAT Agent Malcom Waverly, to board and explore the alien craft. A full briefing of their findings is enclosed as an addendum to this message, which includes our efforts to translate an alien language.

The alien craft subsequently went FTL and disappeared from our sensors. All of Felix's team, with the exception of Agent Waverly, were still aboard the when it disappeared.

Based on all the information on hand, the information gathered by Felix's team, and the extensive information gleaned from the debriefing of returned Marine units (with heavy emphasis on the debrief of Private Lotte), I have decided that our best course of action is to pursue the Daedalus without haste.

If we locate the alien vessel, we will attempt to return it to Alcmene for further study. If we are unable to locate it, it is my intent to order the Nemean *back to Alcmene, where I will give a full report to the President and the Admiralty. It is my hope that you will authorize a return mission to Virgil's Star, to recover the Marines that are still MIA and to potentially open a dialogue with the Structure's inhabitants.*

If this mission has failed in that last regard, the responsibility is mine alone. Despite the extensive work that has been done, I believe that the problem of reliably communicating with a completely alien intelligence is currently beyond our capabilities. This is the one point where I agree with Agent Collins. It is my sincere hope that this mission has provided you with tools, insights and analyses that will help us make a breakthrough in the near future.

This is the personal log of Captain John Benjamin Gregory, aboard the Nemean, *in orbit around Virgil's Star. All other data, ship's telemetry and incidental reports compressed in final addendum.*

Message ends here.

Local time 1330.

--

Searching for *Daedalus*

The captain sat at his command console, examining each departmental report along with attendant notes from his XO.

Standing, he said, "Each station, report on readiness for *Daedalus* jump."

Green lights lit up in his console, indicating that all stations were clear and waiting for his command.

"Commander Peters, confirm go status."

"Go status confirmed, sir."

"Very good. Helm, take us to the *Daedalus* FTL jump point. Engineering, execute Program JUMP once we are in position."

Program JUMP had been developed by the *Nemean*'s engineering team. Once activated, the ship's computer would use the ship's engines and other systems to recreate the exact spatial conditions during the *Daedalus*' jump to FTL, while simultaneously activating her hyperlight pods.

The theory was that the contours and energy gradients of a local portion of space would dictate *how* and *where* an object in that space would move. Setting the four dimensions of space and time, as well as the energy gradients in a given volume of space to specific values would lead to one, and just one, possible destination.

Or, as Doc Smith had summarized the theory when the captain first tried to explain it to him: "Balls roll down hills because hills are steep. Basic thermodynamics."

"Exactly," the captain had replied. "Nature seeks balance, and a ball at the bottom of a hill represents a more stable state than when it's high up on the hill."

"It has always amazed me how the three laws intertwine as elegantly as they do," Smith had said.

The captain had nodded. "Yes, it's an intricate dance. The first law says that energy can neither be created nor destroyed — it can only be transferred or changed from one form to another. In the case of the ball on the hill, when it is high up, has a lot of potential energy. When it rolls down the hill the potential energy is converted into kinetic energy and heat. It does work. Energy has been transformed from one form to another.

"Then, the second law says that in any isolated system, entropy always increases. Higher states of entropy imply fewer states of potential energy waiting for conversion —less work is possible, hence things are in a greater state of equilibrium, as there are fewer opportunities for energy to change from one form to another. So, the ball resting at the bottom of the hill has given up its potential energy and is now in a state of greater equilibrium — if no external force is applied to the ball, it's not going anywhere.

"Reinforcing this, the third law states that the entropy of a system approaches a constant value as the temperature approaches absolute zero…. that is, such systems tend toward having just one energy state with minimum energy — unless energy is introduced into the system from an external source. So that ball at the bottom of the hill represents the lowest energy state for that system.

"And that, in a nutshell, is what we are going to do. We are going to change the environmental variables in a local, small volume of space-time and put it in a new energy state and change its equilibrium. That new configuration will dictate what happens to the ball we place on that hill — in this case, the *Nemean* is the ball and the local space time is the hill. There will be no choice but for us to take a ride down that hill."

The captain was glad to have the doctor's support. He valued his opinion as a friend and trusted unofficial advisor.

"We're at the jump point, sir."

"Very good. Sound alert throughout the ship. Execute JUMP Program on my command."

The captain looked at Commander Peters, who nodded. The rest of the bridge crew looked ready and eager to get this over with.

"Helm, execute JUMP Program *now!*"

The ship lurched, heaved and righted itself again as the space-time topography around it went through a series of changes, eventually settling on the configuration calculated by the *Nemean*'s crew. For several long moments, it appeared as if the *Nemean* had completely gone offline, its sensors dark, the normally constant flow of information processed brought to a halt.

The bridge crew watched the control panels anxiously, minutes ticking by in complete silence.

Suddenly, data began flowing again. The *Nemean* lurched and shook violently, its gravity generators straining to slow the ship as it entered normal space.

"Captain," exclaimed Lieutenant Harris, "I think we made it!"

"Good job, Ms. Harris! Mr. Marker, tactical report?"

"The sensor picture is still developing, sir, said Marker. "But so far I don't see anything to worry about."

"Good. I want a full report on this system. Planets, satellite. Artificial structures…" Turning to Commander Peters, he asked, "Any sign of the Daedalus?"

Scanning his control console, the commander said, "Not yet sir. Our sensors are still sorting out all the contacts in this system. Initial readings suggest there are several habitable moons orbiting a gas giant."

"Let's see it on screen, Commander," said the captain.

Peters called up a three-dimensional display of the system. The primary in this system was a K-type main sequence star. Seven planetary bodies were in nearly circular orbit around the primary. The three closest were rocky planets, while the fourth, fifth and sixth were gas giants with a large number of moonlets in orbit.

Highlighting the innermost gas giant with a red, holographic ring, the commander said, "The gas giant there, fifth planet out from the star…do you see that green dot? That's a small moon about the size of Earth's Io. Sensor readings suggest biosignatures, liquid water, a breathable atmosphere. Gravity is fifty-percent Earth normal."

The doctor entered the bridge and gawked at the view up on the display. "We're still in one piece," he said to the captain. "Congratulations." Indicating the three-dimensional display of the system with his chin, he said, "And what do we have here?"

"We may have inadvertently found a new human-friendly world," said the captain.

The doctor gasped. "What would be the odds of that?"

"Not too bad, Doctor. That's a K-type, main-sequence star," said Peters, zooming in on the point of light at the center of his display. "K-types are actually among the best candidates for hosting planets in the hospitable zone. They're dimmer than the G-types our Union worlds are anchored to but much older, giving more time for life to develop. They are also better behaved, with fewer violent energy releases. So they're less likely to blow away a planet's atmosphere before life can get a foothold."

"We've detected water, a breathable atmosphere, and both oxygen and methane on that small moonlet. Oxygen and methane together don't happen often in nature, as those gases tend to destroy each other. Something must be creating both on an ongoing basis."

"Extraordinary discovery," mumbled the doctor, his eyes still wide. "And the *Daedalus*?"

"No signs yet, Harry," answered the captain. "Helm, take us in for a closer look of that moon."

"Aye sir."

Pressing a button on his console, the captain said, "Engineering. We took a bit of a rattle getting here. How are we looking?"

"All clear, sir. The ship is operating as well as can be expected, especially after the damage we took during the battle and Collins' sabotage. She's a tough ship. We're keeping an eye on everything to make sure things stay that way."

"Very good. Captain out."

Harris guided the *Nemean* into a graceful, high orbit around the gas giant, with the moonlet now orbiting between the *Nemean* and the planet.

"This should allow us to get a better look at that moon," said the captain.

"EVA mission?" asked Peters.

"Possibly. Let's take our time and find out what's down there first."

"Sir, new contact detected," announced Marker.

"The *Daedalus*?"

"No sir. I'm not sure what it is."

An image of the contact came up on the captain's command console. He pressed a button and put the display up for the entire bridge to see.

"What are we looking at?" asked Peters. "That's an odd-looking shape."

The contact had a metallic appearance, with rod-like structures of different lengths and radii protruding around it like spokes on a wheel. It was dark gray in appearance and rotating counterclockwise relative to the *Nemean*.

"How did we miss that on the sensors?" demanded the captain. "That's twice our size and doesn't look friendly."

"Sir, it was in a low orbit around the gas giant. It just crossed the horizon and came into view," replied Marker. "It's now moving up into a higher orbit, probably trying to match ours."

"Helm, gently back us away into a higher orbit around this planet. Let's keep ten thousand kilometers between us and the contact."

"Aye sir. Increasing our orbital distance from the gas giant."

They all watched as the contact continued to spiral into a higher orbit around the giant, quickly closing the distance between it and the *Nemean.*

"Helm, increase speed. Keep that distance between us."

"Sir, I'm trying. Every time I establish a ten kilo distance it increases its speed of ascent."

"Captain, I suggest we deploy the weapons bay and prime cannons," said Peters. "That thing doesn't seem to be getting our message to keep its distance."

"Sir," Marker exclaimed. "New contact. It's the *Daedalus.*"

A new blip appeared in the bridge display, indicating the *Daedalus'* path through space. Presently, it appeared to be headed for the gas giant.

"How did we miss the *Daedalus* too?" asked the Captain. "Are your sensors working properly, Lieutenant?"

"I've been running diagnostics since we entered this system. Sensors are fully functional. The *Daedalus* appears to have completed an orbit around the system's primary star and is now headed this way. My guess is that it was obscured by the star."

"A possibility. But I still want those sensors checked."

The commander took the cue and ordered engineering to manually check the ship's sensor systems and to send a technician to examine the bridge console interfaces.

"Lieutenant Paris, hail the *Daedalus*. See if you can raise Mr. Felix or his team."

"Aye sir. Running through all comm frequencies."

A few moments went by before static began to crackle in the bridge speakers.

"*Nemean,* this is Lance Corporal Eugene Felix. Come in. Over"

"Felix, this is the *Nemean.* We read you," replied Paris.

"Yes! Paris is that you? We thought we lost you guys."

"We're here, Mr. Felix," said the captain. "We followed you through your jump point."

"Captain, I'm not sure that was a good idea. But regardless, we're glad to hear you made it. Is EVAC possible?"

"Stand by on EVAC. We're analyzing your radiation envelope. But it's looking good right now. What do you mean, it wasn't a good idea that we followed you?"

"Captain, we've learned quite a bit about the *Daedalus*. There's a weapon in this system."

"Where?" asked the captain.

"Last we saw it, it crashed into the gas giant, third from the primary. Since we're talking to you, it's probably been destroyed," replied Felix. "We can't see you from here. Where is the *Nemean* located?"

"Mr. Felix, we're in orbit around the gas giant you alluded to. Our sensors have made contact with an object of unknown design. The weapon, I presume?"

"Shit, Captain! Cancel EVAC! Get the hell out of there, now!"

The captain had never heard Felix speak that way, especially to a superior officer. Uncertain of what danger they were really in, he decided to err on the side of caution.

"Helm, break orbit immediately. Take us out one AU from the gas giant."

"Aye sir!"

"Tactical. Deploy weapons bay. Ready all weapons"

"Sir, replied tactical. "Contact's energy readings just spiked."

A general-quarters alarm automatically began ringing throughout the *Nemean*, as the ship's automated systems sensed the dangerous energy spike and went into automatic preservation mode.

Within seconds, bulkheads were reinforced with double doors, the hull began cycling through a series of micro-adjustments designed to better dissipate the type of energy release the computers anticipated, and essential mission data was backed up into hardened, isolated data cubes located in the center of the ship. If the ship were destroyed, the hope was that Naval Command would at least know what had happened.

"Sir, the *Nemean* has just activated APM protocol," shouted Peters over the alarm.

"I know, Commander. Maximum speed, Helm. Get us clear of the blast zone."

"Sub-light drives on full, sir!"

A few seconds later a wave of energy washed over the *Nemean*'s hull, incinerating the sub-light drives and badly damaging her hyperlight pods. The outer layers of her hull began to melt off, as the heat rose tens of thousands of degrees. Cracks formed along her spine, as the extreme temperatures compromised the *Nemean*'s external structural elements.

The *Nemean* began a long arc down towards the gas giant, losing altitude fast as the enormous gravity of the planet overcame the ship's outward momentum. The captain, the bridge staff and the entire crew held on to anything that would give them some level of comfort, as they knew there was no way to recover from this.

Time seemed to slow, as the captain watched the gas giant get bigger and bigger on the view screen, which was somehow still operational, providing the bridge staff with data feeds and crystal-clear views of their final destination.

A moment later, that view changed as the green moonlet swung into view, looming larger than anything Gregory had ever seen, now mere miles away as its orbit brought it between the *Nemean* and the gas giant below.

The *Nemean*'s hull thundered as it made contact with the moonlet's atmosphere, the heat of entry burning more of her hull away and scouring it clean of any Alcmene Naval markings. What fell from the moonlet's sky was a sand-blasted, scorched hulk of metal — a lifeless, shapeless, mangled approximation of a planet's once proud achievement in engineering.

With a surprisingly muffled thud, the *Nemean* skidded onto the surface, sending plumes of dust, smoke and other rocky debris high up into the moonlet's sky, the half gravity making it that much easier for debris to fill the sky many miles away with evidence of the *Nemean*'s demise.

--

"Roll call!" shouted Peters, his body aching from the crash and his uniform torn, burned and stained beyond recognition. "By the numbers! Form up in three columns," he said, pointing to three markers erected around a hastily constructed command center.

Of the original one hundred and fifty crew members and fifty remaining Marines aboard, Peters and his team of people counters had been able to account for one hundred twenty-one, thirty of them Marines and the rest naval personnel.

The thirty Marines had been broken up into six units of five. Two units were assigned to patrol the command center as well as the perimeter of the crash site, three units were aiding in the search for unaccounted crew, and one unit was ordered to recon the general area for food, water, supplies and inhabitants.

Doc Smith and his medical team had set up an emergency triage station, three first aid stations and an intensive care station. The medical team had suffered mostly minor injuries and medical supplies had generally been undamaged, thanks — in part — to the ship's design, which placed emphasis on protecting medical facilities through material reinforcements and facility location, generally somewhere near the center of naval vessels.

Relatively speaking, based on their numbers, the Marines had suffered the most, largely due to the fact that shipboard military facilities, including barracks and training fields, tended to be located away from the ship's core, allowing for faster troop deployment and recovery during military operations.

The bridge suffered heavy damage but was spared complete destruction largely due to luck: The ship had crashed with the bridge on top of the *Nemean* rather than below, where it made contact with the moonlet's surface.

Waverly had suffered a broken arm and a host of cuts, scrapes and bruises, but was well enough to lead a fire brigade struggling to stamp out the fires that still ranged within the *Nemean*'s battered hull.

The hope was that once the fires were put out, what remained of the *Nemean*, which would likely never fly again, could serve as a refuge for the crew — at least until more permanent arrangements could be made.

"State your name and rank," said Peters to the crewman standing before him.

The man looked dazed and was covered in dark streaks of ash, plus other materials that were likely the remnants of his incinerated uniform.

"Andrew Saunders, culinary specialist. Mess hall lounge west and barracks mess."

"How do you feel, Mr. Saunders?" asked Peters.

"I don't know, sir. Not well, I guess."

"Do you have any injuries that will prevent you from working?"

"No sir," Saunders said. "I can work. I just feel exhausted."

"As we all do, crewman. Report to supply officer Reynolds over there. Assist her in inventorying our basic foodstuff."

"Yes sir," replied Saunders, saluting with an arm covered in dirt and dried blood.

"Next in line! State your name and rank," said Peters to the next crewman before him, feeling exhausted; he had been at this for untold hours, after the initial shock of the crash began to fade.

"Amanda Lilbet, medical recovery ward two."

"How do you feel, Ms. Lilbet?"

"As bad as you look, sir," she said, eyeing him from head to foot. She managed a half smile. "That was a joke, sir. I feel like shit. I probably look like shit too."

"You look fine, Ms. Lilbet," replied Peters. "Do you have any injuries that will prevent you from working?"

"None, sir. I took some stims after we crashed and some pain killers an hour after that. I'm fine to work."

Peters nodded. "Doc Smith has set up medical over there," he said, pointing in the general direction of the field hospital quickly erected after the crash. "There's a lot you can do over there to help."

She gave him another half smile and slowly walked towards the field hospital tenting.

"Ms. Lilbet," called Peters. "A favor please? When you get a chance, let me know how the captain is doing."

"I will, sir."

--

Captain Gregory's command console had erupted in flames when the *Nemean* crashed onto the moonlet's surface, which caused severe burn injuries across much of his torso and limbs. Making matters worse, a support pillar directly behind the captain's command area buckled upon impact, falling diagonally across the captain's back, crushing the bones in his left leg and right shoulder.

Commander Peters, Lieutenant Paris and several other bridge officers had struggled to free the captain and managed to take him to safety, where the surviving medical team led by Doc Smith immediately put him under sedation and began treatment with emergency surgery and an injection of medical nanos.

Hours after the surgery, the captain regained consciousness but was unable to stand or walk. At his insistence, the medical team agreed to provide him with a mobile recovery chair, allowing him to move about. He hated the thought of lying in bed while the rest of the crew struggled to rescue trapped crewman, find missing personnel and ensure the security and habitability of the crash site.

He had spent the day after surgery wheeling around in his recovery chair, offering words of support and confidence, issuing orders and conferring with his command staff on next steps.

However, two days after the crash he began to withdraw and started spending spend most of his time in bed, occasionally asking one of the medical staff for updates on their situation.

"I'm certain of it, Commander," said the doctor. "He is severely, *clinically* depressed, and is blaming himself for this." Smith waved an arm across the crash site.

"If there is blame here," replied Peters, "the command staff shares it, starting with me."

Smith held up his hand. "Don't go down that rabbit hole, Commander. I won't debate fault here. The fact of the matter is I *also* told the captain following the *Daedalus* would be the best course of action to take. The issue at hand is that the captain is unable to perform his duties. Physically, I think he'll make a good recovery eventually. Psychologically…right now, I'm not so sure."

"I'm surprised we haven't cured clinical depression yet," said Peters.

"There are things we can do chemically speaking, but my view is that they are temporary measures. And I am loath to use nanos for this. He needs to be walked back by his friends. Like you, Commander."

Peters nodded. "What can I do to help?"

"We have to combat his social withdrawal by engaging him, change his tendency to ruminate about perceived failures by redirecting those energies towards something constructive like organizing our resources, planning next steps and things like that."

--

The next day, at the doctor's incessant prodding, the captain agreed to attend a meeting of the senior staff.

The makeshift command center had been put together using furniture recovered from the *Nemean*, including a large table that came from the barrack's mess hall, along with an assortment of chairs from throughout the ship. A tent had been erected as protection from the elements and to offer a degree of privacy, and the captain's flag had been hoisted to indicate that it was the command center. Other temporary field facilities were erected around the command center and surrounding area, dotting the crash site with tents and other makeshift shelters.

The doctor escorted the captain to the staff meeting, where he was greeted by grim yet friendly welcoming faces.

"Captain, we are happy to see you making such a swift recovery after your surgery," said Peters.

Gregory nodded. "You should thank the doctor, I really didn't do anything."

"No need to thank me," said Smith. "I'm just doing my job. Now, if you'll excuse me..."

The captain seemed uncomfortable with the doctor leaving him alone with the others, but didn't try to stop him. When Smith exited the tent, Peters began.

"Captain, I've prepared a set of status reports and uploaded them to your console. They detail the supplies we've inventoried — food, medical, general use — that we've either managed to remove from the *Nemean* or are certain can be accessed when needed. Another report summarizes our findings regarding this moonlet's biosphere and the flora and fauna contained therein. Regarding equipment—"

The captain interrupted him. "How many did we lose, Ron?

Peters paused for a moment, looked down at his notes, and took a deep breath. "Sir, we have accounted for ninety-one naval personnel and thirty Marines."

"I've lost more than half my crew," mumbled Gregory, the pained look on his face reflecting the turmoil he felt inside.

"Sir. We still have teams searching the *Nemean*," said Peters. "There are areas that are still inaccessible to the search and rescue teams. We believe many of the missing are simply trapped but will be recovered soon. The *Nemean* is a well-designed, tough ship."

"She *was* a tough ship, Commander. Look at her now," Gregory said, pointing to the twisted, melted remains of the *Nemean*. "That ship is never going to fly again."

Peters nodded silently. He glanced at Paris and Harris, who were whispering to each other. They looked like they were about to say something. Peters gestured in their direction, and Harris cleared her throat. "Captain, this really isn't your fault. I had the helm. I crashed the ship."

"And I'm equally at fault," said Paris. "I should have noticed that energy spike sooner. But I didn't."

"Irrelevant," said the captain. "Ms. Harris, you could have pointed the *Nemean* nose down towards the planet and set the drives to maximum and obliterated us all, and it would *still* be my responsibility. Mr. Paris, the *Nemean* went into automatic preservation mode a second before you reported on the energy spike. There's *nothing* you could have done."

"Captain," said Peters, "let's agree that the command staff *all* share degrees of responsibility here. There's no need for you to become a martyr. We need to come together now and plan our next steps."

"Agreed, Commander," said Gregory. "However, I no longer trust my judgement in command matters. Effective immediately, I am placing *you* in command of what's left of this mission. Now, if you don't mind, I really need to get back to bed and get some rest. This has been an exhausting day."

The captain saluted the staff, turned his chair and exited the command center.

Peters shrugged. "I'll speak with the Doctor later. Let's continue this meeting. Our priorities, as I see them, are shelter, food and water, medical facilities and communications. Let's go through each one."

Marker looked down at his console and said, "We have erected a sufficient number of shelters to house every member of the crew. The fires on the *Nemean* have been put out, and if needed most of us could fit inside the cleaned areas to sleep. For now, shelter has been taken care of."

"Very good," said Peters. "Lieutenant Harris, food and water?"

"Reynolds and Saunders report that we have enough food rations to last us six months. Recon Team Six has scouted out to a radius of ten kicks. While they report finding a good variety of edible flora, they have found no obvious evidence of any fauna."

"No animals?" asked Marker. "That's strange."

"None at all," replied Harris. "It seems strange to us, because all Union worlds have both flora and fauna. But that may not be the norm elsewhere in the galaxy. Besides, that's only ten kilometers from our position. We don't know what else is out there."

"The crash could have scared off any animals that were originally in the area," added Peters. "Or maybe they just missed them. We have no idea what native fauna would look like. I would assume they are well adapted to this environment and can conceal themselves if they have to. To them, we are completely alien and potentially dangerous predators."

Harris nodded, indicating she agreed with everything Peters had said. "Regarding the flora that the recon team *did* find, they said much of it appeared familiar, including those that produce fruit and vegetables. One Marine reported taking a bite of something that looked a lot like an apple — and apparently tasted like one too."

"I hadn't heard about that," said Peters. "What's the Marine's name? Do you know?"

"His name is Lotte, I believe." Harris replied. "The other Marines said he felt extremely comfortable here and wasn't concerned with sampling anything."

Peters made a mental note; he would speak to Lotte later.

"Thank you, Ms. Harris. Is there anything else?"

"No sir," she replied.

"Mr. Paris? Your comm report?"

"We have enough working field units for most of the crew," said Paris. "The Marines have their comm built into their suits, so there are no issues there."

"What about long-range comm?" asked Peters.

Paris shook his head. "Negative, sir. Those systems are probably beyond repair, and we don't have enough spare equipment to rig something together. I've been brainstorming with Clara Seung from engineering to see if we can come up with an alternate solution, but nothing so far."

"I want you to keep working on that, Mr. Paris," said Peters. "That remains a top priority. If we don't get long-range comm capability back, we're probably going to be staying here for a long time to come."

Harris looked around and remarked, "It could be a lot worse."

"Yes. We were fortunate," said Peters. "That we definitely were."

--

The moonlet, unofficially designated "Eden" by the crew, was lush with green vegetation, clean, crisp air, bountiful running water, and a temperate climate hovering around 68 °F. Flora included many edibles and medicinals, and were within easy range of the crash site. In many ways, it was an ideal habitat for human life, and that made Lotte wonder.

"You wanted to see me, sir?" asked Lotte.

"Thank you for coming," said Peters. "Have a seat."

Lotte took a chair opposite of Peters and said, "Sir, I know why you wanted to see me. You want to know why I ate that apple, right?"

"That was irresponsible," Peters said. "Look around. Our manpower is down over fifty percent. That apple, or whatever it is, could have killed you."

"It didn't, sir. It was perfectly safe."

"We have protocols in place to ensure the safety of any foodstuff we obtain from this biosphere," said Peters. "I don't want anyone skirting those procedures or encouraging others to do the same. Understood?"

"Yes sir," replied Lotte. "But I think you'll find fruit and vegetables here to be just fine for human consumption."

"Possibly. But we are going to determine that by following protocols," said Peters. "I think I've made myself abundantly clear on the matter."

"You have, sir."

Peters glanced his watch. "I think we're finished here, unless you have something you'd like to add."

Lotte shook his head. "Nothing, sir. I have a few minutes before my duty shift starts. I'm going to visit the captain. If I may speak freely, he has complete confidence in you. That's why he's allowed himself to feel the way he feels right now. It's part of a healing process. If he didn't think so highly of you, he'd keep it all inside where it could do the most harm. You're helping him, sir."

Peters gave Lotte a long, pensive look.

After a few moments, Lotte said, "I know what you're thinking, sir. We can't predict the future, but things will work out as they should."

Peters nodded. "That's a good attitude. Now I have a meeting to attend. Give my regards to the captain."

--

Lotte lazily strolled through the tall green grass around the field hospital, a smile on his face as a mild breeze gently caressed his skin. The area had a sweet, subtle sent and was dotted with patches of color.

Off towards the tree line, one particularly bright patch of orange caught his attention, causing him to take a small detour for a closer look.

It was a beautiful sight — an inflorescence of twelve funnel-shaped flowers sitting on top of leafless stems nearly two-feet tall. The flowers were about six inches in diameter and were shaped like a star; the petals were bright orange with green swirls in their centers.

Lotte carefully plucked one of the flowers and held it to his nose. He was rewarded with a faint citrusy sent that reminded him of a mixture of fresh orange, lemon and lime.

Careful not to damage the flower, he held it in front of him as he made his way to the field hospital. A medic greeted him at the entrance.

"This unit is for serious injuries, soldier," said the medic. "Pardon me, but we are swamped here. The medics at any of the first aid stations can take care of the non-life-threatening stuff."

"I'm fine, Ms. Sciapelli," replied Lotte. "I'm here to see the captain."

"Oh, you know my name? Well, I guess that should be OK. Is that for him?" she asked, pointing to the flower.

"Yes."

"I'm not sure that's a good idea," Ms. Sciapelli said. "We don't want to bring any contaminants into the patient areas."

"The captain has been around the entire area outside and hasn't had any issues," replied Lotte. "This won't hurt him, nor any of your other patients."

Sciapelli looked around, unsure if anyone was within earshot of their conversation. No one seemed to be paying them any attention. The medical staff was short on hands and had too many other things to occupy their attention.

"I guess it's all right," Ms. Sciapelli said. "The captain is in berth nineteen."

"Thank you," said Lotte, smiling at her as he walked past her towards the berths.

Nineteen was about ten meters from the greeting zone, and was separated by the common areas by heavy tarps on four sides. Lotte lifted the tarp hanging at the front of the berth and stepped inside.

The captain was lying in bed with his eyes closed but didn't appear to be asleep.

"Hello, Captain."

Gregory immediately sat up. "Private Lotte? I haven't seen you since we debriefed you. Glad to see you among the survivors."

"Thank you, sir," replied Lotte. "This refuge has enabled all of us to survive."

The captain nodded. "It has. We were fortunate to have found this place."

Lotte held up the flower in his hand. "Keep this by your bedside, Captain," said Lotte. "It will help you get back on your feet."

The captain took the flower from Lotte and held it to his nose. "Watermelon," said the captain. "It smells just like watermelon."

"It's citrusy to me," replied Lotte.

"I've seen these plants all over the Union worlds," said the captain.

"Yes, it looks a lot like amaryllis," replied Lotte. "Although the swirling veins at the center are very unusual."

"It's beautiful."

"On Earth, red amaryllis were frequently offered as gifts during Christmastime," said Lotte. "They are steeped in symbolism."

"Funny what we humans will assign meaning to," commented Gregory. "We tend to give everything some kind of secondary, symbolic meaning, don't we?"

"Yes, we do," Lotte agreed. "Amaryllis has been known to symbolize love, strength, determination and success.

"You seem to know a lot about this plant," said the captain.

Lotte shrugged. "I realized that I had a lot of time to think about things during my time aboard the Structure. Botany has always attracted me, although I never formally studied it."

"Perhaps you should. Tell me, besides flowers, what else did you think about during your time in captivity?"

"I wasn't a captive," Lotte reminded him. "They did not coerce me to stay."

"A subjective point of view," replied Gregory. "One person's captivity is another's voluntary offer of work. I guess it depends who wields the whip."

Before Lotte could reply, Dr. Smith lifted the tarp covering the entrance and entered the captain's berth.

"Mr. Lotte, good to see you," said the doctor. "You look great."

Lotte smiled. "I feel great, doctor. Never felt better."

"Mr. Lotte was kind enough to bring me this flower," said the captain. "Here, have a smell."

The doctor took the flower and smelled it. "Kind of peachy. Very pleasant."

Both Lotte and the captain laughed at that.

"Did I miss the joke?" asked the doctor.

The captain shook his head. "No, Harry. It's just that you said the flower smells like a peach. I thought it smelled like watermelon, while Mr. Lotte smells citrus."

"Interesting," said Smith. "This looks like amaryllis." Turning to Lotte, he asked, "Where did you find this?"

"There's a patch growing about twenty meters outside the hospital, towards the tree line."

"I will have my team analyze this," said the doctor. "Captain, if this is anything like the amaryllis we have on Alcmene, then we may have hit a bit of a medical jackpot here. Certain species of Hippeastrum are high in alkaloids and useful for creating medicines. They are particularly well suited for helping treat things like anxiety and depression."

"'Hippeastrum?'" repeated the captain. "I thought this was amaryllis."

"Hippeastrum is the name of the genus. It means something like 'knight's star'." He looked at Lotte. "Thank you for bringing this to my attention. You are part of the team assigned to recon this moon, right?"

Lotte nodded.

"You obviously have some botanical knowledge. Please, document any local flora you find and send your report to my medical staff. There may be other medically useful plants on this moon."

The captain shook his head. "Why do you need medicinal plants, doctor? Don't the medical nanos do away with the need for medicines?"

"Yes and no," replied the doctor. "The medical nanos can pretty much take the place of almost all chemically-based, injected or ingested medicines. However, there are some things that I won't use nanos for. Like depression, Captain. And, besides, our supply of nanos is limited. Beyond that, in addition to the mechanical work that the nanos do in physically repairing tissues and reversing cell damage, when applied medicinally they can only be programmed to perform like the medicines we know about. There could be hundreds, even thousands, of botanicals with medicinal use here. That could translate into new ways to program the nanos to improve on existing protocols."

"I see," muttered the captain.

"Mr. Lotte, do you mind if I take this with me?" asked Smith.

Lotte shrugged. "I don't mind at all."

"Very good," the doctor replied. "Thank you. Now if you will excuse me gentlemen, I have patients to attend to."

Smith put the flower in his pocket, waved goodbye and left.

"Looks like you've made the doctor a happy man," said the captain, a small smile on his face.

"Happiness is inspiring, isn't it?" replied Lotte.

"Thanks for coming, Mr. Lotte," said the captain.

"My pleasure, sir," Lotte replied, saluting as he pulled the tarp open and stepped through to leave. Before letting it drop back down again, he said, "Oh sir, please don't forget to use some amaryllis. It will make you feel better, guaranteed."

Chapter 10

System: Unknown star

Location: Eden

Marine Patrols One and Two had been assigned to maintain active security around the crash site. Their weapons' compliment consisted of a side arm strapped to their thigh, the Z10 Pistol, and a standard issue M25 plasma assault rifle.

Marine Patrol One was also equipped with shoulder-mounted rocket launchers for use against ground or near air targets, while Marine Patrol Two had three portable surface-to-air missile batteries.

The Marines had also set up sensors in concentric rings one kilometer, half a kilometer, and a quarter kilometer out from the crash site. The sensors listened for activity on the ground and in the air as their reports were synced and processed by a computer located in command central.

The team also had a functional SKYEYE, which could detect activity in near space, up to about two hundred and fifty miles from the surface of a typical terrestrial world.

Peters was taking a break from the day's activities and sipping coffee while reading the recon team's latest report on the moon's flora. It had been a long morning and a sleepless evening, despite the fact that after twenty days on the moonlet, things were beginning to settle into a predictable, relatively stable routine.

The commander felt that once things became sufficiently normal on their new home, they would be in a better position to focus their energies on getting *off* the moon and returning to Alcmene.

Perhaps today could be a lazy day, when he and the rest of the crew could take things a little slower and a much needed and earned break.

However, the SKYEYE had other plans, as it broke the morning's silence with a shrill alarm, amplified by the speakers set up around the crash zone. A fully armored Marine rushed into the command center, nearly tearing down the front of the tent in his rush to find the commander.

"Sir, we've detected a contact two hundred and fifty miles above the surface and closing fast!"

Peters stood up, keyed his comm and said "All Marine units. Take defensive positions. Standard protocol." Turning to the Marine, he said "And make sure everyone heard that alarm!"

"Yes, sir!," replied the Marine, before turning and running back the way he came.

Peters holstered his Z10 pistol and ran to the field hospital, knocking over a medic carrying supplies as he rushed towards berth nineteen. The captain was lying in bed, his eyes closed, the bright orange petals of an amaryllis flower spread out on his chest.

"Captain, we've got company. SKYEYE has detected an incoming contact. I suggest you take cover inside the *Nemean* until we know what's going on."

Gregory hoisted himself up on his elbows and said, "Help me get into my chair."

Peters brought the mobility chair to the side of the captain's bed, helped him sit up and positioned the chair directly below his seat. Gregory reached down and grabbed the chair handles, slowly lowering himself into it.

"Let's go, Commander," the captain said.

Peters was relieved at the captain's willingness to seek shelter in the *Nemean*, as that remained the safest place they knew of on this moon.

"Sir, the *Nemean* is that way," said Peters, pointing towards the opposite direction in which they were going.

"I know," replied the captain, "I won't let the Marines stand alone against this. Did Barracks Master Lauren Vella survive?"

"She did, sir."

"If we survive this visit, I want her to arrange for all naval personnel to receive basic combat and weapons training. We must rebuild our capacity to fight. The Marines have carried a heavy load on this mission, and they need our help."

"Yes sir," replied Peters. The commander managed a small smile, as he heard signs of strength and confidence returning to the captain's voice.

--

The thirty remaining Marines formed a defensive perimeter around the crash site.

Marine Patrols One and Two hid along the nearby tree line and rocky outcroppings, scanning the alien sky with their rocket launchers and surface-to-air missile batteries.

Pre-placed fixed-position gun emplacements camouflaged in short trenches were manned by the three search and rescue team units, while Recon Team Six stood out in the open, just outside the command center, flanking the captain sitting in his mobile recovery chair.

They all watched the sky expectantly, as ISAT Agent Waverly stood off to the side, monitoring a small portable SKYEYE display unit.

"How far is the contact Waverly?" asked the captain.

"A hundred miles above the surface, descending at a rate of ten miles per minute. They are coming in relatively slow."

The captain glanced at the Z10 pistol strapped to Waverly's thigh. "Where did you get that?"

"This?" asked Waverly, putting his hand on the butt of the weapon. "One of my Marine friends, sir."

Looking at Lotte, who was now leading Recon Team Six, Gregory said "Let me have your side arm, solider."

Lotte handed him his Z10, which the captain strapped to the side of his mobility chair.

Lotte's comm piece buzzed. "Understood, Commander. We're ready here."

A few moments later, Peters jogged to the captain's position. Greeting the Marines with a nod, he said, "Captain, all units are in position. We've got everything available pointing towards the sky. Are you certain you want to stay out here in the open?"

"I'm certain, Commander," replied the captain. "We will make our stand, out here, in the open. If that fails, our friends out along the perimeter will make them pay a heavy price for misusing our trust."

The contact is now two minutes out," said Waverly. "We should have visual."

The Marines pointed their SCOPES towards the sky and projected the image to the captain's monitor. The object was small, dull-colored and angular. As the image grew, the Marines could make out wings jutting out from its sides, but no signs of engines or heat exhaust.

A few moments later, a rectangular object the size of a house hovered over the command center in near silence. The captain, Marines and remaining crew watched from the ground, as the wings folded into the structure and the object began a slow descent towards the surface.

Thirty seconds more and the object gently landed, flattening plants and grass as it came to a stop.

The Marines flanking the captain aimed their weapons at the object, but Lotte put up a hand, telling them to stand down.

"Captain," he said. "I don't think there is an immediate threat here."

The captain nodded. "What is that? It somehow looks familiar."

Waverly shook his head. "I can't believe it. It can't be—"

One of the surfaces on the object began to lift, a gentle puff of air escaping, as the atmospheric pressures equalized.

"Captain, I'm so glad to see you here," said a figure masked in the shadow of the object, as it walked down a metal ramp and onto the moon's surface. "I'm sure by now you've had time to consider the error of your ways. You *really* should have listened to me."

"Arrest him," shouted the captain.

All the members of Recon Team Six, except for Lotte, moved in to secure the man.

"Collins," shouted the captain, "I don't know how you made it here, but you are *still* under arrest for sabotage and mutiny. Commander, arrange for a brig to be built for the traitor."

The commander gave the Marines a hand signal and they quickly ushered Collins away into one of the nearby tents. Turning to Lotte, Peters said, "Have your men build a holding cell for the prisoner. The captain and I will want to question that man. See to his basic needs and secure that vessel."

"With respect, sir," said Lotte. "I don't think imprisoning him is the best course of action, given the circumstances. I suggest finding a way to work together. After all, that's why he came here, isn't it?"

"Private Lotte," said the captain. "Right now, we have no idea why he came here. Nor how he found us, or what his motive is. For all we know he could have led the aliens that almost killed *you* back here to finish us all off."

"No, he didn't, Captain," replied Lotte. "I'm sure that's not the case."

Peters could see the anger building in the captain's face. "Private Lotte," he said. "Follow your orders. We will question Collins in short order and then plan our next steps."

"Understood, sir," said Lotte. Saluting, he turned and jogged towards the Marines guarding Collins' tent.

Looking up at Peters, Captain Gregory said, "Since when does a Marine private question the orders of a captain?"

"These are interesting times, Captain," replied Peters. "I suggest that we thoroughly question Collins. He's here for a reason and we may be able to use that to our advantage — possibly getting off this moon and back to Alcmene.

The captain nodded. "One hour, Ron. At the command center. Bring along Waverly and Lotte."

"Aye sir."

--

ISAT Field Agent Collins sat patiently in his seat. Looking around the room, he took a deep breath of air. It was clean, fresh and invigorating, a tremendous improvement over the stale-tasting recycled air he had to put up with during the many weeks after detaching his stateroom from the *Nemean*.

"This place is amazing," he said. "Another Alcmene secret you've been keeping to yourself?"

"No. We were fortunate," replied Peters.

"Mr. Collins," said Gregory. "You have a lot of explaining to do."

Collins looked at the armed Marines flanking him. "Are they really necessary?" he asked.

"They will be, if I decide to shoot you," said the captain. "As you can see, I'm unarmed."

"Ah yes, Captain. You've had better days," Collins said, letting his eyes linger over the mobile recovery chair. "Now…where shall I begin?"

"From the beginning," said Peters. "What happened after you detached your stateroom from the *Nemean*?"

"I went into hiding, Commander," replied Collins. "That wasn't hard to do, as the debris field was large, and my stateroom is rather small. I also took the liberty of disabling your sensors from tracking me. So you would not have been able to see me in any case."

"ISAT staterooms are designed for stealth too," added Waverly. "It would have been hard to find the stateroom, no matter what Mr. Collins did."

"Thank you, Waverly," said Collins. "The bottom line is, had I done nothing, the odds of you detecting me were still going to be small. I simply lowered those odds a bit further, as I was in fear of my life."

"No, you weren't," said Lotte. "You never truly believed that the captain would kill you."

"The captain held me at gunpoint," Collins pointed out.

"You didn't believe he'd use it," said Lotte. "You knew he never had any real intention of killing you."

"That's enough, Mr. Lotte," said the captain. "Mr. Collins, continue."

Collins straightened in his chair, took a sip of water from a cup he found on the table and continued, "I knew you were planning on following the *Daedalus*, and frankly, I thought that was a terrible decision."

"You made that abundantly clear," said the captain.

"Well. Yes, and it didn't make a difference in the end. I realized what you were doing, and I admit I may have left behind a few taps in your internal comm systems, so I was able to corroborate my suspicions with a few snippets of chatter I picked up among the crew."

Waverly whistled, "I had no idea—"

"Mr. Waverly," Collins said to his junior officer. "I *hope* you remember the things I taught you. We are ISAT agents, first and foremost."

Waverly looked at his former mentor but remained silent.

"I tailed the *Nemean* at a safe distance until I was sure of your destination. It knew that once you were ready with the space-time topography calculations, you'd go to the *Daedalus*' jump point. Once there, I reattached my stateroom to the *Nemean*. That was done without your knowledge, as I had already disabled those sensors as well."

"So, you hitched a ride on our backs," said Peters.

"Exactly, Commander. And once we arrived in this system, I detached myself from the *Nemean* and moved off to a safe distance again to collect data and observe. I saw the attack on the *Nemean* and watched you crash. I was doubtful that you'd survive, to be honest. But the fact that so many did is a testament to your planet's engineering talents."

"Spare us the compliments, Collins," said the captain. "How did you avoid getting hit too?"

"A bit of luck," said Collins. "Plus, my stateroom is a lot smaller than the *Nemean*. Most likely, that weapon didn't view me as a threat. Also, I was quite a distance out already when the attack occurred. I stayed out over five hundred thousand kilometers and observed. The weapon follows a semi-regular orbital pattern. It circles the gas giant seven times before dipping into the atmosphere, where it seems to go dormant."

"It might be reenergizing its systems," said Waverly.

"A good possibility," admitted Collins. "Whatever the case, it afforded me with a widow to come in close, and I decided to land and render my assistance. I have supplies —food, water, medical nanos — and other things that can help."

"And what are you asking for in return for your...*assistance*?" asked Peters.

"Safe passage back to ISAT-controlled territory," said Collins. "To any one of our sovereign facilities."

"If we were to do that, then you'd likely escape prosecution by *our* courts," said Gregory.

"Precisely, Captain. I won't hide the fact that I do not want to waste my time with your courts or a lengthy prison sentence. This ill-fated mission presents us, *all of us,* with a lot of work to do, and I don't want to be bogged down with legalities. I did what I felt was right and was within my rights, as an ISAT agent, to do it."

"No, you decidedly were *not* within your rights, " said Peters.

Collins brushed him off. "That would be for a court to decide, and I'm doubtful anyone here wants to waste time on such drawn-out formalities. Plus, does your government really want a diplomatic crisis on its hands? It's election time now on Alcmene, isn't it? My guess is that your President would prefer to be seen shaking hands with a long line of happy partners, like ISAT, rather than get bogged down in dubious legal matters. Who knows what such proceedings could dredge up if they drag on for too long?"

"Even if I were inclined to make such a deal," said the captain, "we are in *no* position to offer you passage anywhere. The *Nemean* is grounded, permanently."

"I know," said Collins. "However, before leaving Virgil's star I sent a message to the ISAT representatives on Alcmene, asking for assistance."

"That's impossible," said Peters. "Even without all the interference put out by that Structure and Virgil's star, we don't have anything capable of sending a coherent message one hundred thirty-nine light years away."

"*You* don't, Commander. But ISAT has been working on such technology," said Collins. "One of my mission objectives was to test precisely such a system, *if the mission called for it*, and this afforded me with such an opportunity."

"What do you mean 'if the mission called for it?'" asked Peters.

"I was to test the system only if we were in distress, as the power output was too much to mask."

"Has anyone received your signal?" asked Gregory. "Is there any way to know?"

"No," replied Collins. "We'll know in about four months, give or take a week or so. That's how long it would theoretically take for the signal to arrive at its destination and for ISAT, or Alcmene Naval Command, to process the signal, plus the transit time needed for a fast naval vessel to travel one hundred thirty-nine light years." My guess is that one of *your* naval vessels will be dispatched, as ISAT doesn't have any interstellar space assets available in your system."

The captain and Peters looked at each other and slowly nodded.

"We might have to add a few days to that estimate," remarked Waverly, "as they will have to make the same jump we did to arrive here."

"Very likely," said Collins, "as this system is unknown to the Union Worlds and they will probably take some precautions before following us."

The captain thought it over for a few minutes. "Agreed, Mr. Collins. If Alcmene Naval Command sends a rescue team, I will do whatever I can to ensure you safe passage to one of your stations. After that, it will be up to the government to decide whether or not to pursue charges against you."

"Very well, Captain. Am I free to go now?" Collins asked, gesturing towards the two guards standing behind him.

The captain gave the Marines a signal and they lowered their weapons, moving away. "Thank you, Captain, Commander," said Collins. "Mr. Waverly, let's catch up soon."

Agent Collins stood, finished the cup of water and walked out of the command center.

"What do you think?" asked the captain of those remaining.

Commander Peters shrugged. "What have we to lose? He's stranded here as much as we are. If he's telling the truth, we have a chance to get back home. If not, then we'll be sharing this moon for a long time to come, and his stateroom supplies will come in handy."

"I agree, sirs," said Waverly. "That stateroom has a lot of technology that could come in very handy, especially if we have to remain here for an extended period of time."

Lotte leaned back in his chair and smiled. "He's telling the truth, Captain. About everything. I think we should make the most of our time here on Eden, before we get back home. As Collins said, there'll be a lot of work waiting to be done."

"Thank you," said the captain. "Waverly, Lotte — you're dismissed. Commander, wait a moment, please."

The captain watched Waverly and Lotte leave the command center. "I actually have a good feeling about this," he told his XO.

"As do I," replied Peters.

"Now here's the thing that's bothering me: Collins, well, he is who he is. He has his motivations. He laid them out here and, frankly, I'm OK with them. I'd like to see him prosecuted, but if we get back home, it will be out of my hands anyway. I can only advise and recommend. Right now, prosecuting Collins doesn't seem like a big priority anymore. What will it gain us? Besides some satisfaction, nothing much."

"It might deter other ISAT agents from behaving in similar fashion," said Peters.

"Unlikely," replied Gregory. "I think Collins, given the same circumstances, would do it again. We've known for some time now that their agents will act according to their own rules, if circumstances call for it. That's not going to change by putting Collins in jail."

Peters nodded. "That's true. Imprisoning Collins is not going to change that dynamic."

"Now, what's been really bothering me is…well, have you noticed Private Lotte lately?" asked Gregory.

Peters returned the captain's look. "He's changed."

"Drastically," said Gregory. "He seems happy, unconcerned with anything and completely at ease with our situation."

"He changed the moment we got here," Peters said. "He really seems to like it here. And lately, he's been displaying a degree of insight. It's something he didn't do before. It's inconsistent with his personality, at least with his old personality.

"We know that his time aboard the Structure changed him," said the captain. "But this place has accelerated that transformation. Let's keep this to ourselves. He's been through a lot — we all have. But he's been through everything we've been through, plus a lot more."

Peters nodded in agreement. "It's confidential, sir. You know, we're treating this as if there's something *wrong*. But maybe we ought to be happy for him. He's a good soldier who found some measure of happiness in a difficult situation. Wouldn't it be great if we could all do that from time to time?"

"I like that way of looking at things," said the captain. "Maybe I'm being paranoid."

"You're not, sir. You've noticed a significant change in a member of your team and are wondering what's going on. That's the sign of a good leader."

"Perhaps, Commander," said Gregory. "Changing the subject, assign a team to inventory Collins' supplies. We'll know in a few months if we've made a good deal."

"Aye sir. We'll see."

Alexander Lotte sat lotus style in the soft green grass. His eyes were closed, and his head turned skyward as a soft breeze gently caressed his face.

He had spent much of his adult life wearing combat armor and relished the freedom the last several weeks afforded him, as his senses were free to experience the world around him directly, organically and naturally.

He took a deep breath and opened his eyes. "Thank you for coming," he said, as he looked out over the faces in front of him.

Eight Marines and twelve naval personnel sat in the same position as he, arranged in five rows, four people deep.

"Now, inhale deeply, hold, and exhale completely."

They all expelled their breath with a sigh.

"Now, inhale for Ohm…"

The group inhaled.

"AAAAAAAAAUUUUUUUUUUUUUUUMMMMMMMMM MMMM"

The sound reverberated around the crash site, somehow amplified by the surrounding trees and the hull of the *Nemean.*

"Now, let's get into a comfortable seat. Bring your hands to heart center. Give thanks to three things you are thankful for. If you wish, you can dedicate today's practice to someone who you feel needs it more than you do."

Several moments passed, as Lotte waited for his students to finish their dedications.

"Great. Now let's begin with some gentle stretches."

Lotte placed his left palm on the floor next to him and raised his right arm in the air. He bent his upper body to the left, while keeping his hips on the ground. His students followed along, bending to their left, according to their ability. Lotte changed directions, now reversing the pose and bending towards the right. The students followed.

Peters and Gregory were sitting in front of the command center, observing Lotte' class from a distance.

"How long has he been holding these classes?" asked the captain.

"He started a few days after Collins' arrival," replied Peters.

"The classes keep getting bigger."

"They are. He's up to around twenty students per class now," said Peters. "I believe he's turned in his weapons to the barracks master. He doesn't want to touch his armor anymore either."

The captain shrugged. "I won't force him to be a Marine if he doesn't want to be one."

"Don't you think it's bad for disciple?" asked Peters. "What if others follow suit?"

"I saw eight Marines in his classes. The rest are navy. Could it happen? Maybe," said the captain. "Hopefully, if Collins' message made it, it won't matter for much longer. These people are ready to go home...*now*."

Lotte's students were in a downward-dog position, their right legs lifted into the air. He made them hold that position for sixty seconds, before instructing them to bring their right leg forward between their hands to then rise into a high-lunge position.

They all moved in approximate unison, as some students were stronger or had better balance than others. The Marines were strong and had no difficulty holding planks and downward-dog positions, although many of them lacked the flexibility of their smaller, less muscular naval counterparts.

"I can see our military incorporating yoga into the existing training regimen," said the Captain. "That might be a good way to ease Mr. Lotte back into Alcmene's armed forces while also helping make our soldiers stronger and more limber."

"That's optimistic thinking," Peters said. "Look at him. Soldiering is the furthest thing from his mind."

They watched the rest of the class in silence, while Lotte would occasionally acknowledge them with a smile or a nod.

Lotte ended the class by saying, "Today I'd like to close our practice by recounting a saying by an ancient Earthman named Dag Hammarskjold. Dag once said that *'the longest journey is the journey inwards. Of him who has chosen his destiny, who has started upon his quest for the source of his being.'* I invite you to think about that as you go about your day." Bowing to the class, he added, "Thank you for allowing me to be your guide in this sacred practice today."

Holding his hands in prayer position, he bowed again, and his students bowed in return. Slowly, the group dispersed.

"Dag Hammarskjold?" asked Peters. "Have you heard of him?"

"Never," said the captain.

A few moments later, Lotte jogged to the command center, greeting both the captain and commander with a wave of his hand.

"Enjoy your class?" asked the captain.

"I did, sir. But my hope is that my students enjoyed it more," Lotte said. Addressing Peters, Lotte said, "Dag Hammarskjold was the second Secretary General of the United Nations on Earth. He thought profoundly and was known as a great stateman. Unfortunately, he died in a plane crash en route to a ceasefire negotiation. It seemed appropriate to quote him today."

Peters and Gregory nodded.

"Thank you, Mr. Lotte," said Gregory. "The commander and I were thinking that it would be great if you were to teach your style of yoga to the Marines back on Alcmene. I can see how this would benefit them. If you'd like, I can put in a recommendation."

"In time, Captain, that would be a wonderful idea," replied Lotte. "But there will be other things to focus on first. Things will be clearer as soon as the rescue ship arrives."

--

Three days later, the SKYEYE alarm sounded, prompting Marine Patrols One and Two to scatter into the tree line again, their shoulder-mounted rocket launchers pointed towards the sky. The rest of the Marines manned the fixed position guns, also pointed their barrels skyward and waited. Some of them ran about the crash site, giving orders and helping naval personnel get to cover.

However, on the far side of the crash site, where the ground was hard and rocky, Lotte, along with four other Marines and three enlisted navy, sat cross legged in a semi-circle, eyes closed, quietly meditating. None of them wore uniforms, preferring instead to wear roughly cut robes adorned with flower petals and small, colorful stones.

So engrossed were they in their meditation that they never bothered to look up as an Alcmene Navy Condor, a large cargo and troop transport vessel, broke through the cloud cover and softly landed alongside the shattered hull of the *Nemean*.

Condors were usually deployed from capital ships and had no hyperlight capabilities of their own, which meant that a larger Alcmene vessel was somewhere in orbit overhead.

The crew erupted in cheers and ran towards the waiting Condor, cautiously followed by the various Marine teams, rifles slung over their shoulders, with just a few keeping a hand on their sidearms.

Gregory, still in his recovery mobility chair, and Peters went toward the center the of the semi-circular ring that had formed around the Condor, followed by the rest of the command staff. A few moments went by before someone in the waiting crowd shouted for the Condor to open its doors, which triggered murmuring and a wave of agitation that rippled through the crew.

The captain raised his arms and told the crew to be patient. "They came a long way to find us and are probably running diagnostics or awaiting orders from their base ship."

Turning to Peters, standing to his right, he whispered, "They *are* taking their time getting that door open, aren't they?"

Peters nodded. "Might be malfunctioning. Their comms are spitting out static too, so they're clearly in need of repairs."

"Captain! Captain!"

The captain wheeled around in his chair. Private Lotte was sprinting full tilt towards the Condor, a rocket launcher in his hands, as the other Marines in his meditation group followed with rifles drawn, aiming for the Condor.

"Captain, that's a shell. An empty shell. Get the people back. Get back!" he shouted as he skidded to a halt, dropped down to one knee and squared the launcher's electronic sight directly on the Condor.

"Lotte what are you doing?" shouted the captain. "Drop that weapon now, soldier. That's an order. Drop it now!"

The crowed around the Condor scattered off in all directions as the Marines drew their weapons and sought cover. Lotte refocused his aim on the Condor, waiting for everyone to get out of the danger zone.

"Lotte! If you don't stand down, I will have the Marines open fire on you the moment you press that trigger."

The Marines were in a difficult position. They didn't want to shoot a fellow Marine, but they also didn't want to disobey orders and possibly lose their only chance of getting home again.

"Lotte, put that weapon down!" Peters shouted. "Please, think about what you are about to do. Put that launcher down."

The captain wheeled himself in front of the Condor, directly in Lotte's line of fire.

"Alexander," said the captain, using the Marine's first name. "Please, talk to us. Why are you doing this? Don't you want to go home?"

"Captain, get clear," shouted Lotte. "There's no time!"

Almost on cue, the Condor's landing ramp extended towards the ground while the cargo door slid open.

A blast of green laser light lanced out of the darkened interior, melted through the back of the captain's chair and came out the front of his chest. The captain slumped to the ground, partially obscured by the smoke smoldering from his chair.

A moment later a tall, angular, metallic humanoid hopped off the ramp and began firing in a seemingly random yet deadly accurate pattern.

The Marines around the Condor returned fire with their rifles, striking the attacker multiple times, causing him to stagger backwards before collapsing in a heap of mangled metal.

Two more humanoids hopped off the ramp, simultaneously firing rapid bursts of green light at the Marines, while another two humanoids emerged carrying heavier weapons that pulverized anything their savage plasma beams touched.

The crash zone erupted in a chaotic sea of crisscrossing laser light and plasma rounds as the Marines struggled to contain the humanoids exiting the Condor, who were now emerging two at a time, lining up shoulder-to-shoulder with the other humanoids, forming an ever-lengthening chain of hostile fire.

The commander and Waverly were crouched behind a boulder, using their Z10 pistols to bolster the Marines' attack. Paris and Harris were scattered about the crash zone with the rest of the Nemean's crew, unarmed and trying to stay out of the crossfire.

Marker and Collins disappeared inside the ISAT agent's stateroom, a few moments before it lifted off and drifted towards the Condor, a gun turret emerging from one of the corners of its structure. Before they could fire the gun, the Condor launched an anti-ship plasma round at the stateroom, causing it to teeter, spin and crash onto the ground.

Meanwhile, Lotte circled around the battle zone looking for a clean shot that would not injure the humans. He flashed several hand signals to the Marines that had been in his meditation group, and they took up new positions but didn't fire their weapons. Lotte stood and ran full speed at the Condor, while the other Marines ran to the fallen captain from the other direction.

From a distance the sprinting figures looked like ghostly blurs as their robes fluttered in the air and their feet stamped out troughs in the tall, green grass.

Like vengeful streaks of light, two of Lotte's Marines dodged around the incoming fire, slowing just enough to take hold of the fallen captain's arms and dragging him to safety, while the other two Marines followed closely behind, firing their weapons and tossing fragmentation grenades at the line of attackers.

Moments later, Lotte shouted, "Cover! Cover! Cover!" before dropping to one knee, fixing his aim on the Condor and firing.

Two rockets streaked out of the twin launcher tubes, striking the Condor a split second apart, causing it to erupt in flames seconds before a deafening explosion engulfed all the mechanical humanoids and scorched the ground clean for twenty meters in all directions.

It was over.

The remaining Marines carefully surveyed the wreckage for any signs of survivors, while medical teams fanned out to treat the injured and care for the wounded. A special medical team led by Doc Smith flooded the captain's system with nanos to stabilize him before performing an emergency surgical procedure to save his life.

--

"How is he, Doctor?" asked Peters.

"He's going to be all right. Luckily, the alien's laser missed his heart by a few millimeters. Had it been a little to the left, I don't think we'd be having this conversation. We're also lucky that the medical facilities on this ship are far more extensive than anything we had on Eden."

Peters nodded. "Thank you, doctor."

"You should also reserve a 'thank you' for Mr. Collins. Had he not supplied us with those nanos, we would have had a hell of a time getting the captain stable enough for surgery."

"He did come through for us," agreed Peters. "I will speak with him later. He might need our help, as ISAT may not approve of him leaving his stateroom behind on Eden."

"I'm sure Lotte and his group will take good care of it," said the doctor.

Peters shrugged. "I was surprised he wanted to stay…that so many of them wanted to stay. We'll check in on them after things settle. Their idea of paradise may be short lived."

"We all need a vacation, commander. Lotte just claimed his earlier than most of us."

Peters laughed. "I'll see you soon, Doctor. I have a mission report to complete."

--

ISAT and Alcmene Naval Command had received Collins' signal and dispatched two Orion class Cruisers, the *Griffin* and the *Pegasus*, to investigate and hopefully recover the *Nemean*'s crew.

The admiral had been extremely generous to Peters and the crew of the *Nemean*. The command staff each received lush personal quarters aboard the *Griffin*, while the enlisted and the Marines bunked in spacious two person rooms. They were given vacation pay and were exempt from any shipboard duties. They had all earned their rest, which started as soon as they boarded the cruisers.

Commander Peters and Admiral Yuri Shinowa sat in the *Griffin*'s officers' lounge, catching up on events at home and exchanging details of their run-ins with the artificial Structure orbiting Virgil's star.

"What I don't understand," said Peters, "is how they got control of one of your Condors."

"Before we made the jump to Eden," explained the admiral, "we decided to see if we could find any of the crewmen you reported MIA aboard the Structure. We sent in a Condor with a small combat team. They encountered mechanized soldiers, much like your first team did, but far fewer of them. Our team succeeded in defeating them and brought one of them back for study. They secured it in the cargo hold and we decided to leave it there for the duration of the trip.

"When we got to Eden, we deployed that same Condor with two pilots aboard. We didn't bother to send a combat team down with them, as this wasn't a combat mission and we wanted to use the space to bring down supplies you might immediately need. We also expected that you'd have many personnel requiring medical EVAC, so that was another consideration.

"After deploying the Condor, we moved off into a much higher orbit in an effort to stay clear of the weapon Collins told us about. We can only speculate on what happened after that. About halfway to Eden, the Condor's comms went dark. The security cams also went dark shortly thereafter, but not before they captured this footage."

Peters looked at the display Admiral Shin brought up on his console. While the footage was grainy, it was clear enough for Peters to see a metallic humanoid approach the pilots' nest from somewhere aft of the ship, violently yanking one out of his chair and throwing him off screen. The footage blacked out before he could see what happened to the second pilot.

"That's all we know for certain," said the admiral. "Both pilots were armed with Z10s, but it doesn't look like they had a chance to use them. Our guess is that the machine wasn't 'killed' in a convention sense. Our Marines probably damaged it enough to put it into some type of dormant state, during which time it repaired itself. It killed our pilots and landed the ship on Eden. By then it had already taken over the ship and probably used the Condor's sensors to see that there were more humans on the surface."

"But where did the rest of them come from?" asked Peters. "You said there was just one aboard. There were at least fifteen of them by the time Lotte blew up the Condor."

"That's the scary part," said the admiral. "Apparently, that one reproduced his cousins somehow — and did so very quickly."

"How do we fight something like that?" asked Peters almost rhetorically.

"Figuring that out is going to be one of our top priorities once we get home," replied the admiral.

Peters nodded. "Any word from the *Daedalus*?" he asked after a moment. "We made brief contact with Lance Corporal Felix and his team aboard that ship moments before the *Nemean* was attacked, so we have no idea what happened after that."

"No, the *Daedalus* was long gone by the time we arrived," replied the admiral. "We did pick up a sensor buoy that Collins had deployed. It captured the *Daedalus'* departure from the Eden system. Our science team is studying the data now. We may be able to follow it again, just as you did."

"Let's hope for a better outcome," said Peters.

The admiral finished his tea and said, "When the captain is up to it, have him come see me. In the meantime, I'm looking forward to reading your final report."

"I'll have that finished soon, Admiral," Peters said.

They stood and shook hands. Peters saluted as the admiral nodded and left the lounge.

--

According to Dr. Smith, with rest Captain Gregory was likely to make a good recovery.

When Peters entered Gregory's room, he thought the captain looked tired and a bit haggard, but hints of his former spirit were returning.

"How is Lotte, Ron? I want to personally thank him for his actions on Eden," said Gregory. "I was close to ordering the Marines to shoot him. Had it not been for that alien….well, things might have turned out a lot worse."

"I'm sorry, sir. Lotte decided to remain on Eden. Ten others stayed with him. Six Marines and four navy.

"All things considered," said Gregory, "that shouldn't surprise me. He did seem happy there."

Peters nodded. "And he was developing a bit of a following. Basically, half of his yoga class stayed on Eden with him. I told him we'd check in on him as soon as we could get back there."

"Will he have enough supplies?" asked Gregory.

"We left him all of our rations and medical supplies, plus he has Collins' stateroom," said Peters. "They'll be fine for a while."

Gregory looked surprised. "Collins allowed his stateroom to remain on Eden?"

"He did, sir," Peters replied. "He 'donated' it to Lotte and his group."

"And this is all in your final mission report, I trust?" Gregory remarked.

Peters nodded.

Gregory gave a small laugh. "Now that is one report I have got to read."

Peters also laughed, adding, "I almost forgot, sir." He reached into a pocket inside his vest. "Here. This is from Lotte. He actually handwrote it."

"Thank you, Ron," said the captain. "I'll read it later. I have a meeting with the admiral in about twenty minutes."

"Understood, sir. Happy to see you back to your normal self. I'll see you at the planning session later today at 13:00.

"Yes, Commander. Waverly, Marker, Harris and Paris will be presenting as well. Should be interesting."

"Ah yes," replied Peters. "These are shaping up to be interesting times."

"Interesting times, indeed," said the captain.

Epilogue I

Lotte's letter to Captain Gregory

Dear Captain Gregory,

I wanted to personally thank you for your efforts during this mission. For the efforts you took to protect and retrieve your crew, and for the commitment you have shown to those who are under your command. Beyond your efforts, I want to thank you for the intent driving your efforts — as that is ultimately more important.

I can attest that the crew of the Nemean, *especially speaking for the members of Marine Company One, look up to you and value your leadership.*

We are now entering a different phase in our development as a people and as a society, and perhaps even a as species.

I have decided to remain on Eden, along with a few members of the Nemean*'s crew. I can assure you that all have remained behind voluntarily. We have enough supplies for probably over a year, and the land is abundant with nutritious foods and medicines.*

The future is yet to be told, but I am confident in the possibilities. If our mission to Virgil's star taught us anything, it's that we are worthy of the time that's been given to us. It's up to us to make the best use of it. We'll make mistakes, trip and fall — and that's okay. We'll just have to get up, dust ourselves off, learn to forgive, and keep moving forward.

I am sure we will meet again.

Sincerely,
Alexander Lotte

PS – Captain, with so many distractions, during our debrief sessions on the Nemean *I neglected to relay the aliens' entire message to you. They also wanted you to know that* Agamemnon *was a hero.*

Epilogue II

Squad 17 commanded by Sergeant Wessler

System: Virgil's star (VGL 191)

Location: Somewhere inside the Structure

Several weeks ago, Sergeant Wessler and his team had emerged from the tunnels into what appeared to be a vast expanse of densely forested woodland. Not unlike the forests of Alcmene or Earth, there was lush, green growth everywhere. The air was clean, refreshing and pure, and the landscape was dotted here and there by swiftly flowing streams of clear, drinkable water.

The Marines saw this as a welcome respite to the constant drudgery of the small confined spaces they had been marching through for the past several weeks, and were finally able to remove their helmets and breathe air that had not been recycled by their EVA suits. Their eyes, accustomed to the dull blue of the tunnels, also rejoiced at the yellow light from the clear, sunlit sky.

This place was like paradise, Rodriguez had commented, and the squad had designated their camp Base Paradise.

The first week at Base Paradise was almost like a vacation for the Marines. While they still maintained the unit on alert status, Wessler decided to create four sentry shifts, with each shift consisting of four Marines fully equipped in their EVA suits. This type of shift rotation ensured that each Marine would get a chance to rest, relax and tend to their equipment, and not be overburdened with excessive sentry duty time.

Lord knew they had been through enough already, and had they not come across this place, Wessler felt that his squad would probably have collapsed from exhaustion.

Unfortunately, their second week was anything but paradise.

On that Monday morning, Wessler roused the squad for morning exercises. While the rest of the squad geared up and lined up for inspection, Tomly had gone into the nearby woods, south of their camp, to relieve himself. They had done this dozens of times during the last week and had even dug a latrine for the squad to use.

Tomly hadn't been wearing his full EVA suit — just the torso section, as he was late rousing to the sergeant's call and hastily put on whatever he could to make rollcall. His plan was to run to the latrine, do his business and get back in time to put his full EVA on before presenting at lineup.

The first person to hear his screams was Rodriguez, who flashed an alarm through the general comm frequency and took the four sentries on combat duty to investigate.

The rest of the squad was still at basecamp, with Wessler hastily forming them up into fireteams.

Meanwhile, Rodriguez and the sentries raced towards Tomly's screams, just in time to see Tomly flailing about as an enormous creature pinned him to the ground, tearing at the torso section of his EVA with razor-sharp claws that sliced the armor from neck to waist in one terrifying, jagged slice.

The beast wasted no time, driving its snout deep into Tomly's exposed chest, devouring the Marine's insides in two bites and tearing what was left of Tomly into pieces, angling its throat down to get the arms and legs in, much like a pelican swallowing a meal.

"Marines, open fire!" shouted Rodriguez, rousing the Marine sentries from the momentary stupor they were in as the reality of watching a fellow Marine being eaten sank in.

The Marines opened fire with their automatic rifles, discharging round after round at the beast.

The beast howled at the onslaught, as plasma rounds sliced through its arms, belly, chest and neck, followed by three shots that slammed into its ghastly skull, felling it right where it had torn open Tomly's chest.

Rodriguez flashed a signal to Wessler, who was just leaving Base Paradise, the rest of the squad formed up into fire teams to search the area for more hostiles.

"Rodriguez!", shouted Wessler into the comm. "SITREP!"

"Tomly is KIA, sir! Some kind of large animal ate him."

"Ate him, Rodriguez?" asked Wessler, somewhat incredulously, although he had no doubt that Rodriguez had reported in correctly.

"Yes sir! We are not alone in Paradise." Just then Rodriquez's comm muffled and Wessler's ears filled with static, as Rodriguez was pounced upon by another beast, this one larger than the first.

The four sentries crouched and opened fire again, but this time the beast seemed to be wearing some kind of protective armor, which was partially deflecting the sentry's fire, but not enough to fully dissipate the rounds. The Marines' continuous fire was clearly causing the beast an enormous amount of pain.

Rodriguez, having seen the first attacker's tactic of pinning down Tomly before ripping him open, rolled out from under the beast before it could cut open his EVA suit and stuck a grenade down the collar of its armored back.

"Cover!" he shouted into the general comm, and the sentries sprinted for cover while Rodriguez took a running leap over a fallen log, landing on his back, shins perpendicular to the floor in the classic Alcmene blast protection posture.

The beast stood and spun around wildly, as the grenade detonator counted down three..two..one…and exploded in a blast that turned its armor into molten slag and incinerated its body.

Wessler and his fire teams made it to the latrine area a few seconds after the explosion, only to see his men taking cover as a group of three beasts bounded over a nearby hill, long curved metallic spears in their enormous hands, their scaly, gray bodies partially covered by glistening long robes.

"Fire at will!" Wessler shouted into the general channel.

The entire squad began firing at the beasts.

Two of the beasts quickly found cover, while the third and largest of the group took several rounds in its left arm and right shoulder. It let out a terrifying roar as grayish goo leaked out from the wounds. Throwing one last look at the Marines, it bounded back behind the hill and disappeared in a thick stand of trees.

"Should we pursue?" asked Young. He commanded Fire Team Three, which was closest to the beasts when the attack ensued.

"Negative," replied Wessler on the general comm. "Recover what we can of Tomly's gear and his tags, take a sample of the gray goo that thing left behind and let's get back to base. We need to find a more defensible position now that we know those things are roaming around."

"Paradise lost," said Rodriguez over the comm, to no one in particular.

"Indeed," Wessler replied absently, as he scanned the line of the beasts' retreat. His HUD could still read residual heat signatures on the tree trunks lining the beasts' escape path, but the creatures were no longer within visible range. That, or they were well camouflaged.

While Young's fire team retrieved what was left of Tomly's tags and gear, Rodriguez and the four sentries carefully approached the hill to scoop up a sample of the gray liquid that had leaked out of the wounded beast.

It was thick and viscous, unlike human blood, and seemed to contain small suspended particles that, at least to Rodriguez's medically untrained eye, could have the ability to scour the inner surfaces of the creature's arteries.

No matter. If, not *when*, Squad 17 linked back with the main force and got off the Structure, the scientists aboard the *Nemean* could figure it out. Rodriguez didn't particularly care whether or not those things had a built-in mechanism to unclog their arteries. He was horrified by what had happened to Tomly, a friend and a fellow Marine. Marines died in battle all the time, but something about being eaten felt — *wrong*.

The sample was sealed in a carbon-titanium biohazard tube, pressure capped and deposited in a small metallic container for safe keeping. It would take a lot of force to break open the biohazard tube, and anything strong enough to do so would likely also kill the Marine carrying the container, so Rodriguez made it his charge to carry the container back to base and aboard the *Nemean*, should they get that far.

Satisfied with Young's and Rodriguez's retrieval efforts, Wessler ordered the squad to head back to Base Paradise, where three fire teams formed a defensive perimeter while the fourth team, along with Rodriguez and Young, were ordered to shut down the base and pack up the squad's gear — and anything useful nearby before heading out on their march through the woodlands to find a better place from which to fight.

Wessler watched the activity from one of the perimeter checkpoints. He was proud of his squad. In his mind, Squad 17 was the best Marine force Alcmene had ever seen. He'd been feeling increasing pangs of guilt for leading his squad away from the main force and into the tunnels in the first place. He should have listened to Duffy's protests instead of his gut feeling. Thinking back, there was probably never any immediate danger of a flanking maneuver that could have come from the tunnels. It had been hours or more before they had even encountered the first set of hostiles, the mini tanks, and they had been well away from the main force when that happened.

He'd made a mistake, and his troops were paying the price for it. And his friend, Tomly, had just paid the ultimate price.

Wessler vowed to get his squad back home, even if it meant his own life. There would be no more casualties on his watch. Not if he could help it.

--

Schwakelutee stood on a butte overlooking an expanse of swamplands below. He brought his far glass to his left eye and surveyed the area. No sign of the diminutive aliens.

His Hunter Troop had first encountered them a light cycle ago and had found them to be rather tasty meals.

However, the aliens had not seemed cognizant of the honor Schwakelutee and his troop had bestowed upon them. Rather, when Schwaktator, his Second, had cornered and devoured one of their number, the little prey animals ran and hid for a few seconds, before emerging from their hideouts to attack his troop. In the ensuring chaos, the little aliens managed to kill two of his brethren with their curiously rhythmic weapons.

In and of themselves, the aliens were no match for Hunters, of that Schwakelutee was certain. They were small, weak and not very fast. Their outer skeleton was hard and strong but could be peeled off with a bit of effort, and their inner covering was so delicate that a slight swipe of a Hunter's claw could tear it to pieces.

However, these creatures seemed to roam in packs, and could be dangerous when formed up in a unit. And their weapons, despite their pleasant, melodic rhythmic thumping, were deadly.

Schwakelutee could attest to that personally, as he had been hit in the arm and shoulder by one of them, and had only managed to survive by the quick work of his Third, who stopped the blood flow and sealed his wounds with one of the med packs they had managed to salvage from the crash site.

For Schwakelutee and his troop of Hunters, this place had been home for many cycles. It had been a boring existence, with nothing to hunt and no honor to be earned among his lazy peers — until yesterday, when the small, tasty aliens showed up.

The Hunters were not certain what these creatures where, or why they were here, or where they came from; they were not even certain if they were truly sentient as the Hunters were, or if they were running on instinct like most other prey animals did.

But it was no matter. The newcomers had revitalized the spirits of his Hunter Troop, giving them something to do, and something better to eat than the crash rations they had been subsisting on since landing here.

Epilogue III

Major Lewis

System: Virgil's star (VGL 191)

Location: Somewhere inside the Structure

Major Lewis crouched behind the metal barrier, his sights on the corridor directly in front of him. He could see glints of light reflecting off their metallic bodies, their gun barrels pointing ominously in his direction.

There were hundreds of them. His motion sensor maxed out at a count of four hundred, but there could have been more, as four hundred was his suit's resolution limit.

They had stopped firing but continued towards him, marching slowly as if keeping in step with a far-off, lazy marching song.

Lotte was still unconscious, while his suit worked hard to stabilize him.

Lewis toyed with the idea of forcing him back to consciousness by injecting him with a rush of nano stimulants but decided against it. No telling what that might do to his system.

Despite the terrible odds, Major Lewis' plan had not changed: He and Lotte were going to get out of here — alive.

Although he had ordered Marine Company One to retreat and get off the Structure, he knew that a search and rescue team would eventually be sent to recover MIAs. And he knew that the first step in any such recovery effort would be to dig through the debris that blocked his escape route.

If he could hold out here long enough, eventually someone would dig through and together they could fight their way off this rock.

But that could be a long time in coming, and time wasn't something he had in abundance now.

A thought came to mind. *"Why am I doing this?"*

Major Lewis shook his head. *"Why don't I leave him behind and flee?"*

He looked over his shoulder. Nothing. Just a wall of debris.

"There, on my right. Ten meters. A small opening in the wall. I can hide there."

He shook his head again. Was he hearing things?

A flash of green light crackled and sizzled as it flew overhead and scorched the rock behind him.

They were firing again.

He returned fire, his rifle set to automatic, firing rhythmically as he launched round after round at the bots.

"You can't win. There are too many and just one of you."

"Do not confuse your superior numbers with my will to destroy you!" shouted Lewis.

Looking down at Lotte, he repositioned him closer to the debris field and leaned the metal sheet against the rock wall, forming a type of lean-to to cover the fallen Marine.

Satisfied, Lewis stood and faced the bots marching towards him.

He primed three frag grenades and reloaded his rifle.

Slowly, he began marching towards the enemy formation, firing his rifle with his right hand while throwing the frag grenades with his left.

The bots returned fire.

Undeterred, Major Lewis continued his march. He still had half a dozen grenades in his belt and ten magazines of ammunition, plus a fully loaded Z10 pistol.

"This is how you choose to end your life?"

"No!" replied Lewis, unsure who had asked the question.

"This is how I lay claim to this chunk of misshapen rock you call home."

--The End--

For news on upcoming books, sign up for K. Constantine's New Release Newsletter at:

www.ConstantineAuthor.com

Book Two: Worthy of Eden

Coming Soon!

Made in the USA
Monee, IL
28 July 2024

62758835R00152